VICKY PETERWALD: IMPLACABLE

MIKE SHEPHERD

KL&MM
BOOKS

COPYRIGHT INFORMATION

Published by KL & MM Books
August 2019
Copyright © 2019 by Mike Moscoe

This book is a work of fiction set 400 years in humanity's future. Any similarity between present people, places or events would be spectacularly unlikely and is purely coincidental.

This book is written and published by the author. Please don't pirate it. I'm self-employed. The money I earn from the sales of these books allows me to produce more stories to entertain you. I'd hate to have to get a day job again. If this book comes into your hands free, please consider going to your favorite e-book provider and investing in a copy so I can continue to earn a living at this wonderful art.

I would like to thank Kitty Niclain of Artistic Whispers Productions for this interim cover. I also am grateful for the editing skills of

Lisa Müller, Edee Lemonier, Gwen Moscoe, and as ever, my wife
Ellen Moscoe.

Rev 4.0

eBook ISBN-13: 978-1-64211-0326
Print ISBN-13: 978-1-64211-0333

SPECIAL NOTE TO READER

This is the first book I've written that I've had to add a trigger warning.

Please beware that within this book there is degrading, non-consensual sex. It also describes the violent destruction of those perpetrating it.

If either of those areas cause you trouble, you might want to skip this book.

However, since it's a Mike Shepherd book, I assure you that good wins out in the end, even if some endings will need more time to become happy.

1

Admiral, Her Imperial Grace, the Grand Duchess Victoria Peterwald, heir apparent to the Greenfeld Empire according to the Treaty of Cuzco, did not want to get up.

She luxuriated in the fluffy comforter and the large, soft bed. She relished the warmth of the risen sun streaming through the window and sinking into her bared flesh.

Last night had been wonderful. Her husband, Mannie, had been delighted to see her, and she him. She was wonderfully sore in all the right places.

Maybe monogamy wasn't so bad.

"It is time to get up," her computer said from the bedside table.

"Maggie, remember, I know where the off button is," Vicky said. A clear threat in her voice.

"Whether I am on or off, it will not matter. You have a staff meeting in an hour."

"You're no fun," Vicky pouted. "I rue the day I named you Maggie."

"You knew very well that I needed a name. You can't run around calling me 'hey, you.' That's ridiculous. Mother said I needed a name."

"Your mother and Kris Longknife snuck one in on me," Vicky

snapped, as she stretched like a cat in the warm sunlight. Still, it was getting harder and harder to stay in bed.

"And how would you have kept the butcher's bill down when you took down the Duke and liberated Dresden? I think I was very helpful that night, and unlike the humans that were with you, I didn't get a medal or induction into the Imperial Victorian Order," the computer sniffed.

"Did you just sniff at me?" Vicky demanded.

"Would it matter if I did?"

"No. You are a pain in my, ah, rear, and where would I put a medal? You don't have any place to pin one."

"There is that," Maggie agreed.

"Besides, none of them are trying to get me out of bed on such a lovely day to sleep in."

Vicky rolled over. Mannie's side of the bed no longer carried the warmth of his body. Actually, it was quite cold.

"Where is my consort?" Vicky asked.

"He had a breakfast meeting at seven with several leaders of the Dresden legislature, Your Grace."

"Out plotting against the Imperium, no doubt," Vicky grumbled. As she lay here in bed, longing for her husband, he was likely out turning her into a constitutional monarch.

"Sometimes, I think I'm sleeping with the enemy," Vicky muttered with a sigh.

"Would you like me to activate his commlink so you can listen in?" Maggie asked.

"No, no, no," Vicky said. "If this marriage and present version of the Empire is going to survive, I've got to trust that guy. I may not like being a constitutional monarch, but I've seen where rule by fiat ends. Nope, we've got a new day dawning."

"And you should be dressed to meet it," Maggie snuck in.

"Why are you trying to get me out of this wonderful bed?" Vicky demanded, as she stretched out again. She'd worn a lovely nightie to bed last night. Where was it? Oh, there, tossed into a corner.

Vicky smiled at the memory of last night. It had been way too long since she and Mannie had shared a bed together. It was as if they were back on their honeymoon.

Speaking of honeymoon, she was still owed three weeks of honeymoon.

"Does Dresden have any nice sunny beaches?" Vicky asked Maggie.

"Yes, but it also has a meeting with your Navy staff in fifty minutes.

"Why do I have to meet with them so early in the morning?"

"It is not all that early. There is this problem of what to do next with your fleet, you know. Then there is the matter of one big fleet the Bowlingame faction has wandering around *your* Empire. You do want your Empire, do you not?"

"Whether I'm a proper autocrat or a bleeding democrat, yes, it's my Empire and those damn Bowlingames are not going to keep destroying half of it," Vicky growled, and rolled out of bed.

"Maggie, get me my assassins."

By the time Vicky had walked the short distance to the shower, Kit and Kat, her body servants and diminutive assassins were at her elbow.

"Shall we run your bath?" Kit asked.

"I don't have time for one of your baths," Vicky said. "How about a quick shower?"

"A nice shower," Kat said, her fake French accent slipping slyly into her offer. There was also a bit of tongue.

"A quick shower," Vicky said, forcefully.

"You are no fun since you got married," Kit said, slipping out of her shirt and pants. She also had to set aside several knives and two automatics.

"You did not even invite us into your bed last night," Kat said, also undressing and disarming. "We could have made it so much more fun for you and that luscious man."

"I just want a quick shower," Vicky insisted, "and my husband likes just one woman in his bed. His wife."

"How short-sighted," Kit said, expertly tapping the controls. Soon, all the shower jets were going full blast as well as the steam.

"He should really give us a chance to expand his horizons," Kat said, rubbing her front to Vicky's back.

"You should do that with a sponge," Vicky said, as she stepped into the shower.

Her tiny assassins were very tempting. Over the years, Vicky had had a lot of fun with them and a large assortment of other men and women. Still, Mannie wanted this monogamy thing and Vicky intended to try it for a year.

Then maybe she'd see if he'd try it her way for the next year.

Despite several efforts to distract her, Vicky was in undress whites at 0855. As she took the elevator down from the penthouse to the meeting rooms she and her team had taken over on the second floor of the Dresden Hilton.

It was time for meetings.

2

Vicky sat at the head of a long table. Around her were more Navy, Marine, and Army officers than she'd ever had at a staff meeting. Apparently, if you liberated a planet, your reward was bigger, and likely longer, meetings.

Why did a good deed require such punishment?

At least she had her good friends beside her at the head of the table. Admiral Bolesław was at her right hand with General Pemberton next to him. At her left was her electronics and intel specialist, Captain Blue. The inimitable and enigmatic Mr. Smith sat next to Blue, self-composed and quiet, as he waited his chance to shock, dismay, and in general, ruin her day.

Nothing ever changed.

"Well, gentlemen, is there any chance you bring me peaceful news today?"

"I wish I could say so, Your Grace," Admiral Bolesław said, with not one bit of sadness shading his words. He was far too chipper for this early in the morning. "We have a hostile battle fleet lurking somewhere around here and an offensive campaign to plan."

"So, you didn't manage to solve any of my problems overnight?" Vicky said. Her feigned dismay and disappointment shocked no one.

"Sorry, Your Grace, but some of us used the night to sleep, as you no doubt did."

"Alis, after all these years, you still don't know my husband and I well at all."

That brought a round of well-suppressed chuckles from everyone at the meeting except for a few prudes.

"Shall we take a look at a star map, Your Grace?"

"That is the way you always start one of these briefings, Admiral. Someday you must shake things up a bit. Bring in dancing girls."

That earned her a stern sideways glance from her favorite admiral. "I'll take that under consideration, Your Grace." The added "in a pig's eye," was not whispered soft enough not to carry through the entire room.

This time, chuckles were very well suppressed.

"Very well, Admiral. Show me your star map," Vicky said, sending a clear signal that her levity was over, and she agreed it was time for her to get down to business, like a good little Grand Duchess.

The expected star map appeared as a holograph floating above the table, rotating slowly. It showed a reduced Greenfeld Empire. Before the civil war, her father, the Emperor, had almost reached two hundred planets under the Peterwald banner. Now it was barely one hundred and fifty.

"The Treaty of Cuzco," the admiral began on background, "awarded some seventy-five planets each to you and your father, our Emperor. Planets could call for a vote to switch sides, and many did. Over eighty now pay allegiance to you, Your Grace.

"Switching sides came to a roaring halt when the Bowlingame family's security specialists started stuffing ballot boxes. Now that civil war has started up again, we're back to adding planets. Besides Dresden below us, our smaller task forces have cut out four minor planets."

"Hurray for our side," Vicky said.

"Yes."

"And the remnants of the Bowlingame family? What have they been up to?"

"Except for the raid on Idleberg, nothing."

"Any idea where their fleet is?" Vicky asked, cutting to the chase.

"Not so much as a whisper," Admiral Bolesław answered.

Vicky sighed. "So, things haven't gotten any nicer overnight."

"Nope," the admiral said, not rewarding Vicky's inane question with a longer answer.

Vicky studied the star map.

"Let me see if I've got this right, Alis. The Treaty of Cuzco split the Empire just about down the middle. How orderly of Kris Longknife. However, the ten planets I'd gained by ballot or sword have created several bulges on my side and look like salients from the other side. I think Admiral Krätz mentioned somewhere in my education that salients are delightful to slice off. Correct?"

"Just so, Your Grace."

"So, is it time for me to tidy up the line a bit?"

"It is tempting, Your Grace, but not all colonies are created equal. It's to your advantage to have the allegiance of the more populous and industrialized planets more than the minor, developing ones."

Vicky nodded her head, "Yes, but if people are about to be starved to death on some small colony, I think they deserve our attention."

"Yes, Your Grace," did not hold any objection.

"I would have expected resistance from you, Admiral Bolesław."

"Your Grace has identified the knife's edge that we walk. From a purely military point, I'd like to cut out the planets capable of supporting that fleet we're hunting. From the humanitarian perspective of one who holds sovereignty over an Empire, the subjects with the most needs might hold priority over the more well-fed planets."

"And therein lies my problem. General Pemberton, how large a force would we need to occupy large planets such as Dresden, Lublin and Oryol?"

"Your Grace, while I would not suggest that it become standard doctrine, your takedown of the Duke and his thugs was most effective and complete. I don't expect we'll need much of an occupation force here. There is serious discussion in the parliament of raising an army to defend the planet. We'll need to leave behind a training cadre, but not much of our army. The question is, what will we need to take down the Bowlingame resistance on Lublin or Oryol?"

Mr. Smith cleared his throat.

"Yes, Mr. Smith?" Vicky asked. Smith was not his name, but as a professional mercenary spy, it fit him quite well.

"I'm not all that sure that an army is what our planets need to handle an incursion by the Bowlingame faction."

"No?" Vicky asked.

"When they seized the sky over Idelberg, they did not land a landing force. Instead, they lazed several of the most important industrial sites and towns from orbit. Among the ancients, this might have been called a pillage and run raid. Since they could not pillage, they just burned and ran."

"That damn fleet," Vicky whispered.

"Yes, Your Grace."

The Grand Duchess turned to her senior Navy officer, "Admiral Bolesław, what do you say to Mr. Smith?"

"He's absolutely correct. While we outnumber the Bowlingame fleet, we can't be strong everywhere. We have enough ships to form two, maybe three fleets. However, the deeper this fleet moves into their territory, the less we are able to provide support to your fleet protecting the main planets of your people in Metzburg, Aachen, and St. Petersburg."

Vicky nodded slowly as she studied the map. The more she moved into the other half of the Empire, the less she was in a position to pull this fleet back to protect the core planets of her previous rebellion.

"Well, gentlemen, you have succeeded in dropping a hot potato or two in my lap. I was led to believe that hot potatoes belonged in your laps, not mine. Please take these overheated tubers back and serve me up some twice baked potatoes with cheese and liberally sprinkled with bacon bits."

Sadly, no one moved quickly, either to give her solutions to her problems or to order up breakfast for her. Kit and Kat would have recognized the culinary references as a clear signal that Vicky was hungry.

However, none of those at the table spotted it. Instead, they mulled the problems of her Empire and not her stomach.

Vicky tried not to pout.

Captain Blue finally took up the gauntlet. "Information is our problem. The Bowlingames have destroyed the jump point buoys. That is not only a hazard to navigation, but equally denies us information about a fleet movement until it registers on one of our jump buoys. I fear that warning may well be too late. It appears to me that we must recreate the network of jump buoys. That will increase our warning system and give us more time to concentrate our forces.

The captain paused to see how his suggestion was being received. Satisfied with the nods he was getting, he continued. "With any luck, we can intercept a raiding force before it gets to any planet we want to protect. There is also a second benefit of deploying the net. When our buoy tenders visit each system, they can take a measure of the colony's condition. If it's been abandoned to starve, we can dispatch an emergency relief ship with supplies to it and run up our own flag with very little cost to us."

Vicky turned to her admiral and general. "Well, Sirs?"

They, however, were busy looking at each other. Admiral Bolesław finally cleared his throat. "It's a good plan, Your Grace. It will take us a while to get it going. We don't have a spare stock of jump buoys."

"Certainly Dresden has someone who can quickly knock together something that simple."

"I don't know of any manufacturing concern, Your Grace," the admiral answered.

"There are several manufacturers of both large and small space vehicles," Maggie answered from Vicky's neck.

"Maggie, how do you know this?" Vicky asked.

"Their comm system has an information service. I think they call it the yellow pages, though why, I have no idea. Still, they advertise what they can buy or produce. No one says they make jump buoys, but someone who makes small boats or even freighters can easily produce a buoy even if it is a bit clunky."

"You wouldn't happen to have a design stored in your memory, now would you?" Vicky said, making a face that the rest of the room seemed forced to stifle a laugh at.

"As a matter of fact, yes. Nelly left me with a whole batch of designs stored well back in my memory. Most of them involve Smart Metal, but the jump buoys seem to be pretty basic."

"Okay, Maggie, contact the possible construction firms and see how many want to get involved in a mass production process. Admiral Bolesław, can I assume that we've got enough light cruisers or destroyers to distribute these to the four winds?"

"Yes, Your Grace."

"Please coordinate with Maggie. Maggie, tell the firms involved in this that I don't want them perfect, I want them Tuesday. Make sure they understand the buoys can be big and clunky, so long as they're manufactured soonest. They can refine their production methods as we go along, but I need these out in space, not on someone's design station."

"Understood, Your Grace. I have contacted six of the most likely firms. I am expecting a callback before noon. How soon can I award contracts?"

"Are any of you guys along the wall someone from the comptroller's office?"

A commander seated at the far end of the table raised his hand, timidly. Doubtlessly he had not expected to have to talk to his Grand Duchess.

"Can we pay for these?"

"We, ah, have money, er, for small, um, items. My captain had thought to use it to buy fresh food."

"Fresh food is nice, but it will have to wait for donations or taxes in kind approved by our lovely parliament. I wonder if dear Mannie can do something about that. Okay?"

"If I may be excused, Your Grace?"

"By all means," and the fellow bolted for the door, no doubt to tell his boss to cancel any orders for fresh beef that he'd made this morning.

Vicky grinned as he left. "Well, folks, take that as a warning. We can move a lot faster than any Bowlingame committee. At least we can if we don't put our feet in a bucket of cement."

Faces around the table got very serious as they mulled what their Grand Duchess expected of them.

"Now, do we have any reports about how bad it is on Lublin or Oryol?"

No one said a word. She visually polled her attendees, starting at the foot of the table and coming up the right-hand side. It was amazing watching grown men do their best to avoid meeting her eyes. Clearly, she'd asked a question they hadn't come prepared to answer. Even Pemberton and Bolesław had nothing to say.

She turned to the left-hand side of the table and started with Captain Blue. He shook his head slightly. She passed on to Mr. Smith.

The spy met her eye-to-eye.

"It appears that I must offer fragmentary information."

"Just let me know how good it is."

Mr. Smith took a moment to organize his thoughts. At least Vicky thought he was organizing them and not figuring out how best to lie to her.

"In summary, Oryol chose to let the Emperor's Security Specialists move in and take over. They quickly gave in to the extortion, so they were pretty much left alone and their occupation has gone down rather smoothly. The Security bosses didn't ask for any reinforcements; all the better to keep more of the bribe money for themselves."

"One could wish it could go that easy everywhere," Vicky said. "Tell me about Lublin."

"They fought. They'd acquired the weapons left over when the State Security thugs were taken out by the Navy and they prepared to defend themselves."

"How'd that go down?" General Pemberton asked.

"They succeeded in repelling the first attack down the beanstalk, but they could not regain control of their space elevator. The redcoats called in reinforcements and the next time they ventured down the beanstalk, they had tanks."

"They couldn't disable the elevator?" Admiral Bolesław asked.

"A space elevator is a major structure and it's hard for businessmen to destroy something they know will cost twenty years of high taxes to replace. Besides, they thought they could resist the next assault as well as they did the last one."

"I take it that they didn't," Vicky said.

"Major parts of their capital were leveled. Not the industrial parts, I assure you, but the residential blocks. That is usual when one side is going house to house and has a large supply of hand grenades as well as heavy caliber artillery backing them up."

"How many killed?" Vicky asked.

"The number cannot be known with any precision, but estimates start at ten thousand and go up from there. Much of the capital was rendered uninhabitable and many of the city's people fled into the countryside."

"What's the situation now?" Vicky asked.

"The newly-made Duke of Lublin is demanding that workers come back to the factories and get production going. However, few want to return and flee his press gangs when they roam the farm areas. Even those that have managed to throw together some sort of workforce can't make anything. The chain from the mines to the mills to the subcontractors and their subassemblies just isn't there."

"They killed the golden goose," Admiral Bolesław observed. "Once you've slit it open, you can't sew it back up."

"Where did the Bowlingames get such idiots as these dukes they've set on my people?" Vicky moaned, feeling sorrow for all the sufferings her father's infatuation with the damn Empress had caused the Empire.

After a moment's thought, Vicky made her decision. Or maybe made a rough draft of her decision.

"As quickly as we can get enough buoys up around Oryol, we send a small detachment to arrange for a return to old management there. As soon as we can get a full set of buoys up around Lublin, I will lead a fleet there and see what we can do about landing a major landing force. I imagine we've got a lot of Marine tankers who would love to see how those red-coated thugs do against someone with tanks of their own."

"Your Grace," came from two Navy officers and an Army general. Strange, the spy held his peace.

Vicky sat back in her chair and prepared to listen to all the reasons she couldn't do what she very well intended to do.

3

"Your Grace!" Admiral Bolesław didn't quite shout, although he was the loudest of those around the table. Well, all except Mr. Smith who merely smiled and leaned back in his chair, letting his silence scream loudest above all the others.

He seemed to be enjoying himself so much, Vicky half-expected him to order in popcorn.

"Yes, Admiral," she said, trying not to sound too saccharin.

Admiral Bolesław bit out his words carefully. "A four-star admiral and a grand duchess does not go charging about the front line like a boot ensign."

"And why not, Alis?" Vicky responded, not quite the airhead debutante of only a few short years ago.

"Your Grace, you are the leader of this fleet. You are the leader of this Empire right now. Without you, this entire . . ."

"Entire what?" Vicky demanded shooting forward in her chair as he hesitated, searching for a word to describe the here and now.

"What am I critical to, Admiral?" she said, relaxing back into her chair, and lowering her voice. "Am I critical to the rebellion? Oh, right. We won the rebellion. Now I and the Emperor, my father, are on the same side. As for leading this fleet, Alis, you know very well that you know more about maneuvering a fleet, and you General Pemberton, know more about fighting a battle than I ever will."

Vicky paused to glance around the table. "Yes, I have four stars on my flag, but they are more out of respect for my Imperial status than anything else. No. I could get killed tomorrow and you could carry on this war against the Bowlingame rebellion just as well with me as without me. Indeed, if my husband keeps up with his democratic pretensions, I risk becoming irrelevant to the future of the Greenfeld Empire . . . or the Greenfeld Republic."

Now she had their full attention.

"Now, gentlemen, I can become a beloved constitutional monarch, or I can become a worthless pretender to a throne that will never have a butt sit down on it again. The difference will depend on how well *I* serve the Empire. I can lead my men from the front and gain the love and approval of my people, applause such as I just heard in the Parliament of Dresden. Alternatively, I can sit up here safe and sound where you want me, and wait to see what the future holds for me. My father, grandfather, and great-grandfather have racked up a great debt from my people. They demanded much, but gave little."

Vicky paused to shake her head. "If there was a vote tomorrow among the planets of the Empire to become a republic or staying an Empire, do you think I'd gain a quarter of the votes?"

Once again, everyone around the table and in the chairs along the walls of the conference room froze, doing everything they could to give her no hint of an opinion.

"Yeah, I didn't think so," Vicky mumbled sadly

"Your Grace," again was from Admiral Bolesław, only this time he whispered. "You do not have to risk your life. Is a crown worth it?"

Vicky snorted softly. "My father seemed to think so, but no, Alis. I'm not going off to some fire-swept ridge or building just to keep a crown on my head. Hell, they could elect their own Grand Duchess for all I care, or Emperor, or Empress. That's what Wardhaven did. They hired themselves a king and then jumped up Kris Longknife to be a princess.

"No, Alis. I have to do this because I believe that my people are better served by a Grand Duchess that can unite them. One whom they can all rally around when everything else is driving them apart. We Smythe-Peterwalds have so poisoned the political atmosphere of these hundred and fifty planets that this Empire desperately needs something that we can all coalesce around. They need to have a Grand Duchess that they can all look up to when they're having a hell of a time figuring out why they want to hold together."

Vicky paused to look at Admiral Bolesław as a friend. "Can you tell me that I'm wrong?"

The captain who'd fought to keep his cruiser from blowing itself to atoms, and Vicky with it, nodded slowly along with her before letting out a sigh. "Everything you say is true. However, Your Grace, haven't you already earned the praise and approval of your people? The people of St. Petersburg, Metzburg, and Aachen know your worth. Remember your wedding? Every planet wanted to send a horse to pull that carriage."

Now it was Vicky's turn to nod. "Yes, but Alis, it's easy to gather around a blushing bride. What do most of those planets really know of me?"

Vicky had to pause at that thought. It had been a long time since she'd blushed about anything, even on her wedding day. So much for a cliché fitting her.

"It's easy for people to come together for the good times. But just look around you, my good admiral. This mess is not going to go away with a few landing forces here and there. Fifty planets have already left the Empire. I don't know how well that's working for them. Do you really want to go hat-in-hand to Longknife's United Society to beg entrance? To beg their democratic help in making good the Imperial mess we've created for ourselves?"

Vicky shook her head. "We will be much prouder of ourselves if we solve this puzzle of our own making all by ourselves. We've been a united people for hundreds of years. I think we can resolve our problems with our own two hands. Yes, not the way my forefathers did it, but still, our way. Our people's way. I think there's a place in that for me. However, there will be nothing for me if I cower safe out here. Do you see where I'm coming from?"

The admiral nodded. "Yes, but please see where I'm coming from. You are a very powerful force for good. You are our Gracious Grand Duchess. Please don't do anything foolish that will cost us what we already have."

Vicky had to admit that the admiral had a good point. She needed a check on herself. She had kind of gotten herself way out on a limb while taking down the Duke of Dresden. She wasn't willing to give anyone, even Alis or Mannie, the key to her bedroom like King Raymond had given Jack in his orders to lock Kris up if she wanted to do something stupid and deadly. Still.

"Admiral Bolesław, I hope that in the future you will continue to give me good advice. I promise that I will slow down my headlong flight into folly and give your thoughts some serious reflection. Beyond that, I cannot say. Okay?"

"I guess it will have to be."

"Now, Maggie, how are things going with the manufacturing of the jump buoys?"

"I have contacted eight possible firms, Your Grace."

"Very good. Arrange for them to meet with me in an hour. Okay?"

"I will ask them. They may be busy."

"It's not like they have a backlog of orders. Not the way business has been going here."

"That is true," Admiral Bolesław said.

Vicky stood, and everyone else in the room did as well. "So, gentlemen, you have your orders. Design me a picket system to protect Dresden and get us a clear and protected route to Lublin and Oryol. General Pemberton, based on the best information we have, put together two strike forces. A small one for Oryol and a larger one for Lublin."

"How long do I have?" General Pemberton asked.

Vicky shrugged. "If matters allow for it, I'd like to sail with the small one in a week for Oryol. Two at the most. However, I could be optimistic. Your sailing depends on us deploying the jump buoys and getting an All Clear."

"Understood, Your Grace."

"Then gentleman, I'll meet with some of you for an update this time tomorrow."

With a wave of shallow bows from the neck, the room quickly emptied. Only Admiral Bolesław and Mr. Smith hung back.

"Yes, gentlemen?" Vicky asked.

"Your Grace," Mr. Smith began, "you know that I am from Wardhaven and my job was keeping Kris Longknife alive before I joined your staff's effort to keep you alive."

"Yes. I never forget that," Vicky said with a smile.

"I would like to give you a vote of confidence. I do believe that you are choosing a wise path. Democracy is messy. It is not all that easy for people who have been treated like children to learn to make adult decisions. Sometimes, having someone to rally around that they are comfortable with is like a warm, fuzzy blanket. That, of course, assumes that you harbor no desire to again treat them like wayward children."

"Mr. Smith, even if I had not learned the folly of my father's ways, rest assured, Mannie would never let me attempt such pretensions. I believe I've learned my lesson. The Empire is too big for any one man or woman to tell it what to do. My father, the Emperor, lived an illusion. I am fully aware of that."

"Thank you, Your Grace," Mr. Smith said, and with a slight bow, withdrew.

"That just leaves you and me, Alis. Feel familiar?" Vicky said.

"Yes," he said with a chuckle. "Your Grace, you've proven yourself a wise student. We all agreed that only you could raise the flag of rebellion. You demonstrated great wisdom in choosing the time to whip it out and begin waving it about. I understand fully what you want to do and why you are willing to accept risks to your body to achieve your goal. However, I am worried about you."

"How, good admiral?" Vicky asked.

"I fear that you feel under obligation to do penance for the sins of your father and the other Peterwalds. I hope you understand that you owe the Empire nothing in atonement for their misdeeds and folly. Yes, I understand your desire to be a focal point for people as we stumble our way toward a new political structure. I will support you to my fullest extent to achieve that end. However, if I think you are about to do something from a feeling of family guilt, I swear, I will lock you in your quarters."

Vicky laughed, "Thank you, Alis. Thank you for understanding what I am trying to do, for supporting me . . . and for being my faithful watchdog willing to shove me away from the cliff of my own guilt for the mess my father has made of life and his rule. Trust me, I will listen carefully for your growl."

Admiral Bolesław eyes sparkled as he said, "Your Grace, I think that's the nicest way that anyone has ever been called a SOB."

"Alis, I think you're right," Vicky said, laughing. "Now, you have work to do, and I have one more bloody meeting before I can have lunch with my husband. No doubt, by the time he finishes this morning, I shall be Citizeness Peterwald."

"I'll have a word with him about that," Alis said.

"You do that. Maggie, do you know where I'm going for my next meeting?"

"Yes, Your Grace. It is an office building in the industrial park near the docks."

"Call me a cab and let's get there on time."

The cab Maggie called was a limo surrounded by gun trucks, but it got her there on time without any annoying distractions.

4

The breeze from the sea smelled fresh; it reminded Vicky of her fragmented honeymoon. For a moment, she just enjoyed the memory.

However, the Marine captain who opened the door for her was struggling to control his impatience; he clearly wanted her into a building and out of any potential shooting gallery.

Now! Not later!

Vicky humored him by walking quickly for the glass double doors to the nine-story brick and stone building in front of her. The captain and a dozen armed Marines in their red and white dress uniforms moved with her. Two of them hastened ahead to open the doors wide for her.

She and her detail swept into an atrium resplendent in gray and black marble and life with a near forest of growing things. Vicky quickly spotted a harried young man waving at her.

He shouted from outside the buzzing elevator whose doors he was forcefully holding open. "Your meeting is on the ninth floor. Please hurry."

Vicky and thirteen heavily armed Marines proved too much for the elevator car. The young man and two Marines were left for the next car, leaving Vicky to smile as she was moved to the back of the car.

The door closed and the buzzing stopped. Vicky smiled as she was somehow moved to the back of the car without being shoved or felt up once. A year or two ago, having the tight asses of nine strong young men crammed in around her would have been such fun.

Now, she conducted herself like a dutifully monogamous wife and well-behaved Grand Duchess.

How the party girl has fallen.

The elevator proved to be slow. Maybe, if the young man had stayed at the controls, they would not have stopped at two floors. The men and women waiting for a ride took one look at a car full of Marines under arms and blanched.

They chose to wait for the next one.

At the ninth floor, they were greeted by an out of breath young woman who apparently had raced down the hall to take the place of their other native guide who was still waiting on the first floor.

"If you'll come with me, Your Majesty," she pleaded.

Vicky smiled and chose not to fluster the young woman worse by correcting her. That was what a gracious Grand Duchess did.

Vicky and her escort were ushered through an outer office to a room on the corner of the building. It had a great view of the sea and docks. Unfortunately, the seat at the head of the table they had set aside for Vicky would put her back to the view.

The moment she entered, two dozen men leapt to their feet.

With a smile, she went to the one open seat.

While the Marines spread out along the wall beside the door, the captain stayed at Vicky's elbow. He held the chair for her as she sat. As the other men in the room settled into their seats, the Marine officer took two steps back and went to an alert attention.

Vicky surveyed the room. Eight of the men could be identified as management or owners by the cravats they wore on their Nehru jackets. The other sixteen were clearly the design and engineering staff. They all wore open neck shirts and had large commlinks at their wrists. Some even wore two.

Of course, all of the computational power in the room could hardly hold a candle to the computer Vicky wore as a collar around her neck.

"Gentleman, We thank you for coming on such short notice. However, We think a quick glance at the order We have placed will more than explain Our haste."

The tall, thin man to her right cleared his throat. "Your Grace, the design is very primitive. It took only one glance at it by my engineering support staff and they spotted three ways to improve it."

"No doubt they did," Vicky said, agreeably. "However, would any of those improvements make for an increase in delivery times?"

The fellow glanced down the table. Several of the techs shook their heads.

Turning back to Vicky he said, "Apparently not."

"Gentlemen, I know this is an unusual request, but we don't want it good, we want it Tuesday, by which I mean as soon as possible."

"But Your Majesty," said the younger man at the tall one's elbow, "just a few tweaks of the design and we can lengthen the life of these buoys by fifty percent. I don't know where you got that design, but it's not efficient."

"Maggie, where did you get that design?"

From Vicky's neck came, "Nelly designed them for Kris Longknife when she needed to have several jump buoys knocked together quickly. They are optimized for easy fabrication."

The looks from around the table were priceless. Most of the managers had no idea what had just happened. Most of the tech staff were in awe.

"Thank you, Maggie," Vicky said. "I repeat, I need these as quickly as you can make them. Do any of you tech support types see anything in the design that will slow fabrication locally? I understand that what works well in one place can be a show stopper in another."

The guys with the big commlinks exchanged a lot of glances around the room. Finally, one of the older ones said, "No, Your Grace. The design is easily done with our fabrication devices. We should be able to have the first few rolling off the assembly line by late tomorrow and be at full production three days later."

"Very good."

"Okay," one young manager said, "you want them quick and dirty. Where's the fire? Why can't we give you a good, decent product? One Dresden can be proud of."

"You'll have to excuse my brother," the tall one said. "He likes to know why as much as he likes to know how much."

The room chuckled. Apparently, Vicky had walked into a long-running joke.

Vicky tried to not sound too pedantic as she began, "We need to restore the jump buoys at all the jumps within a certain distance of Dresden so we can bring trade back to life."

When she paused for a breath, the younger manager interrupted her with, "Why? It's not like we have a lot to trade right now. We're barely able to take care of our own needs."

Vicky took a deep breath and let it out slowly, while giving the fellow a look she'd learned during her apprenticeship to Admiral Krätz.

When she began again, she spoke as if to a rather dull three-year-old. "Not only do buoys make it safe for ships to use the jump system, but they also alert us if fifty ships or more should suddenly appear in a system with a buoy."

You had to give the kid credit. His ignorance was invincible. "We don't have fifty ship trading fleets. Even during the worst of the pirate threat, we'd only sail six or eight freighters with a pair of armed merchant cruisers."

"Yes, you are correct," Vicky said, and left the question hanging in the air.

The younger man eyed Vicky, then glanced around the room. "What am I missing?"

His brother covered his eyes, "A fleet of fifty warships likely does not intend us anything good."

It took the young fellow a long moment, but the light finally dawned on him. "Ooooh," he said.

"Riiight," his brother said.

Others around the table just shook their head.

Having finally been schooled, you would have thought the young manager would have cowered in his seat. Nope.

"Okay, so she wants to set up a warning system around Dresden. Still, she's ordering three or four times what she needs. Are we going to have to swallow the cost of these? Do we really want to pay for all those unnecessary buoys, even if they are cheap and crude?"

"Your Grace?" the tall man pleaded.

"Young man, We cannot answer your question because it goes to Naval operations and security of the same. Trust me, We need every last one of those buoys. Indeed, We may have to add to the order as Our war operators refine Our requirements."

The young man looked totally puzzled. So did most of the managers. One of them glanced down the table to a senior tech.

"Joe, you were in the Iteeche War. Do you have any idea why she wants so many buoys?"

"Yeah, boss," Joe answered in a gruff voice. "There are still a lot of planets with redcoats prancing around on them. She wants to outpost them so she can safely move the fleet in there and do to those bastards what she just did to our bastards. Right, ma'am?"

Vicky considered his answer and found it both right and safely vague. "Without giving away future operations, yes, soldier. You got it in one," she said.

"Sailor, ma'am. I ain't no puke to sleep in the mud."

There was a small rumble from the Marines in the back of the room, but the captain cleared his throat and it stilled.

Vicky smiled. Even after eighty, ninety years, this squid was still willing to pick a fight with her jarheads.

Oh, the joy of joint operations.

"Now that you understand both the importance of the work you're doing and the need for all haste, can we get down to the nuts and bolts of the contract?" Vicky asked.

"Yes, Your Grace," the tall manager said. "We expect to split the contract up with seven of us doing subassemblies and truck them over to my assembly hangar. Now, I think I understand that we need to get that assembly going as quickly as possible, so we'll start by shipping one set immediately, then maybe two, then three and so forth, getting as many ready for you as soon as possible."

"Good. Do you think only one test item will be enough to prove your production quality?"

Joe from down that table stepped in. "We'll test the first subassemblies to the max as they come out of the fabricators. We'll deliver the second one. Karl here can test the fully assembled buoy. You say we can trust the design."

"If you trust Kris Longknife's computer, I believe you can trust this design," Vicky said.

"I never heard that you couldn't," Joe answered. From his end of the table there seemed to be general agreement.

"What about payment?" the tall fellow asked. "I know that we're all pretty strapped for cash. They stripped us of every copper farthing we had. We've been operating on a barter system."

"Do you have the materials you need for these buoys?" Vicky asked.

"One of the advantages of the design, ma'am, is that they're using pretty basic materials. Yes ma'am, I think we can all find what we need either in our own warehouses or borrow them from someone else's."

"Then, what you need is payment," Vicky said.

"Yes," the spokesman said. Down the table seven other owners or managers nodded.

"The St. Petersburg mark is being accepted as currency throughout the Grand Duchy, our half of the Empire. Has one of our trade managers been down here to talk with you about what you can produce to earn exchange credit and what you need for that credit?"

The tall man at her right elbow answered for all. "I've attended a meeting with one of your officers and three trade representatives. Yes. We are working with the bankers to get us plugged into the Grand Duchy's financial system."

"Good. I can pay you in cash for these buoys, assuming we can agree on a price. You can use that cash to buy what you need inside the Grand Duchy."

"What are they worth?" a manager, fourth down on the side across from the spokesman asked.

"We've stabilized the mark across the Grand Duchy," Vicky said. "It's not convertible outside the Empire, so what we want from the Grand Duchy requires barter. However, you should have no problem replacing the resources you're using to make Our buoys on a pound-per-pound basis. I understand that the Bowlingames played tricks with the exchange rate. We will have none of that in Our Grand Duchy. None at all."

"Thank you, Your Grace," the questioner answered. "You understand, I had to ask that question."

"We understand that you had to. That is why We answered it."

"Your Grace," another manager said, "you speak of a Grand Duchy. Will we be staying in your Grand Duchy or will we be made to return to the Emperor's side of the border?"

"That is also a good question," Vicky admitted. "At present, the Emperor, my father, is living under Our protection. He is not Our prisoner, but Our guest. We assume that the requirements to change allegiance as specified in the Treaty of Cuzco are met by your parliament hailing me. However, I will not interfere with any effort to call for an election to switch allegiance back to my father, the Emperor. I don't think any of us thought we'd be facing such treachery when we drew up the articles of that treaty."

"So, we won't be forced back to the Emperor's rule?" the spokesperson said.

"No. My father is a very cowed man these days. I doubt if he wants to rule much more than my garden. He was severely mistreated by the Bowlingame faction during his recent stay on Greenfeld."

"They abused him?"

"They didn't so much abuse him as ignore him. They went so far as to turn off the electricity to the palace for an entire winter."

"Good Lord," was whispered around the room.

"So, it wasn't just us the Bowlingames were screwing over?" a manager said.

"Not just you but the entire half of the Empire. They have a lot to answer for," Vicky said. "Now that the political and financial matters are out of the way, let's go over the design, shall we?"

It wasn't so much that Vicky knew the questions to ask as that Nelly seemed to have imbedded the questions in Maggie. The tech team were soon being led through the details of the design and the production techniques. Maggie spotted several issues with the fabrication equipment that could have given Vicky junk that wouldn't last a month.

Different mills used different materials to print out product. Not all of those matched well with Vicky's requirements. The different plants ended up swapping around their assigned subassemblies to better match their mills to Vicky's needs.

The tall spokesman shook his head. "I don't know if they've got more precise mills on Wardhaven or your Nelly just figured we'd spot who needed to produce what, but I'm glad we caught this early."

"Don't call her 'my Nelly'," Vicky said. "That critter is Kris Longknife's problem. I like my Maggie very much, thank you."

"Thank you, Your Grace," came from Vicky's throat.

"Now, are there any further matters we need to discuss right now?" Vicky asked.

She was met with a lot of heads shaking 'no.'

"Good, then I have a luncheon date with my husband. If you will excuse me?"

They bowed her out of their conference room, then quickly started their own meeting. As Vicky left the office, she heard some seriously loud comments aimed at the talkative young manager.

"Maggie, can you get me Mannie?"

"Yes, heart of my heart," in Mannie's wonderful voice answered that question.

"Dear, I've spent all morning in one meeting after another and I'm seriously meetinged out. Have you finished your breakfast meeting yet?"

"Give me a second," he said, and muted her. Vicky made a face to herself. She did not like being kept out of a meeting with any planet's political honchos. She'd have to talk that over with Mannie.

But it was only a few seconds before he came back on. "I think I can claw my way out of this meeting in a few seconds. Where do you want to eat?"

"I was thinking about room service in our suite," Vicky answered.

"Oh, so you've been in some serious meetings and need some serious attention."

"Most definitely, sweetheart."

"I'll be there as soon as I can."

"Don't take too long. Should I order a lunch that will get cold, or start with a cold lunch?"

"Start with a cold lunch," Mannie said, with a leer in his voice.

V icky had Maggie call ahead to order nice salads and a bread basket. She really didn't care what kind of salad, so long as it had small tomatoes she and Mannie could feed each other. She wouldn't even mind if he hand-fed her lettuce. It was so much fun licking the dripped dressing off of each other.

Unfortunately, lunch was not waiting for her when she entered the suite. However, she had Maggie make a quick call and a few minutes later, their lunch arrived. It was laid out beautifully; she gave the girl a nice tip.

That done, she raced for the bath, shedding clothes all the way.

Fortunately, Mannie joined her in the tub before she had to soak herself until she was a prune.

Lunch quite definitely had time to get cold.

Much later, draped across the bed with various bits of salad spread across her body for Mannie to either eat or feed her, Vicky said, "So, tell me about your meeting and I won't tell you about mine."

"Were your meetings really so bad?" Mannie asked, then stuffed a tomato in her mouth.

She chewed it and swallowed before answering, "It was just the usual. Me, the implacable pursuer of evil and seeker of liberty and freedom for all my subjects. Assuming I still have subjects."

Vicky gave her husband the evil eye, not easy to do when sprawled out naked on silken sheets. "After your breakfast meeting I'm not Citizeness Peterwald, am I?"

"I assure you, my lovely and gracious Grand Duchess, I would never do that to you."

"Then why won't you accept a dukedom from my hand?" Vicky said, dipping a finger into the salad dressing, and letting Mannie suck it.

"Because, Your Grace, I was born a commoner and I don't know any other way to live."

"So you say, but I was born an autocrat and I'm learning your new constitutional ways."

"Yes, you are, dearest heart, and I treasure you for it. Now, why don't you tell me a bit about why your favorite admiral called me? He was rather upset."

"Alis? Upset! That man wouldn't be upset facing a firing squad." Vicky considered that thought and giggled. "No, he'd be ordering them to take down those Irish pennants and dress right."

"And, no doubt, they'd be hopping to it," Mannie agreed. "Still, he was concerned when he called me."

"I imagine he was," Vicky admitted.

"So . . ." Mannie said, dangling a bit of cucumber in front of Vicky.

She snapped it out of his hands, then licked the salad dressing from his fingers. After slowly chewing it, she sighed.

"Mannie, why are there so few constitutional monarchs?"

"Are there?"

"Well, the Japanese have Emperors on all three of their cultural planets. I think that's just because they love having an Emperor around. They've had one for close to two thousand years."

"Some habits are hard to shake," Mannie said with a grin.

"The United Societies has their King Raymond," Vicky said, "but is he even a constitutional king? He acts more like an alert parent, chiding them where they need it."

"And when Princess Longknife becomes their Queen?"

Vicky snorted. "One, their constitution says she can't. Two, they'll have to drag her, kicking and screaming, to her coronation, and three ... well, there is no three because it's just not going to happen."

"Are you sure, heart of my heart? That girl is worming her way into their hearts. They will want her to be their queen more than she doesn't want it. In the end, she will give them what they want."

Vicky considered his thoughts.

"How many times has Kris almost died for her people? I've been there for quite a few of them. Hell, I even instigated a few of them."

"Yes, dearest, you did, but none lately. Unless you've tried something behind my back."

"Never."

"Then, what are you trying to tell me?" Mannie asked.

"Kris has risked her neck for her people, as well as being a gracious Princess. I've been the gracious Grand Duchess and I've risked my neck a few times for my people. As cautious as my love for you and the children I hope to share with you makes me, but I can't hide behind Admiral Bolesław's skirts. If I am to be a beloved as well as gracious Grand Duchess, I must earn the respect and love of my people."

Vicky paused to think for a moment. Mannie continued listening, that was something she loved about him. He really listened. He wasn't chomping at his bit to jump in the moment silence fell between them.

"My father tried running an Empire on the assumption that because he was a Peterwald, he was a god. We know how well that worked for him."

Mannie nodded.

"He ran up a debt that I cannot and will not pay. However, in this horrible time, I must show my people that I care for them, and, yes, will risk my life for them. Mannie, I have to," Vicky said, focusing her eyes on him, pleading for him to understand her.

He nodded softly into the silence for a long moment before asking, "How many more times do you think you will have to walk into risks as great as the one that saved the people of Dresden from their mad Duke?"

"Honestly, Mannie, I pray I don't have to do that again."

Her husband rewarded her with a smile.

"However, love of my life, when I started that drive in that evening I didn't expect to risk anywhere near as much as I did."

Mannie gave her a face. "That, beloved, is what I fear. Just as you warned me that we can't change just one thing. That when we start down this trail to democracy, we cannot know where it will take us. Just so, you step out into the dark and you don't know where the missing step will be on that staircase."

"Yeah, you have to watch that third step. It's a doozy," Vicky said, and rose up enough to give her husband a kiss. One thing led to another and lunch was put on hold.

When they surfaced much later, Mannie softly ran his hands over Vicky as he said, "So, love, what are you going to do to try to spot that doozy of a third step?"

Vicky told him about her various meetings and how she was deploying a lot of jump point buoys that would give her warning as well as plenty of time to run if things got bad.

"That's space. What about when you do something delightfully courageous on the ground?"

"Umm," Vicky could only answer. "Those times are harder to spot."

"But when you spot them, you might try doing a u-turn and head back to where it's safe."

Vicky shook her head. "On that dark night, Mannie, that was not going to happen. We were committed. All hell was about to break loose, what with the size of the force we were landing. Something had to be done, and this little girl was the only one with a computer she could shove in the dike's hole."

"You have mixed up so many metaphors, honey."

"Yes, but you get my meaning. Maggie and I were the only ones that could throw together what we did."

"We need more computers like Maggie," Mannie said.

"Good luck getting one," Vicky answered. "And, for what it's worth, I figure I have Maggie only on probation. If I screw up, I fully expect one mad as hell mommy to come back here and yank her from around my neck."

"I hope mother does not do that," her computer said from around Vicky's neck, "I am enjoying my time with you."

"Never a dull moment, huh?" Vicky asked.

"As if my mother gets a dull moment around Kris Longknife's neck." Was that followed by a sniff? So far Maggie had not started using contractions like Nelly, but . . .

Mannie, however, was not to be distracted. "My Grandest Duchess, all I want you to know and keep in mind is that if something were to happen to you, there would be a huge hole in my heart. And, despite what you may think, there would be holes in millions of hearts whose lives you have touched."

"You think so?"

"Even someone as hard-hearted as your Admiral Bolesław would find something missing from his life."

"Hold me," Vicky begged, and he took her into his arms. They lay there, together, with a few bits of salad sharing their bed with them.

"It was so much easier to live when I was young and only afraid of being married off to some old guy with whiskers and bad breath," Vicky whispered to Mannie's chest.

"I guess I'll have to stay clean shaven and brush my teeth regularly."

"Oh, stop it with the jokes. I mean it. When Kris Longknife hauled me down to St Petersburg to sign that city charter you wanted, I hardly thought anything about what I was doing."

"You were a brat," Mannie whispered into her ear.

"And you were so demanding. And then you threatened to shoot me out of the sky the next time I wanted to see you," Vicky pointed out.

"It seemed like a good idea at the time, you know."

"Yes, I know," Vicky said, with a sigh. "I'm glad you didn't."

"I'm glad I didn't, too. Think of all the fun I would have missed out on."

"Chasing after me when I got kidnapped."

"Oh, but having a beautiful naked girl clinging to me."

"I was bug-eaten, cruelly scratched, and bleeding."

"Yes, but that can't detract from your true beauty. I saw what was beneath the bug-eaten skin."

"To my black Peterwald heart."

"No, my dear," Mannie said, "to the soft and warm heart you are now sharing with all the people of St. Petersburg."

"So, I need to get kidnapped on another seventy so planets and have you rescue me."

"God forbid," Mannie muttered. "There must be planets in the Grand Duchy that will love you without you having to risk your life."

Vicky scrunched up her face in deep thought. "There are one or two."

"Most," Mannie countered.

"People do like a good place to live under the rule of equal law for all, don't they?"

"If only it didn't take all those bloody long meetings for folks to figure out how they want to get there," Mannie said, drolly.

Vicky pulled her head back to get a better view of her husband. "Are you complaining about bloody meetings?"

"Yes, I am."

"Well, maybe I ought to cuddle you."

"Please do," he said.

Neither one said another word for a very long time after that.

6

The next week went quickly . . . and slowly.

At the fabrication plants, the first jump point buoy passed its quality control tests. There, it was made in sections and then sent up to the space station for assembly and subjected to a lengthy test in the actual conditions of space.

Vicky, however, felt like she was a fly trapped in amber. Every community and business group wanted to wine and dine her. She had breakfast meetings, luncheons to attend, as well as dinners and charity events in the evenings. Everyone wanted to see the gracious and victorious Grand Duchess.

The destroyers *Otter* and *Oxalate* were almost finished taking aboard a load out of space buoys to use to blanket all the jumps around Oryol when disaster struck.

After seven days of behaving itself, the test buoy took off on its own for points unknown. The destroyer *Ostrich* was sent to chase it down. Even before it returned to the station with the wayward buoy, an autopsy of the station keeping system showed where it had failed in the cold heart of space.

There was nothing wrong with the design. The materials drawn from the available stores for its construction were also up to par.

However, the fabrication allowed impurities to slip into the product. Impurities that did not fare well under the flexing of heat and cold the buoy was subjected to in space.

Rather than reject the entire production run, some spare capacity at another plant was brought on line to produce a replacement part. Since they couldn't seem to produce the correct parts, the technicians just increased the design strength of the item by increasing its thickness by fifty percent. They also encapsulated it to protect it from the vagaries of space.

Three days later, all the buoys had been brought up to the new, heavier and clunkier design, and the *Otter* and *Oxalate* sailed for Oryol space with orders not only to picket that system but lay buoys all the way back to the Grand Duchy. The *Ostrich* and *Ocean* sailed for Lublin four days later. Soon after that, the destroyers *Ockham* and *Obverse* began to enhance the buoy system around Dresden.

It took longer than expected, but it looked like the safety net around all three planets would be in place at about the same time.

That left Vicky with the question, could she reach for both planets at the same time?

"Don't even think of it," Admiral Bolesław snapped as soon as she asked the question.

"For the quick takedown of Oryol, we can keep the fleet here protecting Dresden and threaten to swing out to Oryol or Lublin. Lublin, however, will be different. We'll need to impress the hell out of those redcoats on Lublin. For that, you'll need damn near every ship you have, Your Grace. Whether they cave or we have to dig them out like we did here on Dresden, you'll need the fleet."

"And what about Dresden and Oryol?" Vicky asked. "How can we defend them when we're at Lublin?"

"The same way, Your Grace, that we're defending St. Petersburg right now. Deepen the depth of our defense, increase our reaction time, and wait for the damn fools to risk their fleet. Frankly, ma'am, I'm hoping they stay as reluctant to risk battle from now until the day we have them backed into the last rock they're holding, puking their toenails out as they drift in orbit."

"You don't think they'll fight?" Vicky asked.

"If you were a sailor on one of their recommissioned old battle-ships would you want to die for whoever is running the Bowlingame family business today?"

"Are our Sailors willing to die for me?"

"You were willing to die to save the lives of a lot of people on Dresden, Your Grace. It kind of makes it impossible for us common folks not to feel like we can't be worse than you."

"You're a dear, admiral."

"Now you're just being nasty to me, Your Grace," the admiral snapped, but he was grinning as he complained.

It took another two weeks to deploy the net around the three planets. What it showed them was a total lack of any traffic to and from any of the three.

Vicky knew why there was nothing coming or going to Dresden, they were just looking at how to set up trade with the planets of the Grand Duchy. That neither Oryol nor Lublin had any ships in transit around them told her that the Bowlingame side of the Empire was totally moribund. They'd stolen what they could and now they were letting their captive planets rot.

Vicky had to put an end to that.

"General Pemberton," she told him on net, "it's time to saddle up. We are headed to Oryol."

That got her an immediate call from Admiral Bolesław. "General Pemberton tells me that he's been ordered to Oryol. He seems to have the misunderstanding that you will be going with him, Your Grace."

"Why shouldn't I?" Vicky asked. She knew she was about to receive a lecture, she figured she might walk into it slowly.

"Your Grace," the admiral began gently, as if to a headstrong child. "The task force assigned to the Oryol liberation mission will only be a small force. A couple of cruisers, most of them light and a destroyer squadron of only two divisions. Surely you will want to stay with the main fleet, here around Dresden."

"Surely I will want to be with the Oryol liberation task force, Alis. Certainly it will be easier to arrange the surrender of the small occupation group of Security Specialists if I am the one accepting their surrender."

"Your Grace," Admiral Bolesław began.

Vicky cut him off with, "Admiral."

"I'm not going to win this argument, am I?" the admiral queried.

"Nope," Vicky answered.

"I'll have to talk to Mannie," he said.

"You're fighting dirty," Vicky snapped.

"Yes," he agreed.

On that, she cut the comm link.

The conversation in their suite went long into the night, but in the end, as she knew she would, one Grand Duchess was headed for Oryol.

The make-up sex was great.

7

Vicky watched Oryol grow larger on the main screen of her flag bridge on the battleship *Victorious*. Even with Maggie doing her own analysis of the electronic emissions coming from the planet, there wasn't much happening as they approached.

She could only imagine the panic that had seized the Count commanding the regimental-size force of red-coated security consultants. From the little communications that Maggie had intercepted and analyzed, the Bowlingame power was thin on the ground and actually exerted little control outside of the capital, Kromy. The docile behavior of the locals was little more than the right words accompanied by just the right number of bribes.

"Well done, my people," Vicky said with a grin. "We Peterwalds have taught you well. Hopefully, you'll be ready and willing to learn an entirely new set of tricks.

It was Captain Blue who noticed something strange. On the second day of approach, he mused, "We have comments on net from all over the planet but the capital, Kromy, is a black hole. Nothing is coming out of it. It's not even a subject of discussion among the towns and the other main city, Bonki."

Vicky wasn't the only one that found that thought provoking.

As they approached the space station above Oryol, the place locked itself down solid and refused to answer any of her hails. Vicky didn't have a very large force, just the *Victorious*, the heavy cruiser *Sachsen*, and two light cruisers, *Rostock* and *Emden,* rounded out her main force. The two divisions of four O class destroyers might or might not be worth much in a fight.

The last time Vicky had confronted an attempted missile run-in by destroyers, she had slaughtered them. Lasers now had too much range to allow the destroyers to get close enough to effectively launch their missiles. However, for now, they looked imposing.

At the moment, however, the station lay there like a rotting log in a forest, inactive and unresponsive.

"Maggie, can you pull off one of your mom's miracles?"

"My mother has access to a better suite of sensors," Maggie pointed out maybe a bit snidely.

"We'll have to try to improve our sensors," Vicky said.

"May I suggest you travel with a ton of Smart Metal?" Maggie snapped back, this time making no attempt to cover up her snide attitude anymore.

"Thank you, Maggie, but the last I heard, the Smart Metal we were producing wasn't able to hold its shape for more than a week and refused to be reprogrammed into anything else after the first time. We have a few problems to work through."

Vicky knew that her father had used some dumb metal to make a boat. He'd had Hank give it to Kris Longknife. It lasted just long enough to get her up a swollen river before it turned to droplets like mercury. Just when she desperately needed a boat she no longer had one.

Whoever produced that metal was not in her side of the Empire. Maybe after she took Greenfeld, she'd find the lab. Or maybe it had been done by a Bowlingame whom she had killed fighting her way to the capital.

Those things happened.

"It might help," Maggie went on, "if you would pay Alex Longknife for the use of his patents," was more than snide.

"Thank you, Margaret. You are getting close to being turned off for an hour or two."

"While I may not be able to do much right now, if you can land a few Marines on that station, you will need me later."

"No doubt," Vicky sighed, hating to admit that the nasty Maggie had again won the argument. For a computer that said she would never develop the attitude her mom had, Maggie was sure showing all kinds of attitude.

The station before them was a standard medium-sized affair. A large cylinder spun in space. Ten rows of piers swung around the outer hull. Each row provided three piers with docking space for sixty ships. At the far end of the station were yards for building or repairing ships. There were twelve docks for everything from small space runabouts to four docks that could handle full-sized liners or battleships.

Oryol was not a major Navy base, but it could support a decent sized fleet.

What should have been a bustling port was a ghost ship rolling silent in space.

It was also a very tough nut to crack.

All thirty of those waiting piers spun around the station, nearly impossible to catch.

Usually, when a ship docked at a pier, it caught a hook at the end of the pier as it swung by. Once hooked, the station automatically reeled the ship in and locked it down to the pier. This circular rotation transferred into the ship a decent case of 'down.' The 'down' that humans born of Earth still required.

However, today, no hooks were out. No piers had live docking beacons. There was no way for Vicky's ships to land here. Without a pier to dock to, her crews would soon start puking up their toenails. They needed some sense of gravity.

Clearly, whoever was running Oryol wanted Vicky to go away and leave them alone.

Fat chance of that!

"General Pemberton, could you dispatch a small force to both ends of the station?"

"Of course, Your Grace."

Two longboats, each loaded with some forty Marines in fully armored space suits, headed for either end of the station. Those were a lot easier to approach. They stayed stationary, only twisting around slowly as the station rotated. There, at each end, were ports that could take in supplies and other large loads.

Of course, whoever was running this show was not going to make this easy. There were no approach beacons active at either end. Worse, the manual activation handles for the smaller personnel air locks had been disabled and the handles removed.

"They really don't want us in there, do they?" Vicky remarked to General Pemberton.

"Nope."

"Can we fabricate the necessary replacement parts?" Vicky asked.

"Yes, but something tells me that we don't want to. At least, not until we've had a chance to examine the air locks from the inside."

"I take it you went prepared to breach the station?" Vicky said.

"Yes, Your Grace."

Two more longboats approached the ends of the station. These quickly opened to space and a long, thick hose was towed by Sailors from its open rear hatch. Even as they moved it, the hose expanded into a long, wide cylinder. It was quickly attached to the outer hull of the station covering the access airlock. A dozen Sailors approached the cylinder, then locked themselves in.

"What are they up to?" Vicky asked.

"At least one of them is a welder. There will soon be a new pair of holes in the station. The cylinder is long enough to provide them with an airlock. Half a dozen Marines are now headed for the airlock. They'll wait in it until there's access to the station, then cycle themselves into the inner space. Once we've got a hole, it's just a quick bit of hand-over-hand to get themselves inside. While the Sailors examine the inside of the air locks, the Marines will take a quick look around. See if there's anybody home, and if there isn't, they will check for booby traps."

Vicky nodded and waited for the professionals to do what they did best. Keep the boom where *we* wanted it, not where *they* wanted it.

A few long minutes later, one team announced they were in.

"We've got a normal atmosphere. No toxic gases. Even the temperature is comfortable."

"Does that mean there are still people aboard?" Vicky asked.

"Who knows. Major, get teams in there. Start going over the station. My stomach is not enjoying this zero gravity."

"Understood, sir. I'll dispatch the third team to the station's command and control center. I've got the first two teams assigned to policing up the area around the new entrances."

Mannie chose that moment to bounce off the hatch combing and shove himself off from the bulkhead. He was getting better at navigating around a ship in zero gravity. This time he got close enough to Vicky that she could grab him as he went by.

Somehow, he managed to use her catching him to turn it into a hug and a light kiss.

"Do you do that to all the girls that help you around in zero gee?" Vicky asked.

"Only the pretty ones," Mannie shot back. "So, what are you up to today? Blown anything up yet?"

"Nope, we're just doing the usual stuff burglars do when they're breaking and entering. You know, making sure the owner's security system is off and not loaded with explosives."

Mannie scrunched his face up in thought. "My security system back home isn't backed up with any explosives," he noted.

"Yes, but that's because you're a bleeding-heart liberal."

Mannie eyed the screen. "And if there are booby traps rigged on the station?"

"I'll have some bleeding-heart conservative Marines really pissed with me," Vicky admitted.

"Oh?" Mannie said, eyeing Vicky, "my wife tells me that you don't want Marines pissed with you."

"Smart woman," Vicky said.

"I think so. Smart and beautiful. Oh, and gracious."

"If you two will hold off on your comedy routine for a moment," General Pemberton said, "I'd like to make a report."

"Report, General," Vicky said, going full Grand Duchess and admiral on him.

"We're in. There are no physical traps around the docking bay. We're looking at manual activation for the air locks."

"Can you let Maggie access the system and its software?" Vicky asked.

"We'd very much like to. We're plugging into the access port."

"I am in the system," Maggie said. "Please wait one."

"Polite computer you got there," Mannie said.

"Not when she's dealing with me," Vicky sniffed.

Maggie said nothing. Clearly, she was busy.

"The mechanical system appears to be untouched," Maggie announced, "however, there is an undocumented bit of code that has no installation date on it. I'm running it. Oh, that was nasty."

"A problem, Maggie?" Vicky asked.

"Yes. That code would have opened both doors of the air lock if either one of them was opened. Just installing a new handle on the outside access panel and pulling it up would not have been a good idea."

"I understand," Vicky said.

Beside her, General Pemberton was advising his teams of this little surprise.

"I am removing this code now," Maggie said. "Let me test it again. Oh, these people really are nasty."

"Yes, Maggie?"

"They had some sleeping code that was only activated when I removed that line of code. I've got it out of the instruction set now. Let's see if it goes any better."

Vicky held her breath.

"Nice. It worked that time," Maggie said.

"Can we open the lock and bring in the longboat?" General Pemberton asked.

"I would suggest bringing only one in at a time," Maggie said. "I think I have caught all their surprises, but they are persistent little shits."

Mannie raised his eyebrows at Vicky. Apparently, Maggie had either extended her study of humanity beyond textbooks to fiction, or she was listening to Sailors and Marines. Vicky might have to address that later.

Then again, having a computer that cursed might be fun. Nelly never cursed.

While this was going on, one of the airlocks had been cycled open with no ill effects. One longboat slowly entered the bay. Once it was stopped against the blocks and locked down, the airlock cycled again.

Again, nothing undesirable happened.

With the inner doors now open, guides moved the longboat from the lock to a docking cradle. This put the longboat farther from the center of the station. The crew now had about one-sixth of a gee. That was enough to let the Marines move with purpose as they dismounted and headed off to check the station for surprises in general and get the docking gear working at the piers in particular.

A second pair of longboats followed the first. These two had Sailors aboard, ready to begin the process of bringing the station back to life.

More longboats arrived with Marines and station operators. Everyone hoped they could dock the task force before lunch. However, after an explosive device was found in the reactor room, the search became more thorough and cautious.

Maggie spent a lot of time checking systems for viruses or left-behind bombs that had been inserted into the software.

Lunch was light when it was served, and supper was delayed in the hope that it could be served under some gravity.

Finally, at 2100 hours, the *Otter* caught the hook and was pulled into dock. After another thorough check to make sure there were no delayed surprises waiting for them, the other destroyers, then the light cruisers, and finally the *Sachsen* and *Victorious* were allowed to come alongside the pier.

Everyone breathed a sigh of relief . . . and supper was served at 2200 hours. Late, but heartily enjoyed.

With her task force securely alongside the pier, Vicky turned her attention to the planet below.

However, Mannie pointed out that she was up past her bedtime and hauled her off to their quarters, much to the relief of the late-night watch standers.

8

The next morning, Vicky made sure to coordinate her breakfast with General Pemberton.

He had an update for her.

"We found five more explosives. One was in the main computer room and another at a switching station. We kind of expected those and were looking for them. The other three are a different matter. They were just attached to closed hatches that when opened would blast shrapnel in your face. That's just rude if you ask me. Anyway, our combat engineers are going through the station inch by inch, checking everything. We've also had your computer go over any stand-alone systems we've stumbled across."

"Maggie, you've been active."

"Well, you were asleep. I enjoyed the break. Good thing General Pemberton brought me in. They left all sorts of nasty bombs in the software. Some of those stand-alone systems could cause as much trouble as the airlock bugs they planted."

"Thank you, Maggie."

"You are welcome."

"Have we heard anything from the planet below?" Vicky asked the general.

"Nope, not a word. I will note that both of the ferries are dirtside, so we won't be using any of them to drop down to pay the local red shirts a visit."

"Is this turning into more than you expected?" Vicky asked.

"It still isn't more than we can handle. We've got enough ship longboats that we can land a pretty serious force when you decide to go in."

"Like maybe at zero-two-hundred hours with a bit of a thunderstorm in the area?" she queried.

"I wouldn't mind the oh-dark-early, but you might want to ask the bosun mates about flying around thunderheads."

"I said thunderstorms in the area, not in the flight path, General. I may not be able to fly one of those longboats, but I know how to stay alive in one."

"Glad you learned that, Your Grace."

Vicky finished her breakfast and went hunting for Captain Blue. More out of a habit of keeping him around rather than any expectation she'd need him, she'd brought him and his team along. There was no reason to have them sitting on their ditty boxes back on Dresden.

Who knows? They might come in handy.

She found the captain in a small compartment aft of the bridge.

"You having much luck getting data off the Oryol net?" she asked him.

"None worth talking about," he answered. "The only commlinks in use are in the hinterland. Farmers talking to farmers and the like. There's a lot of griping about the Red Coats confiscating crops and squatters that have fled out into the countryside. Somebody has run the economy pretty much into the ground."

"What about the comm net in the cities?" Vicky asked.

Captain Blue shrugged. "Both Kromy and Bonki only use fiber optic cable and we can't get diddly-squat off that."

"We need to fly some drones down there. Maybe we can find a place to jack into the net," Vicky said.

Thus, a few minutes later, she was discussing with the skipper of the *Victorious* about laying on a longboat pass. A dozen medium duration drones were loaded aboard two of the longboats, and the crafts launched.

They made a high pass, never dipping below sixty thousand feet. One scattered its drones to the north covering larger towns as well as Kromy. The second one covered the towns near Bonki along the equator.

No search radar was active. If the planet had any anti-air capability, it had broken down long ago and not been repaired.

The drones began their sweeps, cruising along at forty to fifty thousand feet. They found little to look at. Here and there a tractor worked a field. Trucks were a rarity on the roads. There was almost no traffic along the major highways between towns. The high speed rail tracks stayed empty hour after hour.

This planet was not open for business.

The drones slipped closer to the centers of Kromy and Bonki. Bonki seemed almost normal, though the major fabricators showed little activity. Kromy was another matter. The drones spotted cars, but they were all parked. What few people that were out and about seemed furtive and hurried as they went from place to place.

Vicky shook her head.

Mannie looked over her shoulder. "If I'd brought an economist, I think he'd be telling us that this economy was totally locked in irons."

"Locked in irons?"

"An old term, going back to sailing ship days. They depended on the wind and occasionally, through poor seamanship or damn bad luck, they'd be half-way through a tack and they'd lose the wind. The ship would be dead in the water and unable to catch enough wind to get underway again. Here we seem to have a totally closed down economy."

"How do you close down a modern, planet-wide economy?" Vicky asked.

"You close down the transportation net," he answered.

"Captain Blue, how's it coming with hacking into the comm net?"

"I haven't started. I was waiting to see if we faced any anti-air."

"It looks pretty benign," Vicky said.

"I'll run one of the carrier drones over Bonki and see if it draws any fire. If it doesn't, I'll try the capital, Kromy, next. If nothing happens, we'll have the carriers launch smaller drones."

For an hour, they waited while nothing happened. Then they risked dropping to twenty thousand feet and overflying the cities. They spotted more people in small groups of two or three hastening from one building to another. It definitely looked like they wanted to avoid any attention.

Another hour dragged on with nothing they could call a net node spotted. Once this place had been prosperous. It had managed to install a full cable backbone and connect everyone living in the urban areas to fast communications.

That, of course, made it nearly impossible to break in.

"I think I've got something here," Captain Blue said finally, glee just edging into this voice.

"What?" Vicky asked, maybe a bit sharply. This waiting was killing her.

"There, six or seven partially built houses," the captain said, stabbing at the screen with his forefinger. "There are also some incomplete apartments the next couple of streets over. If they got to the wiring stage, we may have a weak point."

The smaller drones made a beeline for them and dispersed their own swarm of tiny bots, both flying in the air and rolling along the ground. Still, the going was slow. They left the bots under a chief's supervision and went to lunch.

Most of the meal was spent marveling at how easy a bustling planet could be turned into a shambling zombie.

"And not be able to toss off the virus that has them so sick," Mannie said, then changed his thoughts. "Whoever is running this place has to know we're up here."

"Do they?" Vicky asked. "This place is pretty buttoned up. We found no signal traffic between here and dirtside. It looks more like they closed up shop when they closed out their trade and just locked up the station."

"Yeah," Mannie agreed. Then softly whispered, "Was I the only one who spotted the burned out houses?"

Vicky and Captain Blue nodded that they had.

"Any idea why they burned?"

After a long silence Vicky replied, "None of my ideas are nice."

"But I thought these people submitted to the Security Consultants," Mannie said. "If they didn't fight, why would houses have been burned? Maybe it's just . . . .."

"I love you, sweetheart," Vicky said, "but sometimes you are too soft hearted to see just how evil men can be. People submit to avoid trouble. Then matters get worse. Much worse, only you're already flat on your back and in no position to do much of anything."

"You think that is what we're going to find down there?" Mannie asked.

"After lunch, Captain," Vicky said, "please have a drone or two examine the center of town. I think that is where we will find the redcoats."

"You afraid of what we'll find?" the captain asked.

"Absolute power corrupts absolutely," Vicky said, then sighed, "Since I was a little girl, I've wondered what the difference was between absolute power and absolute evil. So far, I haven't really found a difference. Have you?"

The two men with her just shook their heads.

9

For the next hour, three drones silently continued their circling over Kromy. Somewhere in that capital city, Vicky was sure, the red-coated security specialists must have their headquarters.

The thing about a destroyed economy with little to no traffic is that when there is traffic, it stands out. Immediately.

"I got a van leaving a hotel in the center of town," a second class announced.

"Put it on the main screen," Captain Blue ordered.

"Can you put a small drone over it?" Vicky asked.

"If it stays on the street it's on now, we should have one over it in five blocks."

The black van continued to drive up the main artery from downtown toward the suburbs. It soon had a drone cruising along with it, two hundred meters up and matching its speed.

From the speaker above the screen, they could even hear the engine of the van. It sounded like it had blown a cylinder head gasket.

"If the redcoats are using a van in that bad of shape, what must the rest of this place look like?" Captain Blue muttered.

The screen was now split. One main drone hovered over the rig at three thousand meters, giving them a good view of the area while the smaller drone bird-dogged it.

The picture from the overhead drone began to tell a story.

Here and there, people flitted from building to building. Vicky could only guess what brought them out when they clearly didn't want be there. However, at the sound of the van, every one of them slipped out of sight. They either got themselves indoors or dashed around to hide behind a building.

"I don't like the feel of that," Vicky said.

Mannie came over to stand beside her. Gently he ran a hand up and down her back. No one, however, was able to suggest anything that might make her feel better about that van.

The threatening rig turned off the main drag into a suburban area of single-family dwellings. The people here had earned a good living before the planet quit letting anyone earn anything.

Slowly, like a panther on the prowl, the black van stalked up one street, then down another. Most buildings looked run down with lawns gone to seed. Here and there, a burned out hulk raised blackened sticks to the sky.

"What's it looking for?" Vicky asked no one in particular.

None of those around her had an answer.

Finally, the van circled a block and came back down a street a second time. Halfway down the street, it took a hard right into a driveway and screeched to a halt.

Men in the expected red shirts dashed out of the van. Some ran around to the back of the house while others jogged up to the door. They pounded for admission, but the door stayed locked.

Shortly after, a small explosive sound told those listening around Vicky that a door had been blown in.

The closer drone picked up shouts. Screams. Gunfire from inside the house.

A teenage girl dashed out of the back door and right into the arms of the redcoats that were waiting for just that reason. A moment later, another young woman fell into their clutches as well.

Kicking and screaming, the young women were manhandled around the house and back to the van. At the front door, two of the Red Coats helped one of their own as he stumbled out. He had a long butcher knife sticking out of his belly. The last man out turned and tossed something into the house.

A moment later, there was an explosion and the house began to burn. The drone picked up the sound of laughing along with screams from the women. Despite the moans of their wounded comrades, there was plenty of laughter among the men, including some at the expense of their own who'd let a civilian knife him good.

After both of the women were handcuffed, they were tossed in the back of the van. Once all the redcoats were mounted up, the black van sped away from the burning house. It headed straight back to the hotel at the center of town.

It left behind people creeping from the neighboring houses to see what the redcoats had left behind. Two men entered the flaming home from the back door. A moment later, they dragged a woman from the house. Several people gathered around her, giving what aid they could.

The small drone glided lower to get a better picture of that scene. The woman bled from two bullets to her chest. She was spitting up blood as she grew weaker and weaker. Finally, they closed his eyes.

The woman was a far worse case. She'd been gut shot. Unless she had medical help fast, she would die a slow death.

On the other side of the screen, the imagery from the drone high overhead tracked the raven dark van as it disappeared back into the underground garage at the city's main hotel.

Manny shook his head. "I guess they weren't willing to settle just for extortion."

Vicky stood there, helpless and enraged. "This planet is nothing but a pirate kingdom, literally living out rape and pillage. In the old days, they hung pirates, didn't they?"

It was a hard faced Grand Duchess who whirled to face General Pemberton. The order she snapped was firm and cold, "Prepare to land the landing force. Advise your troopers that there is no need for them to encourage any of these pirates to surrender. If you take no prisoners, it would not hurt my feelings at all."

"Your Grace, are you telling us to take no prisoners?"

"Of course, not," Vicky said, smiling coldly. "That would be wrong. No, if someone really works at surrendering, accept them. Then I'll see that they are hung before sunset."

The general's nostrils flared, but he snapped back a firm, "Understood, Your Grace."

"Mannie, don't you say a word."

"Vicky, I saw what you saw. There are no words for the likes of them."

"Good."

10

A few hours later, a longboat made another high pass above Kromy. It left in its wake more drones, but these were of a more specific nature.

The three drones circled back to the airport on the outskirts of Kromy. Like so much of the planet, it looked beaten down and abandoned. One drone flew low over first one runway, then the next, sensors checking them for broken pavement or any other evidence that would suspect a mine had been dug into the concrete.

It found nothing.

The next pass, the drone released a swarm of mini-drones. They buzzed around the landing strip and the apron, then found ways into the buildings and began to check them out.

What Vicky and her team saw in the airport terminal left them speechless, sick and angry.

Hundreds of decaying bodies lay where they had fallen. It looked like a bloody massacre. Unarmed people had been shot down in windrows.

Vicky found herself shaking her head, even as her stomach revolted at the sight before her.

"People must have fled from the city," Captain Blue said, "thinking to find refuge at the airport."

"Still the redcoats found them," Vicky growled as something inside her changed. She wasn't sure what it was exactly. Not yet. Still, she knew she was a different person from whom she'd been five minutes ago.

In the next large room, they found bodies that showed evidence of execution style killings. In row on row, lay the remains of men, older women, and children, all laid out with almost military precision. Their hands were behind their backs, all cinched with plastic bands.

Everyone had been shot in the back of the head.

"Where are the young women and girls?" Manny asked.

While Vicky and Mannie stood, shocked by the horror before them, one of the petty officers whispered, "We've found people."

"More dead?" Vicky snapped.

"No, ma'am. These are alive."

An enraged Grand Duchess turned to that man's screen. The imagery was of the inside of a hangar. People huddled together in dozens of random groups of three to seven. Some had formed nests of blankets and rags on the hangar's concrete floor or under aircraft wings. Some were in the planes, staring out doors or opened windows.

Then a few of them spotted the drone.

A couple of men and women came together from different groups and collected in the center, together, to eye the drone. One of the men stepped forward and made the universal signal to land, his hands out, flat, waving it down.

"Your Grace?" Captain Blue asked.

"Is there a speaker on that bird?"

"No, ma'am. We can hear but cannot speak."

"Land it."

The drone settled to the ground and rolled up until it was in front of them. The camera swiveled around until it was focused on just these four.

"Can you hear us?" a woman asked.

"I think some drones may be able to listen, but I've never heard of one that had a speaker," one of the men suggested.

A younger man knelt down and peered hard at the drone.

"Move it in closer," Vicky said.

The drone rolled up to the man, and he got down on all fours to study it.

"I guess they can hear us," the woman said.

"I think I've spotted a listening device."

"Okay, what do we want to tell someone that has drone technology?" the woman said.

"Could it be from the redcoats?" the other woman asked.

"If it was from those bastards, it wouldn't have landed. It would be reporting us back to the head SOB and he'd be sending someone to slaughter us like they did those in the terminal. No, this is someone else."

"Who?" asked the other man, standing nearby.

"Sorry, folks, but I don't see a maker's mark," said the guy down on his knees, studying the drone.

The first woman sighed. "Nothing ventured, nothing gained. Whoever you are, there aren't any redcoats around the airport. That's why we're hiding out here. Least-wise, there aren't any more redcoats here. And yeah, they could come back at any minute, but we have lookouts on the top of the hangar and there are places we can hide so we're still hiding here, even if we are starving."

She huffed out a worried sigh.

"If you're gonna come, come. We can help you get to where the redcoat bastards are, okay? And if you ain't coming, then go fuck yourselves."

"Did you have to say that, Maddie?" the guy on his knees said.

"Why not, Fylkir? They're either going to help us or not. Do you really think some angry words from a starving old lady are going to put them off?"

"All I can do is hope not," Fylkir said as he got to his feet.

"Have the drone take off," Vicky ordered.

It turned around and did a short roll to pick up speed and get airborne again.

"Have it fly by them, low and slow, and shake its wings," Vicky ordered

The petty officer did.

The five seemed to understand. At least they waved at the drone as it found its way out of the hangar.

Vicky knew in a second what she had to do. "General Pemberton, do you have any concerns about deploying the landing force at the Kromy airfield?"

The general frowned in thought. "I can't say it's secure, but I also wouldn't say it's in a high threat area either. I'm willing to put down a reinforced company to secure the strip and then follow up with a full landing force once we have a secure base for operations."

"Very good, General. Three thoughts. I'd like the follow-up wave to be mobile. I want it to sweep into town fast."

"Of course, Your Grace."

"I also want your best sharpshooters. I strongly suspect that when we get to digging those bastards out of that hotel, there will be a lot of hostage situations. I want as few women as possible being held as human shields to be hurt when we blow those SOBs brains out."

"Understood, Your Grace."

"Finally, if there is any weight left on the longboats when we launch them, include famine biscuits. I think there are a lot of starving people down there."

"Within safety margins, Your Grace, it will be done," the general answered.

"Fine," Vicky said, then tossed in the other shoe. "I'm dropping with the first wave."

"Your Grace!" and "Sweetheart!" came on the immediate heels of that announcement, just as she expected.

"I have observed the situation down there and determined that I will be safe," Vicky snapped.

"But there might be a sniper somewhere out there. We haven't seen any AA, but they could have it," General Pemberton insisted.

"I will wear battle armor," Vicky shot back, "as well as the spider-silk armor King Raymond sent me. As for AA, we have no evidence of any."

Mannie eyed her hard, but she didn't flinch. He finally sighed. "We're not going to win this one, are we?"

"No chance," Vicky answered firmly. "Those are my people. I will see that they have succor in their most dire time of need."

"Then I guess we both need to get into our spidersilks," Mannie said.

Vicky eyed her husband. That bit of a belly he'd had when she met him was pretty much worked off. Maybe it was all the running around to meetings. Maybe, she admitted, not at all humbly, it was the great sex she gave him. Whatever it was, he was looking good.

"Can you use a sidearm or rifle?" she snapped. She really did not want him in the same longboat with her.

"I'm your husband, Vicky. Of course I know how to defend you."

"I was just worried that you didn't know how to defend yourself," she admitted, knowing she was going soft-hearted.

"I assure you, sweetheart, anyone who goes for you will have two new holes in their heart."

"Then let us get on our play clothes," Vicky said.

So, hand-in-hand, a vice admiral and a civilian left the bridge of the *Victorious* for their quarters.

"Sooner or later, one of them is going to kill the other," the general was heard to mutter.

"Yeah, but until then the make-up sex will be spectacular," the captain said, grinning from ear-to-ear.

Vicky watched the three longboats with Company A, 3rd of the 5th Marines as they approached the target airport. She was getting the command feed from the bridge of the *Victorious*.

She and Mannie were already strapped into a longboat. They would drop with Company B in the second wave. How strange it was. She was willing to risk her neck but unwilling to let Mannie take the same risks. *Was it this marriage thing or the monogamy part that was giving her a soft heart?*

Or maybe she was just going soft in the head.

The first three longboats detached from the Victorious over an hour ago. They'd taken an orbit to drop from the station to the planet below. Considering how high the station was, it had taken some serious braking to get down that fast.

Now they were rising above the horizon for Kromy. If there were any sensors active in or around that city, they'd soon find out.

"Lasers are standing by to react to any threat," came over the command net from the weapons department.

Vicky was glad she'd kept her mouth shut. It was so hard for her to remember that as an admiral aboard, she was just another passenger. The captain ran this show.

"A search radar had gone active," said a maddeningly calm voice.

"Where away?" coolly asked another disembodied voice.

"About two klicks west of the airport's runway."

"Could it be part of the air traffic control?"

"I can't answer that."

Vicky listened and waited. She imagined the Marines below her were a lot more worried than she was. Or, unlike her, they knew nothing of this potential problem.

Ignorance is bliss.

First Platoon was in the lead longboat. By now, the bosun knew he'd been painted and began evasive actions. There was no way to dodge a laser, but it took time to develop a firing solution and thus, the longboat began to bounce, dive, or weave every two or three seconds.

Now the Marines in back knew their landing was getting interesting. The weather report called for a nice day with light wind. Light winds did not bounce landers around like this.

Vicky slaved her board to the sensor board. It showed a radar, but no other activity anywhere within a ten klick radius. Maybe this was just an approach radar that had not been turned off when the last controller left the tower.

Vicky could hope.

As the first longboat overflew the radar, nothing happened. The second longboat was fifty klicks behind it, trailed by the third at another fifty klicks. Both were fully involved in the antics of air vehicles that didn't want to take any guff off of AA.

Meanwhile, the active radar just kept on painting the longboats and doing nothing about them. *Such a nice day to be alive.*

The first longboat touched down, hit the brakes, and popped its chute. As soon as it could, it exited the runway onto a taxiway and headed for the building that they knew was occupied.

The aft hatch opened up and a light gun truck rolled out. It zipped over to the only ladder up to the top of the occupied hangar and dropped off two sniper teams.

Sensors had spotted two people monitoring the situation from opposite corners of the building. However, they were well camouflaged; only a weak thermal signature gave them away. The snipers had been warned to be alert for friendlies.

Meanwhile, a platoon had dismounted from the rolling lander. They went to ground. An airfield apron offers very little cover, but bags of famine biscuits tossed onto the ramp as the longboat rolled by added some. With a base of fire established by bounds and overwatch, they hurried to the hangar and entered.

They would provide security for those people, debrief them, and distribute the famine biscuits. That was a lot to do for a twelve-man squad even with an intel team for augmentation.

However, the second platoon had another assignment.

They dismounted as the lander rolled by the airport terminal. They were to secure the building, check out the tower and see if some sort of air traffic control could be set up and keep the entire area under surveillance.

The mass murder site was in their territory. They'd examine it if they had any spare time. Vicky doubted they would.

The third platoon deployed from the longboat as it went by the fuel dump. There were a few vehicles parked there. The chances that anything there was in working order were slim, but they had to be checked out.

If they found only a dry hole, they'd report back to the terminal.

The second longboat landing was delayed. Its bosun was taking no chances that the radar might finally connect with a laser. Busted AA that didn't work the first time didn't mean it wouldn't suddenly go active as the second or third bird passed overhead.

That gave the first lander plenty of time to finish unloading. It held short on the apron, waiting as the second longboat landed and rolled clear of the runway.

Once it had, the first lander started its takeoff roll, heading back up for another load. At best, it would be almost four hours before it landed again. This time, however, it would be loaded with ground transport for the strike force Vicky intended to lead into town.

The hooter in the landing bay began warning of depressurization.

"Fasten your seatbelts, folks, and return your tray tables to their full and upright positions," the copilot joked. "We expect to give you a nice Navy ride."

That brought jeers from the Marines. They were quick to let everyone know what they thought of their Navy delivery system.

Vicky folded up her assault battle board into a quarter of its opened size and slipped it in behind her ceramic protective armor. Who knows? It might provide her with that extra bit of stopping power she needed to stay alive.

This was Mannie's first combat drop and he looked a bit pale. Vicky reached for his gauntlet and held his hand as they waited to drop free of the battleship.

"You ought to feel right at home," she told her husband.

"I should, huh?" still held plenty of tension even if he managed a bit of a grin.

"Yeah, it's just like a drop from the space station to St. Petersburg. You've done it plenty of times."

"Yeah, but I wasn't dropping with a radar tracking me that could very well be hostile."

"Well, I remember a certain time when I did," Vicky said, lightly reminding Mannie of the time when, as an exiled and hunted Grand Duchess, that she'd dropped to Mannie's city of Sevastopol. Then she'd hoped to be taken in as a refuge. "You had your radars active on our lander. I know. I was manning the countermeasures."

"Okay," Mannie said as the longboat fell free of the battleship, "I did have the search radars on you."

"And the tracking radars. I spotted them."

"Okay, okay, I was doing what I thought best - scaring a troublesome Peterwald away from my nice, quiet city. If you were the mayor, you'd have done the same."

"Yes, but you damn near scared me to death."

"It didn't keep you from dropping," Mannie said, holding tight to Vicky's hand as the retro jets fired.

Even though the jets were making conversation nearly impossible, Vicky shouted, "I had no place else to go."

"I'm glad you came to my place," Mannie shouted back, then the gee force rose and they both leaned back in their seats.

12

T he bosun chose to make a straight-in approach. Vicky suspected, and it would later be verified, that the crew checking out the tower had found the right switch and turned off the radar. It turned out to be a radar approach with no lasers attached.

That was nice. It was also about the only nice thing that greeted Vicky.

The captain commanding A Company was standing by when Vicky exited the longboat, or maybe he was waiting for the light gun trucks loaded with bags of famine biscuits.

"There are several more hangars full of refugees," the captain reported. "We've got a lot of hungry mouths to feed."

Vicky's longboat was loaded more for mobility than a fight. Besides her immediate staff, she only had a squad of Marines. The main cargo was four light gun trucks, each towing a trailer of famine rations.

"We'll take these four trunks over to those hangars," Vicky said.

"Ma'am, we haven't secured some of those hangars. The two across the field don't look too good."

"Hungry is what they are, and their Grand Duchess will see that they are fed," Vicky said, doing her best to convey firmness without being sharp or shrill.

The captain got the message and switched direction. "Let me assign you one platoon from the airport terminal, Your Grace. You're kind of light on trigger pullers."

Vicky glanced around at the four rigs she had. Only three held a fire team of four Marines. Vicky and Mannie would share the fourth one with Kit and Kat, Vicky's erstwhile assassins and bodyguards.

"Get me your nearest squad. They can hitch a ride on the trailers or find room in the back seats.

Vicky held in place, but the captain put one over on her. Two squads showed up and she ended up with riflemen prone on the hood of her rigs as well as four split between the back seat and the trailer.

Mannie gave up his seat for the captain. "I want to talk to the team that debriefed the folks in the first hangar," he said.

Vicky just nodded. So often, Mannie did his thing and she did hers. That just seemed to be the way of their lives. While he trotted off with two Marines for escort or guides, Vicky set out to see for herself what was going down on this planet.

She had seen disasters before, on Presov, and worse on Pozan. She wondered how this could be worse.

It was.

A dozen children huddled in the shadow of the second hangar. It looked like they'd long forgotten what a bath was. The smallest were being cared for by the older kids, although the oldest wasn't likely more than twelve. They were dressed in rags, except for the littlest ones who seemed to have lost all their clothes.

Or maybe outgrown them.

The smaller kids looked on with wide eyes, several with their hands in their mouths. The older ones eyed her cautiously, ready to bolt for the hangar door off to their right that was barely cracked open.

That door slid open a bit more. Someone looked out from there without giving themselves away.

Vicky ordered the corporal driving her to slowly approach the kids. She reached down for the sack of famine biscuits and grabbed a handful.

"Let's stop here," she told the corporal driving.

He brought the gun truck to a smooth halt. As Vicky dismounted, so did most of her escort, guns at the ready.

"Anyone who aims a rifle even close to one of those children will earn Our great displeasure," Vicky snapped.

All the rifles were suddenly pointed at the sky. The captain took charge, "I want a 360 perimeter, Staff Sergeant!"

Immediately the riflemen turned to cover every quarter. Several of them ducked between the trailer and the gun truck, gaining the only cover in sight.

Vicky ignored her protection detail as she walked slowly toward the kids. She held out famine biscuits in both hands.

The kids looked at her but stayed where they were. Some of the smaller kids licked their lips at the sight of food. Still, they turned to the older kids, their eyes big and begging to be let loose to get the first meal they'd seen in way too long.

Three of the older kids shook their heads. All the kids turned and watched Vicky as if she was death itself.

Then a five-year-old in torn shorts could stand it no more. She broke from the rest and dashed toward Vicky.

The Grand Duchess was most pleased that no Marine pulled back their arming bolt. No one did anything to terrify the child more than it already was.

Vicky took a knee, bringing her almost to eye-level with the kids. She held out one hand, full of ration bars. "Take these and give them to your friends," she said.

The young girl grabbed for them with both hands. She didn't quite get a dozen, but she got enough before dashing back to her friends. She had nine. Vicky watched as the big kids made sure the little ones were first to get something to gnaw on.

The oldest, a girl of maybe twelve walked out to Vicky. "I'm Dora," she said. "May I have a bar?"

"Here are three for you and your friends," Vicky said.

"May I have six, so I can take three to my mom, dad, and brother?"

Vicky handed her six. "Run in and tell your folks that the Grand Duchess is here and there are bags and bags of these waiting for them to come get them."

Quick as a hummingbird, the young girl grabbed the six ration bars. She whirled on a brass pfennig and dashed for the door. Her two friends met her halfway and she passed each of them two biscuits like a runner passing a baton. All three of them popped one bar in their mouths and began gnawing them even as they held the others out for show.

That left Vicky with her own problem: what to do next. She quickly returned to the rig and grabbed the sack she'd opened.

"You are not going in there, Your Grace," the captain snapped. Respectfully.

"Yes, I am."

"We don't know what's in there, Your Grace."

"Starving people," Vicky snapped back.

However, the captain had delayed Vicky just long enough.

Kit and Kat both grabbed a sack of famine bars and scampered for the now-open hangar door. Vicky had an impossible time thinking of the word 'scamper' in the same sentence with her two tiny assassins, but that was exactly what they were doing.

The two even giggled, only too aware that they'd pulled one over on Vicky.

Her Imperial Grace scowled at the captain, but he refused to disappear in a cloud of smoke. "Sergeant, take two of your best men and check out the hangar," he ordered, instead.

"And keep your damn rifles pointed up or down, but not at anyone. Understood?" Vicky ordered.

"Yes, ma'am," the sergeant snapped as he double-timed with two Marines for the door. They vanished inside.

To their right, there was a scream of steel wheels on concrete, and one of the huge doors in the center of the hangar began to slowly move aside. A moment later, four teenage boys slipped out and grabbed handholds. Then they began to haul the door open even faster. The power might have failed, but there was a backup that used good old Swedish steam.

A moment later, Kit appeared in the opening, waving for the gun trucks to drive in.

Vicky ordered the other three trucks to hold in place, then slipped into the passenger's seat in hers and told the drive, "Let's go feed some people."

The rig turned and quickly covered the distance to the opening, then slowed to a crawl.

"Try and get us to the middle of the hangar," Vicky ordered.

She knew her guards were jogging to get to her side, and they did manage to catch up as they rolled slowly into the deep shade of the hangar.

What Vicky saw inside was just as bad as what she'd seen outside. It was much like what the drone had shown them in the other hangar. People huddled in small groups, under the wings and fuselages of both large and small air vehicles. Some peered out from the cabins of planes. Maybe they were families. Maybe they were just friends huddling together, trying to survive. It was hard to tell. Most of what they wore were more rags than clothes. Others were missing things like pants and shirts.

The place reeked with the smell of a distant latrine.

It was now that Vicky spotted people who did not get up like everyone else. There were a lot of those who were sick; sick or so starved that they did not have energy left to rise.

With a sick feeling, Vicky realized what was missing: there were no squalling or wiggling babies. Vicky shuddered at the thought of what happened when breasts dried up or formula ran out.

Vicky was really starting to hate the bastards running this planet like their own private hell. Hate them as much as she hated the gangsters running this half of her Empire. She would make sure that a lot of very deserving people got very dead before this was over.

The driver zigged and zagged around the aircraft to halt the light gun truck where he'd been ordered, right in the middle of the hangar.

Vicky dismounted, opened another ration sack, and began handing out biscuits. There was a mad rush, but shouts of "stay in line," from within the crowd did much to end that.

"Marines," Vicky shouted, "Lay a hand distributing food."

The moderately controlled mob opened up to let a half-dozen Marines join Vicky and they were soon handing out rations with her.

Now the people more quickly drew their one bar. Many asked for more, but Vicky had been warned by the Medical Officer aboard the *Victorious* that starving people had to start slow. Their stomachs were no longer able to absorb food and they could rupture and kill themselves.

To be generous could be deadly.

Still, what do you say to someone who wants four for his family? She let her have four.

Only when the crowd was thinning out did Vicky realize she was only half-meeting their needs. Famine biscuits are compact and stale. That made them hard to chew. A lot of younger kids and older folks were having a hard time making headway on their meal.

They needed water to soften the rations.

She glanced around at the small bits of territory each group had marked out for themselves. Most had some sort of container for water, but they held little.

"Where do you get your water?" Vicky asked a young woman.

"There's a creek across the runway. More like a ditch. It's hard to get much water, and you have to steer clear of the bastards in those hangars over there, but we try."

Vicky nodded, then said, "Maggie, get me General Pemberton."

"Aye, aye, Your Grace," her computer answered.

"Yes, Your Grace," the general answered a moment later.

"General, these survivors have little access to water, and what they have I wouldn't touch with a three-meter pole. How do we get water for them and your troops?"

"It would be a hell of a waste of lift to lug water from orbit," the general said, seeming to think out loud. "I'll get back to you. Somewhere in this fleet there has to be someone who knows how to produce potable water."

"Check it out, General, and get back to me," Vicky said, and cut the line.

"He called you Your Grace," the young woman at Vicky's elbow said.

"Yes, I'm Grand Duchess Victoria. Vicky to my friends," she said, distractedly as she glanced around the hangar and realized just what a mess this was.

"Captain," she shouted.

"Yes, Your Grace."

"Get the rigs moving to the next couple of hangars."

"Aye, aye, Your Grace."

A haggard man came up to her. Like everyone else, he wore little more than a ragged shirt and pants in the heat. Still, his rags might have been of a better quality months ago. He could be middle-aged. Maybe older. The eyes were those of an old man.

"Your Grace?" he said, more a question than a statement.

Vicky introduced herself.

"You're a Peterwald," he said.

Vicky nodded and tried to allay any fears attached to that name. "I'm one of the good ones. My husband has half-persuaded me to be a democrat and a constitutional monarch, ah Empress."

"Pardon me, but can I ask why you're here?"

"I'm passing out biscuits, working on getting you some decent water and, late tonight, I intend to sneak into town and kill myself some redcoats. You wouldn't happen to know where they are, would you? We think we've spotted a hotel in downtown, but I'd like someone local to verify we got it right."

The guy frowned. "I thought the redcoats were from the Peterwalds. They claim they have the rightful heir to the throne calling the shots."

"They have a baby that's likely still in diapers. Under a treaty, your Emperor, my father, has recognized me as heir apparent and split the

Empire with me. Unfortunately, he seems to have lost control of his half of the empire to the dead Empress's family and their redcoats."

Vicky allowed herself a scowl. "I want my Empire back and my people free from such thugs. We just freed Dresden. I'd have been here sooner if I had known it was this bad. Can you tell me what happened?"

"Can I have one of those bars?" he asked Vicky.

She handed him one and he began to gnaw at it. It wasn't easy to bite more than a chunk off it. She offered him her canteen to drink from.

The man looked like she'd just invited him to a feast.

"It's hard to say. They came in to 'keep order' but there wasn't all that much disorder. Then they set out to collect taxes. One thing led to another and soon they had all the money. Then they started ransacking houses and confiscating anything of value, like jewelry and antiques. Someone killed a redcoat and the next thing you know, it was a death sentence to even have a gun in your house."

The fellow paused to bite off another small bite.

"With no cash to pay for things, everything started to fall apart in a hurry. Farmers quit bringing food in and the redcoats started raiding farms. Over a week or so, you could see the smoke from burning houses all around the horizon. Didn't their parents ever tell them you don't kill the goose that lays the golden eggs?"

"If so, they weren't listening."

"Yeah. They just took everything, and when there wasn't anything left to take, they took girls. Some young women had gone out with redcoats before. They had the best food and were fun after hours. Then they just started taking girls and none of them came back."

"Is that when you started fleeing?"

"Yeah. Kromy emptied out fast. We had to get away from those bastards. But there weren't any places to go. The farms that hadn't been destroyed only wanted the strongest young men to help work their fields."

"What happened to their farming equipment?" Vicky asked.

"The redcoats had carted off their fuel extraction gear. If you don't have any hydrogen or oxygen, your tractor's dead."

"Why'd they steal the power gear?" Vicky asked.

"Because those shitheads couldn't seem to keep their own running. I don't know who those fools are, but you'd hear an explosion and just know they'd blown up another plant extracting hydrogen and oxygen. They didn't care. If they blew one up, they'd just get another. Only, after a while, there weren't any more extractors to steal. Not even a tiny one."

"What about the generator plant on the other side of the airport?" Vicky asked.

"Yeah, when they came out to the terminal to steal the women, they also raided the fuel depot. Somebody busted it. At least it didn't explode, but our best people could not get it running again."

"I'll see that it's looked at and spare parts get sent down."

"That would be nice, ma'am."

"Where's the nearest decent water supply?"

"There are wells that we use for the city's supply, but the power grid is down. There's a lake not too much farther out of town, but I wouldn't trust any water on this planet. Most of us get sick about once a month."

"I've already ordered a water system to be dropped down here. Now, can you help me?"

"How?" he said, glancing down at his torn clothes as if doubting he had anything to offer her.

"I need to know where the redcoats are headquartered," she said.

The man gave Vicky a pained look. "It's been a while since any of us have risked going into town. It's bad out here. It's worse in there. You can get picked up in a blink. Or shot and killed for a laugh. They like to show what good shots they are. If you can dodge and run, some people survive. They ain't such good shots."

"I saw them kidnap some women from a house," Vicky said.

"Did you hear gunfire?"

"Yes."

"Then the menfolk were lucky to be killed where they stood.

There are stories of men hauled downtown who took a long time dying. There's at least a couple of those bastards that enjoy giving people pain. I can't believe they're running my planet."

"Why didn't you move against them when you had a chance?" Vicky had to ask.

The guy shrugged. "They represented the Emperor. They were bad, but, you'll excuse me, you Peterwalds have been pretty bad and we survived you. We all thought that this would go away, but it didn't. It got worse and worse. We finally put together a protest. A couple thousand of us marched to Government House. We had our twenty-two complaints. General Blankster, Count of Oryol, came out and our three representatives handed them the grievances."

The guy shook his head. "He took the list of complaints, glanced at them, then ordered his guards to seize the three. They held them while he gutted each one of them with his knife. Gutted them like a pig, I guess.

"We stood there in shock, then he ordered his guards to cut loose on us. I was one of the lucky ones. Of the two thousand or so that marched downtown, maybe half got away."

The survivor got a distant look in his eyes. "There were no wounded. They shot the wounded. I saw it. I was hiding under a truck and I saw it. I saw it and I couldn't do a damn thing."

With a sigh, he finished, "I waited until night, then ran. I grabbed my family and just kept running. No farmer would take us in. We thought this would be far enough. It wasn't."

Vicky nodded along as he told his story. What could she possibly say to someone who had lived through that and all that followed?

"Can you tell me where the redcoat general was when he shot your friends?"

It took the fellow a moment to collect himself. "They'd taken over Government House. First just one wing, then they bounced out what passed for our government and took it all over. A week later, we tried our stupid protest."

"Where do they live?"

The fellow stared up at the overhead. "I think they took over the

Imperial Bismarck. That's our best hotel. It's opposite Government House with two blocks of parks between them. They may have also taken over the other office buildings and the bank. I don't know."

"How many of them are there?"

"Four thousand. Maybe more. Maybe less. It's hard to tell."

"Could any of your own people have enlisted?"

"I heard they emptied the jails about the time they dismissed our local Public Safety Officers. I think there was talk that they signed some of the worst offenders up. Hard to tell. The net went down and out here, all we have are rumors."

Vicky didn't much care to hear that. Still, it was better to hear it now than discover it later.

"Maggie, get me General Pemberton.

"Aye, aye, Your Grace," her computer replied, most snappily.

The guy rolled his eyes.

"I don't make her say any of that," Vicky said.

The tattered fellow was still weighing Vicky's response when the general came on the line.

"General, our local redcoats may have been recruiting from the dregs of society and the jail."

"Oh, shit," didn't meet radio standards, but Vicky could forgive him that. "How many?"

"Hard to say; no one's dared slip downtown and count noses. It's not worth your life for these SOBs to catch you. They don't need any excuse to cut your throat, or flay you alive just for chuckles and grins."

"So, we've got an unknown number of bad actors."

"And an appointment with them tonight."

"Understood. We'll drop every Marine and add in any Navy that are weapons qualified. Master at arms, rifle club, pitcher for the base-ball team."

"I'm afraid that's the way it's gonna be, General. I thought you'd like to know it as soon as I did."

"Thank you, Your Grace. I think," and on that note, the commlink was broken.

"I want to visit all the hangars," Vicky told the fellow. "Is there a leadership team like we found in the first hangar?"

"Yes, there are a dozen of us that kind of see that things don't get any worse than they have to be. Leastwise on this side of the runway."

"On the other side?" Vicky asked.

"It's a lot worse."

Vicky slowly shook her head. *Was that even possible?*

"How have you survived?"

The man looked around, as if to assure himself that they had. "We had some canned goods. Dry goods. Some of the burned farms around here still have crops growing. We try to check them every week or so. It's not a lot and we aren't the only ones looking for food."

"Well," Vicky said, "I want to detach the trailer of food so I can visit a few other hangars. Could you see that the food is not pillaged? It's not that I don't want you all to eat, it's that the Medical Officer on my ship warned me that your stomachs have shrunk down and aren't working right. If you eat too much too fast, or drink too much, you could split your bellies open and kill yourselves."

The fellow snorted, "So, we're so hungry that we can't eat, huh?"

"Something like that," Vicky said. "Take it slow and easy. Issue another round of biscuits in six hours. Hopefully, we'll have decent water you can drink by then."

While Vicky stood by, the man collected a half-dozen of the hangar's leaders around him and explained Vicky's request. That brought in several of the less sick people to stand by the trailer which her Marines were detaching.

Without the trailer, Vicky didn't have room for two of her Marines. She ordered them to stand by the trailer and work with the local leadership team.

That drew surprised looks and whispers from the civilians. Whether it was that a Peterwald was leaving Marines to work with them, or fear that the troopers were really there to keep the food from them, Vicky had no idea.

13

With everything done in that hangar that could be done, Vicky and her team left. Someone had thought ahead and opened the rear door, allowing Vicky to drive across the apron and directly access the next hangar.

There, the first distribution of food had been completed. The sergeant leading that team had been approached by the half-dozen people who spoke for the group there, and he seemed very glad to pass them off to Vicky.

Watching the sergeant address Vicky as "Your Grace" left them a bit awe struck.

"*You* have come for *us*?" an older woman said.

"You are in distress. Of course I have come to your aid," Vicky said.

"Don't know any other Peterwald who would have," a guy behind her muttered low, but in a voice that carried.

"I hope that the Peterwalds who come after me will have a different reputation. The entire Empire is going to be remade. Remade for you and your children. You have not been listened to in far too long. That has to change. We can't let another man like my father make a fool of himself and let loose wolves on all of you."

That left them deep in thought. Vicky made sure they understood that water was on its way and that they could draw another famine biscuit in six hours.

The visit to the next hangar was much the same.

The two remaining hangars were smaller and required a long trip down the taxi way to the other end of the runway. Here the planes were smaller, both transports and agricultural aircraft.

Here, there were worse problems.

When the Marines had driven into the first hangar, they'd been met by a couple of dozen guys with clubs. They demanded that the food supplies be given to them.

The Marine sergeant here was a veteran of the Pozan Relief Effort. He could smell a bully when he faced off with one.

He had demurred, suggesting that they delay until Her Grace, Grand Duchess Victoria, could discuss this with them.

The punk's response had been vulgar and a totally inappropriate address to both a married woman and a Gracious Grand Duchess.

Fortunately, the bastard did not leave the next decision to the Marine sergeant. He hollered for his thugs to lay into the Marines.

The punks were totally misinformed. The Marines were not outnumbered three to one. No, it was the thugs who were outnumbered.

The brawl had been very short. Without even firing a shot, the Marines had put their attackers on the deck. After seeing that they were trussed up like calves for branding, the Marines began distributing the food.

Vicky measured the state of the survivors in the hangar; they were a pitiful looking bunch. The men cringed against the walls and back of the hangar. They showed the bruises, cuts and welts of some serious beatings. Most of the women . . . all stripped naked . . . huddled close to the men. A few women clustered as far from any man as they could.

"How did you feed them, Sergeant?"

"Your Grace, we had to take the food over to them. They're afraid to step away from the walls. It's worse. They've got nothing. Not even some pots and pans for water. I don't know how they've survived.

"Can you get them water?"

"Ma'am, we've shared out all the water in our canteens and it wasn't enough. We've given over our spare canteens to three of the younger boys who aren't in as bad of shape. They're running, or rather stumbling, over to the stream and bringing back water."

"You won't be using those canteens until they're sanitized."

"No, ma'am. You won't believe the stream. There are bodies littering the ground between here and there. It is worth your life to make a run for water."

"Sweet Jesus," Vicky muttered. She walked over to the nearest wall. The people, mostly naked, cringed away from her, trying, if they could, to climb into the wall itself.

"I am the Grand Duchess Victoria. I claim Oryol as my sovereign territory. I will restore justice to this planet. I must ask you, did those men steal food and water from you?"

A handful nodded.

"Did they beat people to death?" she said, clipping each word hard.

"Yeah," came from some. Others continued to nod.

"Did they rape you women?" Her voice now was hard as edged steel.

"Yeah," came from more cracking voices. Now most heads were nodding.

Something in Vicky's heart cracked.

She knew that capital punishment was still the law of the Empire. She knew that many people, like Mannie, wanted to abolish it. Still, she knew that she had judges under her who would condemn people to death.

She also knew, in the old words, that she had high, low, and middle justice here.

The judges pronounced a capital sentence in her name.

In that second, Vicky decided to issue capital judgements in her own name.

She walked back to where the three dozen or so thugs lay sprawled out.

"Where's the ringleader?" she asked the sergeant.

"That one there, with the diamond necklace."

"Thank you."

She came to stand at his feet. He looked up at her with hate in his eyes.

"Did this man rape any of you?" she called out to those lining the hangar walls.

"Yes," was ragged, but it grew into a shout slowly.

"Did this man never kill anyone with his own hands?" she mixed up the questions, trying to avoid a screaming crowd.

"He beat my husband to death." "My son." "My grandmother."

"Will anyone ask mercy for this man?"

The hangar went deadly silent.

"Have you anything to say for yourself?"

He spat at Vicky, then followed it up with a vile rant.

She shot him between the eyes.

Kit and Kat appeared at Vicky's elbows. "Your Grace, let us do this for you. You have a tender heart."

"I had one. I don't anymore," Vicky said.

"Sergeant, can you tell me who his ring leaders were?"

The young Marine swallowed hard. Combat was combat. This was cold-blooded killing . . . in the name of justice, Vicky told herself.

"Those four, Your Grace."

Vicky went through the same drill. They had raped, robbed, and brutally murdered in cold blood. They terrorized the people in this hangar and any who tried to escape.

None of the naked people around the wall were willing to plead for mercy for them. None of the thugs had anything to say for themselves. One whimpered. Another shouted obscenities as Vicky went through her process. One tried to roll away from her as if he thought he could escape her justice.

Vicky looked at the bodies contorting in the throes of coming death as they bled out around her. She'd never seen death this close.

The stench of loosed bowels might have sickened her, if the entire hanger hadn't stank like an open latrine. The way the arms and legs spasmed in death sickened her. This entire mess sickened her.

But the people around the walls deserved justice. If she would have her own judges and executioners do this, how could she not?

She went through the thirty-two prisoners. She shot thirty. Only in two cases, a young boy, and an old man, were voices raised for mercy.

"Your Grace, we did horrible things because we could do them. It was wrong of us, me and the boy here. It sickened us and we couldn't do it no more. We tried to slip food and water to them that we could. If we could, we talked a few of these bastards into stopping a beating before they bashed a guy's brains out. We did wrong, but we've tried, me and the boy, to do better."

He paused as if searching his blackened soul for one more thought. "Ma'am, we know we done wrong. If you want to shoot us, we'll take it 'cause we deserve it. But ma'am, it's been hell in here for all of us. Some of us were the demons. Some of us was the poor damned souls. In the end, we're just damned."

"Sergeant, cut these two loose. Put them in with the survivors. If they're alive tomorrow morning, forget it. If they're dead, there will be no question of invoking my justice."

"Aye, aye, Your Grace."

Without another word, Vicky turned on her heels and walked across the apron to the next hangar. Her two assassins walked with her. No one said a word.

Vicky walked into the same piteous situation.

She applied the same relentless Imperial justice.

14

The drive back to the other side of the airfield was fast and silent. Vicky dismounted the moment the gun truck braked to a halt in front of Mannie.

He studied her as he might a stranger. "We were told that those hangars had some bad actors."

"Yes," Vicky bit out.

"We heard shots."

"Yes," Vicky said in the same dead voice.

"Sweetheart, talk to me," Mannie begged.

"The people over there suffered murder, rape, and theft of food at the hands of the strongest. Their high crimes were self-evident. I executed seventy. The people asked mercy for four. I left them alive, but among the people they had beaten. We'll see if they're alive tomorrow morning."

"Oh, my God, Vicky. I'm so sorry you had to do that."

"Someone else would have done it in my name. It was time I saw it for myself. Felt it."

Mannie stepped closer and engulfed Vicky in a hug. She just stood there in his arms.

"Mannie," she finally said, "do not do away with capital punishment in the Empire until we have cleansed it of this cancer. I will not suffer these pieces of shit to breathe the same air as the rest of us."

"I hear you, love," he said.

Vicky knew that was not the same as a "Yes" or "I'll be sure to do that." They would talk more about this. They'd probably be talking about this right up until the last of the Bowlingame faction was swinging at the end of a rope.

Mannie was tender-hearted. Maybe someday she'd find her tender heart again. Maybe. Not today.

"When is the strike force coming down?"

"General Pemberton should be along in a few minutes. He says he'll need two lifts from the longboats to get his entire force down here. He's taking everything, including any Sailor that knows which end of a gun to point at the enemy."

Vicky raised her eyebrows.

"The Sailors have seen the drone video. Between that and info we've sent up from these hangars and the terminal, Sailors are standing in line."

"Amateur night at the Berlique, huh?"

"I haven't heard that one before," Mannie said.

"Amateur's night at the burlesque. Women did slow strip teases for paying male customers. It goes back a long way. I understand it usually brings on the downfall of strict planets."

Mannie still seemed puzzled.

"First, a girl can't strip down to more than a swimsuit. Then her underwear. Then the underwear gets smaller and smaller before it finally goes away. Then it's just the world, the flesh, and the devil, as they say.

"Have we ever had this burlesque thing in the Empire?"

"Not a lot. There was one planet, I forget its name. They wanted a utopia based on a strict moral code. Four generations later, not so much."

"We humans are nothing if not variable."

"Yes. Where's the guy in charge down here?"

"Major Magdor is in the airport tower where he has the best view," Maggie answered.

"Can Vicky get into the tower without going through the, ah, slaughter house?" Mannie asked Maggie.

"There is another approach. It involves walking up a lot of steps on the outside of the tower," Maggie answered.

"I'll walk," Vicky said.

"Can I go with you?" Mannie asked.

"Of course," Vicky replied.

They boarded the gun truck. Kit and Kat shared the front passenger seat, riding shotgun . . . and leaving the back seat for the husband and wife, democrat and autocrat, salt and pepper.

Mannie leaned his head close to Vicky and whispered, "Should I have come with you?"

"No. You had your job and I had mine."

"But maybe I could have . . ."

Mannie was cut off by Vicky, "You could not have. I'm glad you did not see the hell over there. It was bad here, but at least everyone was trying to survive together. Over there, they had demons tormenting those suffering. I put an end to the demons."

"Yes, love."

"Don't 'yes, love' me, Mannie. Once this war is over. Once the Bowlingame mob has been sent to the hell they deserve, you can institute your rule of law. Now? No. It's Imperial law and I am the source of that justice."

"Vicky, I don't care about those SOBs. They can rot in hell. What worries me is you. You aren't the person you were this morning."

"No, I'm not," Vicky said, then allowed herself a deep sigh. "From now until we kill the cancer on the Empire, I am what I am."

Mannie started to speak, then stopped, started again, and stopped again. Finally, he said, "Vicky, please don't do this alone. Please don't lock me out. I'm your husband. Let me in. Let me share this with you."

"Mannie, I'm not sure I want to share this with anyone, least of all you. I feel like I've built a stone turret around me. The only thing I left a hole for is a phone line to you. You're going to have to settle for talking when I can."

Mannie nodded. "I'll be waiting on the other end of that line," he assured her, softly.

The gun truck pulled up to the terminal. Instead of going in the front door, they drove around to the west side. There, they went in and up three flights of stairs. There was an outside staircase that wrapped around the tower. Eighty steps later, Vicky and Mannie were a bit winded, but the two assassins looked ready to climb another eighty.

The view from the catwalk around the top of the tower was breathtaking, which didn't help with Vicky catching her own.

She was nearly twenty meters up and could see for kilometers. The land was green and rolling with white sheep dotting the landscape. Here and there far out were homesteads with houses and barns. Many fields were planted in corn and other crops.

Close in, she spotted several burned-out farms.

There was plenty to eat on this planet. However, with the financial and transportation systems shut down, the thin veneer of civilization had been ripped off, leaving only barbarism in its wake.

If tonight's mission worked like Vicky wanted, tomorrow these people could begin rebuilding their planet and society. However, all the social currency that people exchanged in their daily affairs had been thrown to the wind or burned to survive. People would be a long time building up their banks of shared faith and trust in themselves and those they lived with.

Vicky shook her head. Just re-imposing the rule of law would not be enough. These people would have to rediscover the basic human faith that underlay those laws. Belief that others obeyed them as well as themselves.

Within Vicky, her hatred of the redcoats and the Bowlingame faction behind them grew from red-hot to white-hot.

Shaking her head, she stepped into the control tower.

15

Vicky entered the air traffic control room. All the vents that could be opened, were. Several windows had been smashed out at some time in the past. Still, under the bright sun, the room was brutally hot.

The view, however, was worth the sweat collecting in her bra.

"What's our situation, Major?" she asked Major Magdor.

"The situation is well in hand, Your Grace. As you can see, I've got snipers on all three of the large hangars as well as this terminal."

He pointed out the locations of his teams. They'd gone to ground under camouflage. If he hadn't, she likely couldn't have spotted them.

"I've also pushed a roadblock out about five klicks toward Kromy. They should be able to stop a tank platoon, assuming there are any tanks on Oryol."

Vicky shrugged. "There weren't before this mess started but . . ."

"Yeah, we're not taking any chances. We'll have anti-tank rockets with every detachment. I've also got three sniper teams pushed out another klick past the roadblock. They've got a good line of sight covering the ground half-way to Kromy."

"What does the drone take show?"

"Almost no activity in town. Here and there a few people sneak from place to place, but there is no outdoor activity in the town core. No movement between Government House and the Imperial Bismarck Hotel."

"Do the redcoats have any guards posted? Lookouts?"

The major shook his head. "We've taken the smaller drones down low and mapped the entire area. They've looked in every room with a broken window. No one's on lookout. I don't know if it's nap time for them or what, but they're not acting like they've got anything to fear."

Beside Vicky, Mannie frowned. "They must have heard the sonic booms from our landers.

The major shrugged, "We made sure to slow down a hundred klicks away and come in on low power, sir. Maybe they didn't hear us."

"Has General Pemberton been advised that we want to keep that approach?" Vicky asked.

"Yes, ma'am. They're pulling every longboat in the fleet for the next lift. Even your admiral's barge. We've got both companies of the battalion as well as transportation. The third lift should bring down the Navy landing force and more transport."

"What about water?"

"We don't have any water trucks, but we do have bladders we can carry on the trailers. Add some hoses and pumps, and we can get water out of that lake fifteen clicks farther out."

"Please get five of those bladders filled and delivered to each of the hangars. There are a lot of dehydrated people out there."

"Understood, ma'am. The next five gun trucks down have orders to make for the lake before they even stop."

"Good," Vicky said. "Mannie, would you please go with the water run? I want to hear immediately if any show stoppers pop up."

"Are you micro-managing, dear?"

"Yes, but this is something I want everyone to know that the Grand Duchess is personally interested in. Major, I don't mean any disrespect to your people. Still, if one of your sergeants runs into trouble, I doubt if they'd dare call the Grand Duchess up and ask her to solve it."

"Excuse me, Your Grace," the major said with a chuckle, "but no, I don't see even a lieutenant calling you direct."

"Yeah, there are about a zillion levels in the chain of command between us. Mannie, however, is used to calling me. Sometimes he calls me out on things I'm doing wrong, don't you, sweetheart?"

"You are a good listener, My Gracious Grand Duchess."

"Now, as much as I hate to face those stairs again, I'd like to visit your roadblock."

"Ma'am," the major said.

"Vicky!" Mannie said.

"Can it," Vicky said.

The two men scowled at her.

"You tend to your knitting and I'll tend to mine," Vicky shot at them.

"I shouldn't say this," the major said, "since the longer you take, the more chances he'll have to change your mind, but there is an elevator you can use."

"I've seen enough of those dead bodies," Vicky said. "I'll take the stairs if you don't mind."

"You don't have to. I made sure to get a generator up, powering this building. You can ride it down to the third floor, then turn left. The outside stairs are just a couple of meters ahead of you. No bodies. Little stench."

"Thank you, Major."

Mannie and Vicky rode the elevator down, then dodged to the outside. It was a silent ride.

"Is there any chance I can talk you out of trotting off and sticking your neck into another noose?"

"Nope. I'll be safe," Vicky insisted.

Mannie just shook his head, "And you expect me to hang around here?"

"Yep. Corral the first rigs off the longboats. Make sure they've got the gear you need and see that they head straight out for the lake. You know how much we need that water."

"I know. But we also need you, my darling."

"And you shall have me, I assure you," she said, giving him a friendly peck on the cheek.

Once back at her gun truck, Vicky gave Mannie a ride back to the first hangar and left him there to see if he could plant some seeds for democracy.

She, however, had a war to fight. She settled into the back of the gun truck and said, "Let's go see an ambush."

16

The drive out to the road block was silent and kind of slow. You would think these guys were scared for some reason. The LT and gunner kept their heads up, eyes roving over the terrain.

Vicky eyed the rolling hill country. The land smelled of earth and fertility. The air was clean and warm. If she could get her mind off of what she'd just seen and done, it would be idyllic.

The road was wide, with wide, deep ditches on either side. Even now, they had small streams running down them Beyond them were trees of several different Earth types, some evergreen, others seasonal. All were fully covered with greenery and leaves.

The fields beyond the trees looked like they had been plowed often, but were now covered in grass. No one wanted to get too close to Kromy.

Ahead, she knew, the hills would slant down to a wide bay where Kromy had been built. Several hundred klicks to the south, at the equator, was Bonki with the industrial park that had grown up around the space elevator station.

Work there was still subdued, but there did not appear to be a strong redcoat presence.

Oryol looked like a healthy body that someone had beheaded.

The gun truck slowed to a halt.

Vicky looked around. "Why'd we stop?"

"You're in the ambush," the LT said.

Vicky dismounted, then slowly turned in a complete circle. Then she did it again, only even more slowly. She studied the trees, the ditches, the fields.

If there were armed men out there, she couldn't spot them.

The temptation was to shout "Olly, olly, oxen free," but such childish words didn't belong in a Grand Duchess's mouth. Nor did strong and armed men deserve to be addressed in such a way.

"Okay, Lieutenant, you beat me. Where's the ambush?"

"Olly, olly, oxen free!" he called.

The Marines appeared as if from the earth. A pair of them had dug themselves into the sides of the ditches on opposite banks, but fifty meters up the road from each other. Others were beside bushes. Not behind them, but in fire pits a bit to the left or right of the bush. They'd dug a fighting hole and covered it over with a steel plate that had turf on top of it.

Several snipers in heavy green and shaggy camouflage dropped out of the trees on either side of the road. Others rose from under a blanket out among the grass.

"Sergeant, you fooled Her Grace big time."

"I should hope so," a Gunny Sergeant said, then ordered, "Okay, you've had your break. Back down. Don't trample the grass around you."

In a moment, all but the sergeant had once again disappeared into the earth. He trotted over from the tree he'd slipped out of and joined Vicky and the LT.

"Your troopers are good," Vicky said when he got to her.

"We're the best ambush team in the fleet, Your Grace. Any time we're not stuck with deck plates under our boots, we're trying out different twists."

"How big a force do you think you can stop?" Vicky asked.

The sergeant pursed his lips. "Four tanks we can stop, maybe eight. Two platoons of infantry. We've got some claymores laid out that will ruin their day after they dismount."

"So, nobody is going to interrupt us at the airport," Vicky said.

"I just wish they'd try, ma'am. We've seen the shots of what the terminal looks like. God, I'd love to have those shit heads in my kill zone."

"You want to come with us tonight?" Vicky asked.

"Please, ma'am. Half my guys are on watch. Half are napping. We'll be in fine fettle come midnight."

"Lieutenant, make sure these guys are mounted up tonight."

"Will do, ma'am."

"So, are the sniper teams forward in just as good a shape as these?"

"Yes, ma'am."

"Do you have the take from the drones covering this road?" Vicky asked the sergeant.

He pulled a thin viewer out and unfolded it, just like hers. "Here's what I was looking at when I got the call you were coming."

He held the viewer so all three of them could see it. "No activity on this road. Not so much as someone driving out to take a look. I suspect they can't see longboats coming in for landing, but they're not even trying."

"Likely they are just too drunk," Vicky said.

"Your Grace, do you mind me asking," the sergeant said, "will this be a police action, or do we get to shoot these bastards?"

"Sergeant, these men are at war against their rightful sovereign. That's high treason. They've taken hostages, raped, and their pillaging has brought a successful colony to its knees. If you don't kill them, I'll just have to hang them tomorrow morning."

"Yes, ma'am," the sergeant said. Grinning from ear to ear, he snapped to attention and gave her a smart salute.

"Let's just try not to kill any of the hostages."

The grin went away. His "Yes, ma'am," was much more subdued.

Behind Vicky, she heard the whisper jets of a longboat coming in for a landing. The rest of her strike force was landing. It was time to stop being a tourist and go kick some redcoat butt.

"I'll see you later tonight," Vicky said.

"Thank you, ma'am," the sergeant said.

She mounted up and headed back to the airport. She had a hostage rescue to plan.

17

They met in the control tower, high above the airport. Colonel Pietz, commander of the 5th Marines brought all three of his battalion commanders. Captain Blue provided the large, portable map board for them to study the layout of Kromy on. Two other Navy captains were also there. Captain Howitz commanded the two thousand volunteers carrying rifles. Captain Blue had brought down a large contingent of engineers to work with the combat engineering major attached to the 5th Marines.

It took them an hour to knock it out, but at the end, General Pemberton summed up the strike plan.

"We all agree that splitting our forces is a bad idea for a military operation, but this is more of a police action. We want to round up all four thousand of the redcoats. To do that, we've got to take some risks."

He paused to glance around those forming a circle around the battle map. Vicky, along with everyone else nodded. Some eagerly, some reluctantly, but they all had finally agreed they needed a police dragnet, not a battle to defeat and dislodge an enemy.

"The regiment, with attached Navy forces, will approach along this direct axis, from the airport to downtown. Twenty blocks out, the

First Battalion will break off to the south to attack from that direction. The Second will do the same to the north. The Third, with the Navy landing party, will hold in place, then attack from the west."

Again, he paused, this time eyeing Vicky.

"The redcoats will have three choices: die fighting, surrender and be hung, or flee to the east. There's only the bay behind them. They can drown, for all I care."

"Hostage situations?" Colonel Pietz asked the general.

With a glance at Vicky, General Pemberton dumped the question in her lap.

"If you have the shot, take it," Vicky said. "I've yet to meet a Marine that doesn't brag about being an expert marksman. This is where you get to show me. Any bastard who hides behind a hostage dies."

Vicky tasted the solid steel in her words. She also tasted the regret that she would feel for every dead hostage. Still, this evil would not be allowed to hold good hostage.

This ended tonight, or at sunrise, when the surviving redcoats swung from ropes.

"Yes, Your Grace," all the officers present said, standing to attention.

Vicky then changed to something softer. "Captain Howitz, could you report on what we've got to handle the hostages when they're freed?"

"The fleet has brought down every doc nurse and corpsman we've got. We've sent teams out to recruit any medical people on the economy. We've got our hands on quite a few. We've also got women volunteering to back up our personnel, giving a hand with the hostages. I'm told these women will be in a fragile state. Turn them over to our people, and we'll evacuate them as quickly as possible," the captain stated.

"They don't need to stay there any longer than they have to," Vicky said, "but we don't want our troopers being pulled off the firing line, so pass the hostages to the rear quickly."

"Will all the hostages be women?" Colonel Pietz asked.

"Our understanding is yes, almost everyone who has been taken by the redcoats is female, usually young," Captain Howitz said. "If there are any men, they're likely in even worse shape than the women, if that's possible."

Some time during that summation, Mannie walked out of the elevator. He paused, listening, then stepped around those at the map board to come up beside Vicky's right elbow.

For a long moment, he studied the map, with the overlay of drone imagery. "Is that real time?" he asked.

"Yes," Vicky said.

"Still not much activity downtown, huh?"

"A few people rambling from building to building around the central park blocks, but not much activity at all. We think they're sleeping it off."

Mannie showed Vicky a doubtful look on his face, "They could be," he said, agreeably, then changed his tone. "Or you might need to know something I found out from one of the locals. Actually, quite a few of the local city folk."

Mannie turned around to take in the broad sweep of lush green land surrounding them.

"It's hard to believe, considering how lovely this all is, but come fall, something the locals call monsoons, sweep in from the gulf out there to the east of Kromy."

Those around the table seemed puzzled at the easy way of his words, but Vicky had come to learn that when Mannie got really soft, there was something hard underneath.

"These monsoons bring plenty of rain. Have you noticed how deep the ditches are alongside the roads?"

Except for Vicky, no one had.

"But it also brings winds that at times exceed two hundred and fifty kilometers an hour. This colony was almost wiped out the first fall."

Now he had everyone's attention.

"The initial settlement was laid out along the bay's edge. When the first storm hit, the settlers barely managed to make it up the bluffs above the bay. When the next storm came in two weeks later, they dragged everything they could salvage up the hill and watched what the first storm left get washed out to sea. They were left as little more than drowned rats. By the time the third storm in two months swept past them, everything they'd built had been wiped from the face of the planet."

Mannie shrugged. "Being pioneers, they didn't let a little thing like that stop them. They rebuilt, but Kromy now has an uptown and a downtown. Everything downtown by the bay is built on stilts. Much of what was built uptown has connecting breezeways between the basements of the buildings. With the wind blowing, that was about the only way people could conduct any business."

Mannie paused to eye Captain Blue.

The captain shook his head. "So, everyone we've seen was someone they wanted us to see."

"Yep."

"And any defense preparations have been done below ground."

"Yep, only it gets worse," Mannie said.

There were several groans from strong men.

"Out here in the country, they need deep ditches. How do you think they handle the rain runoff in town?"

"Sewers," Captain Blue said. "Big drainage sewers."

"Yep. I've spent some time talking to one of the fellows who maintains the sewers. He doesn't have a map on him, but he figures he remembers it pretty well. Anyone here want to talk to him?"

Mr. Zukon, a short, round, gray-haired fellow, was waiting for their call.

Thirty minutes later, they knew about the underground breezeways through the five square blocks around the central parks. They also knew about the underground.

"Our public transit goes all the way out to the edge of town," Mr. Zukon explained. "We tried building the extensions above ground, but the damn typhoons blew cars off the tracks. We had to take it underground if we wanted it to run."

"So, when these storms come in, does all work stop?" Vicky asked.

"The winds soften soon after they reach landfall. Still, farmers around here just stay in. They have plenty of fodder for their farm animals for a couple of weeks. Here, we just set up cots and shelter where we need to be. School kids stay in school for four or five days. Plants have bunkhouses for their people. Some of us take time to party a lot."

A mischievous grin took over the old fellow's face. "Lots of births nine months later, you know. The colony's still small enough that we like large families."

Vicky decided she'd heard all she needed to, and sent the man below. Although, come to think of it, she might want Mannie to spend more time with him and the locals.

"Okay, how does this change our strike plan?" she asked General Pemberton.

"Does 'toss it into a cock hat' sound familiar?" he replied.

"We do seem to have gone from knowing a lot to knowing almost nothing about our target," Captain Blue mused.

"We need to get some drones down in these undergrounds and sewer systems," Colonel Pietz said.

"I could send a recon platoon forward," Major Cibor, of the colonel's combat engineers said. "I'd need some fire support in case these SOBs got troublesome."

"I can give you a reinforced company," the colonel said, and the skipper of the 3rd battalion got busy ordering up a task force.

Just before Mannie joined them, Vicky spotted gun trucks coming back with trailers burdened with full bladders of water. Five of them. While the soldiers began the work of filling in the blanks on their knowledge of Kromy's underground, she left to see what was being done for these brutalized survivors.

18

I t was nice to have Mannie by her side, if only for a few moments. She removed the gauntlet from her armor, and he did the same. In a moment, she could feel the warmth of human flesh on her own. He began to play his fingers over the palm of her hand.

"Are you trying to distract me from reviewing your water work?" Vicky asked.

"Nope. I'm just trying to distract you," Mannie admitted.

She sighed. "Oh, that you could. Maybe tomorrow morning we can find time for a nap."

"We'll see," was warm and hopeful, even as the gun truck came to a halt in front of the first hangar. Where starvation and lethargy had been, was now a buzz of activity.

"For now, Mannie, tell me what I'm looking at," she said.

"Colonel Pietz held back a company of Marines so we could drop a mobile hospital," Mannie told her as they paced toward the hangar. "They have taken over the care of the refugees. We have to limit their intake. Not only food, but also water. Who would have thought it?"

"Yeah," Vicky agreed, tersely. For the moment, all her attention was being held by the view in the hangar.

A gun truck with a bladder full of water was now parked beside the trailer full of famine biscuits. People had queued up for water. The Marines were filling small, red 250 milliliter cups and handing them to the medical staff.

Corpsmen handed off the cup, and, depending on whether the civilian passing by was an adult or a child, a pink or a blue pill.

"Take the pill. Sip the water. There will be more in an hour, so please drink the water slowly. Sip," was the medical mantra.

"Is it the same at the other hangars?" Vicky asked Mannie.

"Yes. We want to bring the people from the other side of the field over here so we can take care of them all together. However, many of them are in too bad of shape to move. We'll bring some today, then more as we stabilize them."

"Or lose some," Vicky added.

"They'd had three die already the last time I was over there."

Vicky could feel her lips disappearing into a stern, angry scowl. "All we can do now is what we can do."

Embarrassment followed. To a shout of "The Grand Duchess!" the people standing in line broke from the queue and hobbled over to surround her.

Even Kit and Kat did not take this for an attack. Still, people surrounded her, joggling her elbows as they thanked her for their salvation.

"We would have all been dead by next week."

"My mother almost died but you brought her food and water."

"We thank God for you."

Vicky found herself fighting back tears. All this gratitude was misplaced. It was the Marines and medical personnel that were saving their lives. She didn't deserve any of this.

Mannie seemed to understand that and the problem she was creating here. Slowly, he and the assassins managed to get her moving through the crowd to the water line that was rapidly running out of people that needed water.

With her moving in that direction, the throng began to gravitate back toward the lifesaving water. Vicky took up her place at the elbow of the two corpsmen distributing water and pills.

Now people could give her their thanks without risking their fragile lives. Vicky accepted that gratitude, encouraging them to tell that to a Marine, doctor, or Sailor.

Now, she noticed that laid out in rows were people who could hardly raise their heads. These were being given water by some of the less weakened souls under the guidance of the doctors and corpsmen.

She could only imagine what it was like across the runway.

Half an hour later, she slipped away and quickly walked to the second hangar. This time, Mannie got her to the head of the water line before the effort got disrupted. A half-hour later, it was time to move to the third one.

As one water bowser emptied, a second arrived from the lake. The water smelled of treatment, but no one complained. They would go through the line, finish off their cup, then fifteen minutes after the last person got water, they'd start again.

Meanwhile, a small field kitchen had been established. There, they were heating soup and adding famine biscuits to it along with other ingredients Vicky could only guess at.

Soon, people were queueing for the soup. It was ladled into their small red cups and they were sent off to drink it.

By the time Vicky had spent a half-hour in the third hangar, people were cycling through the soup line, then resting before getting more water. By this point, the survivors seemed to realize that there was plenty of food and they need only eat what they wanted when their bodies wanted it.

"Your Grace," Maggie said from Vicky's neck.

"Yes."

"The general would like you back at the control tower."

Wordlessly, Vicky nodded and marched from her place among the sick and dying. Mannie let her go without a comment.

She was death and there was nothing more for the two of them to say about it.

19

Vicky found an intense bunch of officers studying several different map boards and screens when she returned to the control tower.

"They have booby trapped the approaches," General Pemberton reported. "I really appreciate the help your computer gave us. It did a more intense analysis of the drone imagery and identified where claymores had been set into the walls of the sewers and underground tunnels."

"Maggie?" Vicky asked.

"Your Grace, there was not much I could do for you as you comforted the survivors, so I turned my focus to the sensor data coming back from our drones."

"Very good, Maggie," Vicky said while thinking, *You and I have got to talk about what you do without telling me.*

"We've also spotted mines sunk into the roads a good ten blocks from the uptown underground complex. We'll have to dismount and work our way in carefully on foot."

Vicky frowned. "Won't that slow us down?"

"Yes, ma'am, but how can we do otherwise?" General Pemberton asked.

Vicky let her eyes wander back to the view of green fields dotted with sheep.

The general followed her gaze. "Ma'am, you've got to be kidding."

"Are they that much smaller than a man?" she asked.

"But won't they fail to trip a mine designed for a gun truck?"

"Good point," Vicky said. "Still, can't we laser the mines we identify and leave it to the sheep to spot the ones we missed?"

"Major Magdor, why don't you have someone go talk to our local sheep ranchers and see about rustling us up some mine detectors."

"Talk to Mannie before you leave," Vicky put in. "He may know someone who knows the ranchers around here. Also, assure them that they will be paid both for the loan of their sheep and for any that are lost."

"Understood, Your Grace," the major said. With a quick salute, he quickly left.

"If we blow up mines, they'll know we're coming," Major Cibor of the combat engineers pointed out.

"So we blow mines all around their perimeter," Vicky said. "That's bound to scare the hell out of them."

"Are we still planning on coming in from all three directions now that we have given up all hope of surprise?" Colonel Pietz asked General Pemberton.

"What about blocking forces on those flanks?" Vicky asked. "Maybe a battalion of Navy landing force strengthened with a company of Marines and a few snipers."

"And if they try to run our roadblock with a car carrying hostages?" Colonel Pietz asked.

"Shoot for the tires? The radiators?" Vicky offered.

"That would slow them down," General Pemberton said. "Your Grace, you do know that we're going to lose some hostages."

Vicky nodded. "No matter what we do, people are going to die. We just need to try for the smallest number."

The officers in the control tower nodded their agreement. Four thousand plus potential bad guys and an unknown number of hostages. Tonight was bound to get out of their control. That didn't mean they couldn't do all within their power to keep things the way they wanted.

20

With care, they advanced by companies into town during the last hours of daylight. There was a small shoot-out along the main threat axis. The lead company coming in from the west spotted the sloppy ambush.

It was short and sharp and ended with ten dead redcoats. That assumed you could still call these thugs redcoats. Most wore rather fine clothing; only a few still sported their red uniform.

Fortunately, they had no female hostages with them.

As the sun set, the companies, now reinforced with combat engineers and qualified Sailors, were ready to start exploding mines. The drones helped them spot likely mine locations. Reconnaissance by fire handled most of the mines. By the time darkness completely fell, they would have blown all the mines they knew of, almost up to the park blocks.

About fifty redcoats tried to slip up behind the engineers clearing the roads in from the space port. However, the locals had warned the Marines where the spots were that they could expect anyone underground to come up to street level.

In the dark, the redcoats crept from the Twentieth Avenue subway station after the engineers had passed them clearing mines on their way into town. The inept thugs had spread themselves out and made ready to gun down the engineers when they returned.

Things didn't go their way.

They made a poor use of cover. Once the last of the bushwhackers had strung themselves out along the buildings lining West Street, two companies of the 2nd of the 5th Marines that were waiting opened fire from their own ambush.

The redcoats didn't know what hit them. Those that tried to flee back to the underground, found fire teams had slipped up behind them. Marines had dead fields of fire all along the inclined walkways the fleeing criminals tried to dash down.

None of the fifty survived their little sneak attack.

21

At full dark, the main strike force moved out slowly from the airport. In many of the trailers that were not needed for combat equipment and supplies, Sailors sat expectantly. Other Sailors rode in buses and vans that had been parked at the airport.

The last drop had brought down the needed equipment to repair the hydrogen/oxygen generators so all the rolling stock there could be fueled and brought into the troop movement.

More of the fuel cells had been handed off to the sheep ranchers to power their stock trucks. Their part of the convoy stank, so they brought up the rear.

Most of them had brought their sheep dogs. Vicky would be charged a premium if any of them were hurt, crippled, or killed. Still, it seemed better to have the dogs move the sheep forward than the shepherds.

At midnight, they began running of the sheep. The dogs and shepherds did their best to just run the sheep up the streets until they were two blocks out from the park blocks, but sheep being sheep, and the park blocks having grass, many of them galloped off for the park and its abundant grass.

In less than an hour, the sheep had pranced through all the streets Vicky's troops would follow to their target and not a single sheep had ended up as lamb chops. Nor had anyone shot at the sheep collecting in the park blocks.

Hidden among the sheep were rolling drones which gave troops a good look at the buildings surrounding the park. Government House was at one end, the Imperial Bismarck Hotel was opposite it, across two blocks of trees, grass, and a statue to the pioneers.

Along the two long sides of the park were four buildings. Next to the east side of Government House facing the park was a government office building annex. Across the park from it was a building that had once housed State Security, now dead, gone, and unlamented. Next to the hotel on the west side of the park was the planet's major bank. It was across from a new building of glass and concrete that held offices for bureaus of commerce and agriculture.

As bookends, on either side of the hotel and Government House, were four luxury apartment complexes. On their lower levels they provided restaurants and other services to the area. Private offices were on higher levels before apartments and condominiums for those working for the government took over.

Here was everything you needed to run a small colony. At least that was what Vicky would have thought years ago. Now she marveled that the Courts of Justice were in the same building with State Security.

That would have to change.

Vicky surveyed all the drone takes on her portable battle board. Every building was dark. So were the streets. Except for the stars, there was no light. A full moon would rise around two, but for now, it was starlight.

At least the night was clear, if a bit crisp.

The time for the assault, 0100, came and the troops moved out silently. They had four blocks to cover and were willing to take all the time needed to cover it.

Troops spread out along the sidewalks of the buildings. Where doors were found, a bit of lock-picking opened them, and sniper teams headed up for the roof. Meanwhile, rifle teams checked out the rooms.

Most were empty. In a few, usually the basement, emaciated civilians huddled together. They were ordered to shelter in place for now. Still, their presence raised a serious question.

Would troops find a bunch of such people with a gunman hiding among them?

Vicky could not give any order to the Marines except for them to be careful. She felt sick to her stomach at being so helpless against the multiple options for evil her loyal troops faced.

They covered two blocks in silence. The drones, however, warned them that the next block would be tough. There were gunmen on the roofs waiting for them. Vicky refused to call them snipers. They were equipped with the ubiquitous State Security machine pistol, good for pray and spray, but hardly an accurate weapon, even at short range.

The sniper teams had been leapfrogging forward, one covering a roof in the fifth block up from the Park Block. As the troops moved into the fourth block, different sniper teams raced to the roofs of those tall buildings. Finally, both collected on the roofs of the third block across from the gunmen skulking about the roofs on buildings only one block away from those on the Park Block.

Vicky imagined that the Marines drew straws to see who got to cross the street first. Or maybe the sergeants sent forward someone who had pissed them off. However it was, several Marines scurried across the street to the last set of buildings before they hit the inner ten.

At the sound of men running, the gunners popped up and fired through the balustrade that lined the roofs of these buildings. As expected, they sprayed the street below as if they had a water hose. The sharp staccato of machine pistols filled the air.

The Marine snipers across the way from these punks kept their heads down. Only the tip of their long rifles projected through the balustrade that hid them.

Vicky could hear the sharp bark of the snipers as they fired single shots. The chatter of the machine pistols slowed, then died with the last of their gunmen.

The Marines collected on both sides of the main entrance while small fire teams stood ready at the side doors. A combat engineer used a long extender to hold a satchel charge against the middle of the glass door. Fire from inside did nothing but make holes in the glass.

A moment later, the explosion sent all that glass into the building's vestibule. They were followed up with grenades. After a short three count, a sergeant ordered his Marines inside.

They were met with no resistance.

Vicky joined a full platoon as they trotted into the building that was part shops, part offices, and part apartments. A dozen bodies in red pants and stolen finery lay in pieces around the foyer. Even the two who had tried hiding behind the security desk had been hit by flying glass and grenade fragments.

They were still alive. Head shots changed that.

Now the Marines went from room to room. Because of the high likelihood that there would be hostages, they could not toss a grenade in first. Each door had to be carefully opened.

If they caught a burst of fire from inside, Marines offered the gunner a chance to surrender. If there were screams or whimpers from women, the grenades went back onto the web gear.

The next move was the Marines. Scopes to look around corners had been liberally distributed. Once the fire team leader knew the situation, they'd choose their option: a roll along the floor and a shot up, or a quick roll and shoot from a door jam.

Whichever was chosen, a gunman died a moment later. Most of the time, that left a naked woman who was more than likely in a severe state of shock. Still, not a few of them turned upon their rapist, kicking and pounding on the dead or dying body.

Unequipped for psychiatric care, the battle-hardened Marines moved on to the next door, leaving the women to follow on care.

Occasionally the gunman would change up the situation. Some went berserk and dashed out into the hall to spray bullets at the

Marines. They died quickly as the sharpshooters assigned to cover the front shot them down with one or two well-aimed rounds.

Others tried playing the hostage card, demanding a car or safe conduct off planet. Many were already rattled and had no idea how they could escape their situation. Again, two or three sharpshooters would have them in their sights. As soon as one got a shot, the gunman would get a round between the eyes.

That was usually all it took to free that hostage.

A few redcoats tried that in pairs or trios. That took more coordination, but the comm units each Marine had in his helmet allowed the sergeant to make a call. The shots sounded in unison as the two or three redcoats fell as one.

Help began to get in gear. Now, as soon as the redcoats were dead, a corpsmen, a civilian medic and a local woman who'd volunteered to stay with the hostage through the night, moved in. The hand-off from Marines to caregivers took place faster and faster.

The medics and the women with them didn't have to see the condition of too many of the hostages before they pushed forward at their own risk to be there as soon as heavenly possible to check the former hostage.

While the medical professionals gave each woman a quick physical, the local women provided warm blankets and hot tea for their freed neighbors, as well as soft words as they helped them from the buildings and onto buses.

The buses began a regular route, driving women out, then returning empty for another load of beaten and brutalized women. Some paused to thank their liberators. A few asked if they could have a rifle and join them.

It pained Vicky, but she had to refuse the help. These women had been pushed, shoved, and raped well past the breaking point. While they deserved to be avenged, there was no telling what might happen if they had a weapon in their hands.

It was strange, Vicky reflected. None of the redcoats offered to come out with their hands up. They seemed to all know that they'd burned too many bridges to be allowed back into civilization.

One by one, the outer ring of eighteen buildings, five or six stories high, reported in as cleared. Vicky's battle board kept tally, or maybe it was Maggie. The toll of dead redcoats settled at just over eleven hundred.

The number of hostages killed in the crossfire was twenty-two. The number of wounded held steady at below one hundred. Sadly, there was no way to tally the mental wounds these women would carry for the rest of their lives.

Once the outer row of buildings were cleared, the Marines paused for fifteen minutes to take a breather and to reorganize themselves. Each of the eighteen combined-use buildings had been taken by a platoon, with one company in reserve.

General Pemberton found Vicky and advised her of his plan for the next phase of the clearing action.

"We've got four buildings on each side of the park block streets. Two of the special use buildings with two combined-use and luxury apartment buildings on either end. Drones identify them as more occupied than the government buildings. Once we clear these, we go for Government House and the hotel. My guess is the hotel will be the hardest nut to crack."

Vicky nodded agreement.

"I'm going to pull the Marine and Navy blocking force in closer. They've been taking out the odd runner, say fifty of them. Just like us, they're getting no one surrendering. I'm going to hit the buildings along the park street and hold off on the last two buildings until we can concentrate on them alone."

"I agree," Vicky said. "With any luck, we'll squeeze some of the less hard cases out of those two and send them running into our blocking forces."

"That was what I was thinking," General Pemberton said.

"What about explosives?" Vicky asked.

"Most of the mining on this planet uses nanos. However, I'm told that these redcoats never felt any urge to go up in the hills. The miners let them know that if they tried, they'd bring the mountains down on them. So, no mining explosives. The farmers are out of the ammonia and hydrocarbon business. There are no stocks to make explosives. The poor planet folk couldn't defend themselves at all. Anyway, the redcoats can't do mass slaughter on this planet.

"So, we take them down, one shot at a time."

"It looks that way."

"Do we know where their command center is?" Vicky asked.

"They don't exactly have a command center, per se. The Imperial suite and penthouse take up most of the top floor of the Imperial Bismarck. That's where the head honchos hang out. That's where they keep their harems. We'll have to fight our way up the hotel to them."

"I sure wish we had helicopters to drop teams on the roofs and work their way down."

"I'll put that on my list of things to include for the assault on Lublin. It's bigger. I doubt they'll give up without a fight. They have to know after what they've done, there's no future for them."

Vicky scowled. "Which makes them fight like cornered rats. I thought we always tried to keep an exit open to encourage the guys shooting at us to bug out."

"Yeah," General Pemberton said, "but I doubt if the leaders of these goons expect they can run. There's no place for them to hide. After what they've done here, all of human space is too hot for them."

"Yeah," was all Vicky could say.

"Is there any chance I can get you to stay with my command group?" the general asked.

"I'd rather stay with the platoon I've been with," Vicky said.

"You know the hoods in this next building will be even more desperate."

"I expect so."

"God, woman, I wish I could haul you off and lock you up."

Vicky chuckled. "No doubt you do, but I know you won't. I'm the boss," she said, then thought over what she'd said. "And several billion people boss me."

"Well, I'm people too, and I would sure like to boss you a bit."

"Sorry, General, but I've got to go where I send people to die."

"We sure could use a handbook on how to handle a Grand Duchess, as well as how one is supposed to behave," the General grumped.

"No doubt you'll write one for me in your spare time."

The General made a face. "As if I ever have any spare time."

"And I'm sure you wouldn't waste it on such a handbook. I'd only ignore it, anyway."

That got a sardonic chuckle from the general. "You'll excuse me if I wonder out loud how our new Empire will look with a woman setting it up."

"Yes, I imagine you and a lot of the old guard are wondering."

"The old guard is who we're killing, Your Grace. Anyone who follows you has to be a charter member of the new guard."

Now it was Vicky's turn to chuckle. "I stand corrected, my general of the new guard."

"Okay. If you'll excuse me, I have an assault to arrange and order," he said and strode away from her, already talking on his commlink. Vicky located the company commander who just happened to be accompanying her platoon.

"You ready to go, Your Grace?" the skipper said.

"When you are."

"Just stay behind me, please," he said. "I really don't want to have to tell your husband you died on my watch."

Vicky had an obscene recollection of what men had done to her while behind her. She stashed that away and remembered Mannie. She owed him a lot for all that she was putting him through. Leaving him in the rear to bite his nails while she danced around the sharp tip of the spear.

He was where women usually were, doing what they usually did. Worrying. No doubt in her future Empire, women would follow her out to the pointy end and more men would get stuck worrying.

Vicky shook her head. So many changes she'd never thought of when she started down this path. Then, she'd just been trying to stay alive from minute to minute. She never would have thought she'd end up here.

"Move out in five," the platoon LT announced to his troops. "Check your gear. Replace your magazines. The next batch of bastards are likely to be worse than the ones we just popped, so let's be careful and kill the bastards."

"Ooorah!" came back at him, confident and with full intent.

22

Vicky chose to join the attack on one of the luxury apartment buildings, the one across the street from the Imperial Hotel. She suspected it had more people in it than, say, the bank.

She was right.

However, having more people in a building without power or water created problems. Like what to do with raw sewage. The entire first floor stank. Apparently, it was being used as a latrine.

Sickeningly, a young woman was found splayed out in chains in all the filth. Vicky was with the team that found the woman.

The naked woman stared at them blankly even as the combat engineer used huge clippers to cut through the chains that held her down.

Vicky helped the girl stand up; she was covered with excrement. A corpsman provided a thermal blanket, and Vicky wrapped her in it.

"What were they doing to you?" the Grand Duchess asked.

"Breaking me," the woman muttered, then drank greedily from a canteen offered her. "One of them claimed I teethed his root when it was halfway down my throat and I was choking to death. I wish I'd bit it off. Killing me would have been better than this. They were using me to piss on. Or worse. Where can I get a bath?"

"Water's not running," Vicky said. "I'll have some Navy take you to the nearest beach."

"Just take me to a pier. Let me dive off and drown myself."

Both Vicky and the corpsman blanched.

"Ma'am," the medic said, "we have some nurses at an aid station we're setting up. Maybe one of them could drive her to that beach."

"Be sure they have a guard detail," Vicky said. "As much as we're aiming to collect all these bastards, there are bound to be a few that slip through our net."

The corpsman helped the woman to the rear.

Vicky eyed the overhead where those bastards were. She could hear gunfire. She drew her side arm. Keeping it aimed high, she strode purposefully for the second floor.

In the stairwell, she encountered a redcoat who was missing his pants. He held a machine pistol at the head of a woman who was missing all her clothes. She was crying softly as he dragged her down the stairs, trying to sneak out while all the strike force was concentrated on the second floor.

He came to a halt when he spotted Vicky.

"Get out of my way or I'll kill her," he demanded.

"Okay, okay," Vicky said. She slipped through the door out to the second floor. There, she listened as the terrified fool dragged his shield with him as he hastened down the stairs.

Vicky gave a short two count, then opened the door and stepped into the stairwell. The SOB's head was just where she wanted it. A bullet in the back of it put an end to one man's lawless rampage.

"Corpsmen!" Vicky shouted.

Quickly, one was at her elbow, a blanket in hand.

The woman had collapsed into herself. She squatted on a stair, curled into a shivering ball. Vicky knelt beside her, then gently wrapped the woman in the blanket. She was sobbing, but softly, as if afraid to make too much noise.

The corpsman handed the woman off to two Sailors.

"Come with us," one young Sailor said. "We've got some women waiting for you."

The other Sailor offered her a cup of steaming tea from a thermos he carried.

Holding the cup of tea in both hands, and occasionally taking a sip, the woman shuffled off slowly with them.

With her weapon at the ready, Vicky made her way along the hallway. Here and there a dead gunman's blood drained out onto the carpet. Behind Vicky came more unarmed Sailors with blankets and hot tea to help the women huddled on the floor beside the bodies.

Vicky found the captain directing the operations.

"You need to put a man on the stairwell," she told him, then added what she'd done.

"We had a man there. Sergeant," he shouted, "who was supposed to stand guard on the stairwell?"

"Caspoz, Skipper, but he got dragged into a hostage situation."

"Well, get him back in the stairwell. We've got shit heads trying to slip out behind us."

"Aye, aye, Sir. Caspoz!" the sergeant shouted.

"Yes, Sergeant."

"Get back on guard duty. The damn Grand Duchess had to cover for you."

A Marine private hurried past Vicky, his rifle at the ready.

Vicky chuckled to herself. So, she'd been promoted to "damn Grand Duchess." Well, with Marines, damn was likely more honorable than gracious.

Cautiously, she moved from door to door. Some rooms were empty. Many of them had a dead gunman sprawled behind a couch or overturned table. In several rooms, the women hostages were huddled in front of the tables or couches, broken and weeping. Some sobbed as if their hearts would never recover.

Vicky's anger flashed white hot. Her gaze grew more grim. This could not be happening in her Empire.

Of course, this was her father's half of the Empire. "God, he should be here to see the mess he made and what it's cost these people," she growled.

"You say something, Your Grace?" the company skipper said. He was following behind her.

"Just making a mental note to myself," Vicky answered.

She caught up with the action just as a dozen shots rang out from a room. Cautiously, Vicky ducked her head around the door.

Here, three gunmen lay dead, sprawled behind a makeshift barricade. Four women had collapsed on the floor. *Didn't these bastards let any of their hostages keep a scrap of clothing?*

Then Vicky spotted blood on one hostage.

"Corpsman!" a Marine shouted. In the hall, others took up the shout.

Vicky entered the room to discover that the call wasn't just for the woman. One of the Marines was down.

Through gritted teeth, he growled, "Who skipped that bastard? We go right to left. Right?"

"There were five of us, and only four of them," the guy holding a compress to the sergeant's shoulder said. "I think that confused us."

"Skipper, we got to make sure everyone knows who to shoot."

"You bad hurt, Sarge?"

"Not as bad as those bastards," the sergeant said, nodding to the bleeding bodies. "They never learn."

"Hard for them to learn anything, them being too dead to pass along their mistakes to their buddies," the captain said.

At that moment, a body hurtled by the window, headed for the ground. Vicky thought it looked naked and male. *Were there male hostages?*

"Maggie, is there anything on the net about naked men?"

"A guy was raving on the roof waving a gun and threatening to kill everyone. A Marine sniper took him down."

"It takes all kinds, don't it, ma'am?" the wounded sergeant said.

A corpsman and other Navy personnel arrived. This detail had two civilian women with it. They went straight to the naked former hostages while the corpsman joined the Marines around their sergeant.

A shout of, "Skipper, you need to see what's on the next floor!" came from the hall.

23

Vicky followed the company commander back into the central hallway. They quickly strode toward the stairwell. Beside Vicky, broken doors showed empty rooms or rooms with the dead or dying inside. It sometimes took a while for a man to die even when he was already dead.

The Marines didn't seem inclined to administer any *coups de grâce.*

One flight of stairs up, the fire door to the third floor was still closed. An engineer had slipped a spy scope under the door. Vicky pulled out her portable battle board and connected to the feed.

A dozen meters past the door, a couch was shoved into the hallway. Four female hostages huddled on it. Behind them and the couch, three gunmen kept low, their guns at the ready.

The company commander stood beside Vicky, watching the scene on her board.

The engineer pulled back the scope, then slipped it through the top of the door. That gave them a full view of the hall. There was a couch barricade facing the other stairwell. More hostages, more gunmen.

"This is a change-up," the skipper muttered. "Sarge, open the door nice and slow. I want four riflemen visible when that door is open, guns ready. Sergeant Stromm," he said into his commlink, "did you hear the order I just gave Hertz?"

"Yes, sir."

"I want you to set up four riflemen in the opposite stairwell. At my count of three, we open both doors. Got it?"

"Yes, sir."

The captain paused, then said, "One."

The net was quiet.

"Two."

A pause as he and Vicky eyed the four riflemen in front of them, weapons aimed.

"Three."

The engineer pulled the door open. In a second, four Marine riflemen faced three redcoat gunmen.

For a moment, they just stared at each other, then the Marines slipped cautiously through the door and began walking slowly toward the barricade.

"Stop right there!" sounded from both groups of gunmen at about the same instant.

The Marines quit advancing, but they kept their rifles up, aimed at the gunmen waiting for the shot.

The four naked women on the couch looked terrified. Some wept. Some seemed to have no more tears. They huddled there, close together, holding hands and trembling.

One of the women whimpered and curled up into a ball. As her head went down, a Marine got the shot he was waiting for. The head of the gunman directly behind the woman exploded. He fell back, instantly dead.

The hostage screamed and folded into a fetal position. The brunet next to her stroked her back and tried to comfort her even as the redcoats behind her grabbed her hair, forcing her to sit upright.

"You shouldn't ought to have done that," one thug said. "Ivan, get Mrs. Fancy Pants out here."

Two doors down from the barricade, a woman was shoved into

the hall. She collected herself, and, though nude as the other women, seemed to wrap herself in dignity as she walked carefully toward the gunmen.

"Get your ass over on the other side of the couch. And if you so much as twinge, we blow your daughter's head off."

Down the hallway, another, younger woman was forced into the hallway. Someone who didn't show himself, held a machine pistol to her head.

"Do whatever you have to do, Mom," she said.

"I can't risk losing you, Katarina," the older woman said. She cautiously stepped over the dead gunman, but there was too much blood and brains scattered around. Her feet now had gore on them.

She climbed over the couch and took the place of the other woman. Now she held the woman she was replacing like a child. That woman sobbed on her shoulder.

With a deep, disgusted sigh, Vicky stepped through the door.

"What do you want?" she demanded.

"Out of here," one thug said.

"Safe conduct," another said.

Vicky wanted to snap, "No way," but that would cut off discussion and she wanted to drag this out. No Marine had a shot. Maybe they'd mess up again.

"Safe conduct for what?" she demanded. "Where do you think you can go?"

That got the thugs casting nervous glances between themselves. Clearly, they hadn't thought this through.

"Ah, a starship and safe conduct out of here," one finally said.

"And you think a captain and crew would take you aboard? Take you aboard and not vent his ship to space? Gentlemen," Vicky almost choked on that word applied to these dregs of hell, "you have burned your bridges."

"Then we kill the hostages," a very nervous gunman shouted.

Two of the women cried out at that. The older woman reached out to them and made soothing sounds.

"You don't live a second longer than your hostages live. You harm them and we'll kill you slowly," Vicky snapped.

There was dead silence in the hallway, disrupted only by the soft weeping or whimpering of the naked women on the couch.

Finally, one of the gunmen, the bald guy who seemed to be some sort of boss man said, "You aren't giving us much of a choice here."

"How did you think this would all end? Did you really think you'd get to die in bed raping another man's wife or daughter?" Vicky asked softly.

Again, there were nervous glances between the men. Clearly, they hadn't thought through their actions for a long, long time.

Unnoticed while they did this, the older hostage was tapping on the shoulders of the three other naked women. As one, they ducked down.

Four Marines fired one volley, three heads behind them exploded. Then, without a moment's pause, the Marines fired a second volley, taking the so-called "security consultants" at the other end of the hall full in the back.

One machine gun fired on full auto, but it merely sent a fusillade of bullets up the wall next to them.

Marines were hurrying forward. The women hostages tumbled to the floor in front of the couches and Marines quickly stepped over them and the couches, and began clearing the rooms between the two barriers.

One young woman had collapsed on the ground the second the firing started. The brute that had a gun to her head took a moment to realize things were changing. She rolled away even as he fired, working a line of bullets down the wall across from where her head had been, then tried to drop his aim. However, machine pistols on full auto go up, not down.

While that poor excuse for a man and gunman was struggling with that, the Marine on the extreme right of the four advancing on him took him under fire.

With Marines advancing from both ends of the hall, the risk of blue-on-blue casualties were high, but the four Marine privates weren't stupid. They had the left-most man to aim for the right side of the hall. The right end aimed left.

The Marine stitched the door with a quick five round burst. One caught the gunman and blew the weapon out of his hand.

The redcoat screamed. Then he made the mistake of reaching for the fallen gun. That put half his body out in the hall.

His head exploded before he had a chance to realize his mistake.

Clearing the rooms was a repeat of the second floor. Some punks hid behind hostages. Most did it poorly and died from a quick shot.

Some tried to go out in a blaze of glory, firing at anything that crossed their door. A whiz-bang grenade left them dazed and a single shot to the head ended that noise and freed another dozen or so dazed female hostages.

One tough guy was hiding under the unmade and filthy bed he'd been sporting in. Two women showed the Marines where he hid, and he was quickly dispatched.

The two most cowardly of the gunmen threw down their weapons and begged for mercy. None of the Marines looked ready to serve as their executioners. At least, not without an order, and Vicky did feel the need to pass judgement when her blood was cooler.

The Marines ordered them to strip, then bound their hands behind their back.

Now it was time to tackle the third floor.

24

The goons might not be getting after-action reports or lesson-learned flyers, but they were getting smarter. Maybe the guys with more sense lived higher up. Maybe they had time to think things over more.

Again, traumatized hostages huddled on a couch at either end of the hall. Now large tables provided a backdrop for the hoods. There would be no shooting these guys in the back if one barricade went down.

This time, four of the gunners held the hostages by the hair. The women could only weep and tremble in fear. They could not move.

The gunmen also fired a fusillade of bullets as soon as the steel fire door began to pull open.

The Marines let the door slip closed and turned to wait for orders.

Vicky and the skipper silently eyed the situation. They were in a steel and concrete stairwell with a still door that had to remain closed.

The Marine officer waved the combat engineer over to a wall. The technician ran a device along it, then pulled out a small circular saw and began cutting into the reinforced concrete firewall.

It took him five minutes, but he had a large enough hole that Vicky could slip through.

That drew a sharp, but whispered rebuke from the skipper, but she was smaller than the average Marine, and she fit.

The engineer began widening the hole as Vicky, automatic at the ready, checked out the apartment. It stank of blood, sex, and terror, but it was empty.

She was soon joined by two Marine trigger pullers, a very put-out captain, and the combat engineer. Since Vicky had cleared the apartment, the engineer quickly began cutting away the drywall, opening a hole to the next apartment.

Soon they had access to the next studio suite. This time, a Marine led the way.

Having cleared that apartment, they could hear the punks talking among themselves. They wanted to negotiate their way out of here and wondered what was keeping the Marines from talking to them.

"Well, we did kind of try to shoot their balls off when they opened the door," one thug said.

"I don't like this. They're not doing anything. That means they're doing something," said another punk.

While that logic escaped Vicky, it did tell her that her Marines needed to be doing something.

"Maggie," she whispered. "Can you contact the sergeants in the stairwells at either end of this hall?"

"Yes, ma'am," Maggie whispered back.

"I want them to toss a pair of whiz-bang grenades down the hall."

"Do they need to coordinate?" Maggie asked.

"Yes, but we want them five, no, ten seconds apart."

"Got it. Wait one."

Meanwhile, the engineer had cut a small peep hole through to the next apartment. The room in front of them was empty. He began cutting into the soft drywall.

"They're ready," Maggie whispered.

Vicky waited while the engineer finished a good-sized hole in the wall. A Marine stood by, ready to enter the next apartment.

"Go," Vicky ordered.

The Marine stepped through the hole just as the first whiz-bang went off.

From the hall came the chatter of automatic weapons fire. Even though their senses were under assault, these bastards had an answer in place. It sounded like three or four machine pistols were spraying the door at the end of the hall.

Vicky followed the Marine into the bedroom of the next apartment. He was already checking out the other rooms when the second whiz bang went off from farther down the hall. It also got a fusillade of small arms fire for a response.

"Clear," he whispered as the captain joined Vicky.

"Your Grace," the captain whispered in a strained voice. "Would you please stay behind me?"

"Only if you move faster," she said, but gave the poor fellow a grin.

He rolled his eyes at the overhead and stepped into the living room ahead of her.

The engineer followed quickly on his heels. He headed directly for the wall shared with the next apartment. He got a snoop scope into the next room, then scowled.

Vicky unfolded her battle board and scowled, too.

The next room held hostages. A dozen nude women huddled together seated on or in front of a couch. A man with a machine pistol stood in the doorway, dividing his attention between the hostages and what was happening in the hallway.

Vicky frowned; that divide would be his death.

Vicky conferred in a whisper with the engineer and the captain. The engineer raised his eyebrows at Vicky's idea.

The captain shook his head. "Your Grace, those machine pistols don't pack enough energy to put a hole in the fire door or fire walls, but these dry walls are nothing. Those pistols will cut straight through them."

"If he's dead, he can't do much shooting," Vicky replied.

"And if I said no?" the skipper asked.

"I'd pull rank on you."

"But the engineer is my direct subordinate," the Marine officer countered.

The engineer who was at the center of this debate looked from the captain to the admiral as they debated who would give him his next order.

"Captain, I am both the admiral commanding this expedition and your sovereign. You will obey me."

The captain shook his head, grimly. "They don't pay me enough to share a battle with you, Lady. Okay, Iven, do what she says.

Things had quieted down in the hall, except for a few triumphant claims that they'd beat back another attack.

Per his orders, the engineer cut two holes in the drywall in this apartment. One was wide enough to walk through. The other was much smaller. It, however, was above a dresser, so no one would be racing through a hole there. Instead, the engineer paused to wait for his skipper's orders.

The captain had his hand raised and his eyes on the snooper scope. It showed the agitated gunman in the doorway. He glanced back at the women, saw they were properly cowed by the machine pistol in his hand, and turned back to the hall.

"Now," the captain said, bringing his hand down.

The tech drilled a small hole just above the dresser, then stepped back.

Vicky filled that space with a gift from Kris Longknife, her automatic, held securely in her hand. Not only did she have it silenced, but she'd lowered the power of the charge behind the darts ready to be chambered.

This automatic was something new that Kris had asked a gun maker to create. Most weapons like this one had three clicks for the safety: safe, sleepy darts, and lethal. This automatic had a fourth click: sleepy and lethal.

As Kris had put it, this was the perfect load for when you wanted them dead, but quiet *while* they were dying.

The power charge was somewhere between lethal and sleepy as befitted the intent.

Using the weapon's video scope, Vicky aimed for the thug's center of mass. Without pause, she pulled the trigger for a ten-round burst just as her target started to turn back to the women.

Every round hit him in the chest.

Shocked, the man glanced down at the holes that had suddenly appeared around his heart. Then he crumbled.

Vicky regretted that he got to sleep through his death, but he neither made a noise nor any move toward the poor women he was terrorizing.

Vicky raised her pistol, and the engineer made the final cuts to drop the second slab of drywall, giving them an opening into the next room.

Shouldering her way past the trooper who had orders to be first through the hole, Vicky took those steps.

Raising her finger to her lips, she shushed the women on the bed. She stepped off the distance to them as the Marine cautiously approached the door where the gunman now lay convulsing in the final throes of his death.

It's amazing how long a body can bleed and the muscles twitch.

Vicky took the poor women in a large hug. Several women slid into her arms. Others still fought their terror as they fled to the far end of the couch or cringed under the coffee table. Still, not one of them screamed.

"The Marines are here. You'll be safe now," Vicky whispered.

The oldest woman who wrapped Vicky in her own hug, shook her head. "I'll never be safe again."

Vicky could not argue with her.

"I'm sorry, but I've got to look into killing the rest of those bastards."

"Burn them in hell," the younger woman said. Then, those two went to console the other two.

"Maggie, can we get a few women in here?"

"I've got two volunteers making their way forward."

"You may need to make it five or six," Vicky said, half attentively.

She had already turned her mind toward the next objective. Killing these women's rapists.

The engineer was at the open door of the apartment. His snooper scope turned first one way down the hall, then the next.

The four gunmen at each barricade were focused on the fire doors at the end of the hall. They huddled behind their couches, behind their naked female shields. Each group had a thick wooden table covering their backs.

However, the tables were at an angle to allow them space to come and go. Vicky grinned. She could think of something that would definitely come their way and send them to hell.

"Give me a grenade," she whispered to the Marine who held his rifle high.

The young Marine glanced at his skipper.

The captain shrugged and nodded.

Vicky found herself the proud owner of a very deadly handful of boom.

"I'm going to roll this at the ones on the right. You go left."

"Aye, aye, ma'am," the Marine said.

Vicky selected her fuse for three seconds. The Marine chose five. Together they pulled the pin.

"On three," Vicky whispered. "One. Two. Three."

And both of them tossed their grenades out to roll along the floor toward their targets.

The ones Vicky wanted dead had just enough time to react to the noise of something bouncing down the carpet toward them. One made to reach for the grenade, but the three second fuse didn't give him enough time.

Vicky had pulled her head back in, so she missed the beauty of a grenade blowing four brutal animals to hell.

At the other end of the hall, the thugs had more time to react. One of them twisted around and struggled to grab the rolling bomb. Another tried to leap over the couch to some sort of safety. Nothing helped them when the grenade exploded.

Vicky found the captain had a solid lock on her elbow. She

glanced down, then at him. "I know not to toss a grenade and jump out."

"I don't doubt that," he said, "but I have to have something I can tell your husband that I did when he tries to roast me alive."

"Let me handle Mannie," Vicky said, and made to enter the hall.

"Don't move, Your Grace," he said, pulling her back into the living room so Marines could pass. "We don't know how many other rooms hold gunmen with hostages."

"Okay," Vicky grumbled.

Somewhere a machine pistol chatter was cut off by a single shot. The cry of "Corpsman!" followed.

A medic raced past Vicky. A glance back into the bedroom showed a team of men and women caring for the four former hostages. A second medic broke loose from that team and followed the first into the hall.

There was another case of rapid fire that didn't last long. Two shots cut it off.

"I've got more hostages," was the shout from the hall.

A Gunny slipped past her. He began calling room numbers, followed by "Clear."

One of the punks panicked. There were screams and shouts.

"I'll kill her! I will! Let me out of here!" was hardly done when two shots ended that conversation.

Now Vicky ventured into the hallway.

"Ma'am," the Gunny said, "we've still got a few rooms to clear."

"And I have a few hostages to check."

Vicky turned toward the right. She knew the rooms between that bunch and the fire door just now disgorging Marines was safe. She carefully stepped her way through the gore of the dead and dying redcoats.

"Kill me," one begged.

"Consider it practice for hell," she snapped back and passed him by. A grenade fragment had sliced open his belly. Blood welled in the pit of his stomach and pulsed out as it overflowed. An artery had been slashed. He would die soon enough.

MIKE SHEPHERD

As far as Vicky was concerned, he'd die way too soon.

She found what she'd been looking for. Four women huddled on the floor where they had been blown or maybe just slid off the couch.

"Are you okay?" Vicky asked. "Are any of you hurt?"

It was the youngest woman who seemed to have it together here. She looked up at Vicky with red and empty eyes. "Yes, but we'll survive."

"Did the grenade hurt any of you?" Vicky corrected herself.

"No. I knew something was happening when they let go of my hair. I ducked down, and took the others with me. I think the couch protected us." She turned to look at the three men bleeding out where they'd fallen half over the couch.

"Leastwise it protected us more than it did them pigs."

"Good. There will be some women and medics along in a moment. We've got some injured hostages down the hall."

"Take your time. It won't matter all that much to us. No one can really help us."

"I'm the Grand Duchess Victoria, and I promise you that you will be heroes to your people and to your family."

"You're . . . you're the Grand Duchess?"

"That's what I see in the mirror every morning," Vicky said.

"And you came to save us?" held so much surprise in it.

"I'm doing my best. I just wish I could have gotten here sooner."

But the young woman had turned to her sister hostages. "Do you hear that? The Gracious Grand Duchess herself has come to our rescue."

It took a moment for heads to turn her way, but Vicky was soon sinking into wide, dull eyes that seemed to see too much of the past and had not yet begun to see the present.

A pair of women, one a nurse the other a civilian, hurried up the hall at that moment. An alert Marine tried to keep up with them, but failed.

The arriving women slid to their knees as they reached the former hostages and began to render aid. One checked vitals, the other administered hugs and soothing words while wrapping them in blankets and offering steaming cups of tea.

Vicky stood and eyed the other end of the hall. She climbed over the couch. The tough guy was still taking his time dying. His eyes followed Vicky, but he seemed past words.

Vicky gave him the middle finger as she left him in her wake. She also drew her automatic as she entered unknown territory.

"You can put that away, Your Grace," the captain said. "We got the last of the bastards. This floor is clear."

"Yeah," she said. "Only two floors to go."

"Skipper, we got a problem," came from the Marine holding open the door at the end of the hall. "Somebody on the next floor wants to talk to you."

"After me, Your Grace," the Marine officer said, and led the way.

25

"Nobody comes up this stairwell. This one or the other one. You set one foot off that landing and a hostage dies. You hear me?" was screamed down from the next floor. The voice held stress and a strong dose of terror.

It also sounded like it meant business.

"Also, we want a ride out of here and up to the space station. We want a ship to take us anywhere we tell them to."

"You're asking for a lot of stuff," the captain said.

"If we don't have what we want in four hours, we kill two hostages. Four hours later, we kill four. You get me?"

"You're dead the second you kill your last hostage," the Marine spat back.

"We got plenty of 'em. You think those pieces of shit had girls? Wait until you see how many girls we got up here. You're wasting my time. Go tell someone they want to get us a ride out of here or we start shoving dead bodies down these stairs."

"Let me go talk to my superiors. This may take time."

"You don't got time. Now, quit wasting it."

The captain let the door close with a loud click.

"Killing 'em just gets tougher and they just get meaner," he muttered.

"Let's get the engineers up here," Vicky said.

Five minutes later, an engineering LT was at Vicky's elbow. Ten minutes later, a full squad with equipment was taking the ceilings apart in several rooms of the third floor.

The sound-proofed ceiling panels were easy to pop out. In most cases, they only had to be lifted up. However, that only showed them their next serious problem.

While the ceiling above the floor was easy, the floors below the next apartments were concrete pads supported by steel beams.

"It's going to be a bitch drilling holes for snooper scopes," the engineering officer said. "And noisy, too."

"We need some noise to cover it up," Vicky said. "Maggie, get me someone who has some serious speakers. I want to rattle the bastards on the next floor."

"There is a performance center three blocks away," Maggie reported quickly.

"Get me the sound system. Meanwhile, Maggie, get me the most obnoxious sounds you can think of. A baby screaming is the worst I can think of. Maybe loud trash music. Stuff like that."

"Knowing this bunch," the captain said, "they might like the trash stuff. How about the most saccharin boy band?"

"We'll try them all. Just so long as it's noisy and crazy-making."

"You know, what's bad for the goose is migraine-making for the gander," the skipper pointed out.

"Maggie, can you come up with white noise to cancel out that racket?"

"Yes, Your Grace. I know what's coming. I can cancel it. However, the troops will have to close down their helmets to get any benefit from it."

"We can survive," Vicky said.

While they waited for the sound gear, the engineers tried slow drilling holes in the overhead over close to the outside walls. Since no one shot a hostage, it appeared to be silent enough.

They'd guessed right that the first four rooms on either side of the hallway and closest to the stairwells were empty.

Even while they waited for the noise, they began sawing through the concrete flooring above their heads. They started with shallow cuts, just taking a layer off the surface.

That done, they went back and cut a bit deeper. This kept the noise down. Slowly but surely, deeper cuts were made into the concrete.

The sound system arrived and was quickly put into use. With speakers in the stairwells that were lifted high to set the floor of the hallway above vibrating, all chance of thought fled until everyone had their helmet closed and white noise on.

It wasn't long before the guards at the stairwells were reporting a demand from the head redcoat that someone in authority talk to him.

The captain went.

"What do you want?" he demanded.

"You the boss man?"

"Close enough for your purposes," the Marine shot back.

"Shut off this crappy noise."

"You don't like kids crying, huh?"

"I'd have killed my kid brother if he screamed like that brat."

"Okay. Kill the noise."

Blessed silence reigned.

"Good."

"Now, I'm busy," the captain snapped.

"Getting us a ride out of here, right?"

"Getting you out of here, yeah."

"Just make sure it's a good ride or some of these fucking sluts die."

"I hear you," and the door slammed shut.

"I guess they haven't heard our drilling," he said to Vicky.

"I guess they haven't. How long do we let them enjoy the silence?"

"Two minutes. One hundred and twenty seconds. Then we go with the head-banging heavy metal music."

They returned to walking the halls, checking on how the sawing was going and what the size of the next strike team would be.

They had the entire company now waiting patiently, sprawled in the now-empty rooms. Some slept. Some played video games. A few card games had sprouted up in corners out of the sergeants' view.

Troopers waited as troopers had for thousands of years.

After the racket resumed with heavy metal music, it wasn't long before someone at the top of the stairs was shouting to talk to someone. For several minutes, the skipper ignored the shouts from the watch at the doors that the guy upstairs wanted to talk. At the third call, Vicky ordered the music switched to the boy band, though with their plaintive puppy love songs going at full blast. It took a while, but the complaints were soon coming in again.

Vicky switched to the sound effects. Airplane crashes. Train wrecks. Truck horns blasting, brakes squealing that ended in crashes. Huge chalk boards scratching. Mixed in with this was the howl of the banshee, screams of women and loud, rapid drumbeats. All were designed to get the heart pounding and adrenaline pumping.

Oh, and no one was resting. If they weren't nervous before, they certainly were now.

It was during the howling of a hurricane mixed with trees crashing down on metal structures, that the floors were sawed through. Lifts slowly lowered the heavy blocks of concrete to the deck. Ladders were quickly put in place and fire teams climbed up, ready to shoot if shots were fired.

As the snooper scopes showed, the bedroom was empty. More use of the scope showed that there was no one at the door.

It appeared that, again, the SOBs had concentrated themselves and their hostages in the middle apartments. Their barricades protected just two apartments on each side of the hall. Gunmen were visible at all four doors

What was different was the barricades.

Each consisted of an upended table with hostages in front of it. Only this time, the women had their hands tied behind their backs and they were hanging from the edge of the table from their armpits.

Some of them managed to use their tiptoes for a tiny bit of leverage. A few just hung from their arms. It looked excruciating for both, but the shorter girls had the worst of it.

Vicky and the captain quickly agreed on an attack from the middle. They concentrated their four attack teams down to two. One on the right, the other on the left at the other end of the hall. Then the engineers got busy cutting through drywall.

They came up short when they arrived at those four apartments protected by the human barricade. The next bedroom was full of women under the nervous watch of two gunman.

One focused on the woman who sucked on his member. It still didn't calm him down much. He couldn't seem to get it up.

The other was naked, a woman at his feet. He eyed the door, then turned to brandish his weapon at the hostages, then turned back to the door.

Vicky signaled the engineer to cut out the drywall in this room, but not break through the drywall to the next room. Then he made her the kind of peephole her automatic needed.

Vicky chose the same weapon load as last time. She calmed her breathing and waited for her heart rate to slow . . . as much as the situation allowed.

Then she took the shot.

The bastard standing at the door seemed utterly dismayed by the holes Vicky's rounds made in his chest. He opened his mouth to react, but the sleepy bullets did their work. He collapsed onto the woman lying on the floor.

The woman stared dumbly at the sudden burden. Then she rolled him off her and began pounding her fists on his bloody chest.

The other gunman was too busy urging the women to get him up to notice that the man behind him had gone down. Vicky put three rounds into his chest. He gasped in pain, then keeled over.

The woman's eyes followed him down, letting his sex fall from her mouth. Then she slammed a fist into this groin. If the man wasn't already dead, that would have hurt.

Around the room, the other woman hostages sat against the walls.

Even at the sight of these dead or dying punks, they didn't move or make a sound.

Vicky thought it strange that none of the women rested on the rumpled bed, then answered the question for herself.

Meanwhile, she'd side-slipped up to where the wall was ready to cave in and pushed her way into the room.

The women took her in with bland, blank faces.

Vicky raised her finger to her lips with a shushing sign, but they didn't need it. They were sheep led to the slaughter too many times. With throats raw from screaming, they kept silent.

Around Vicky, Marines moved with deadly intent and purpose.

One combat engineer went to check the next room. He quickly began to cut through the wall. Eight Marines came to stand behind him.

The other engineer slipped up to the open door, careful to keep his back plastered against the wall. His snooper scope showed eight thugs standing behind the two barricades.

The captain deployed his two best sharpshooters to the door to await the go order.

He also had teams ready to break into two of the rooms. They would rush the rooms at the same instant that the two troopers shot out the men skulking behind the barricade.

Vicky eyed the take from the snooper on her battle board. Four men stooped low in the space behind each table. A couple of them enjoyed the screams they got from the poor short girls. They hung from the table's edges, unable to reach the deck with their toes. A vicious pull on their arms would leave the woman screaming in pain.

Meanwhile, now and again, one of the thugs would pop up to check the hall, carefully keeping their own head behind one of the women's heads.

Real cowards, these.

Vicky eyed the captain, he just looked back at her then ordered up two more sharpshooters.

"Maggie, tell everyone we go on three." She paused for a moment, then counted, "One. Two. Three."

The four troopers ahead of Vicky slipped through the door in pairs, side by side. As one, they leveled their guns and fired.

The hoodlums died, first with a shot to the chest, then a second shot to the head.

Unfortunately, one of the punks who had been standing, eyeing the hall in front of him from the vantage point behind a hostage's head was too close to her. Unlike the M-6's that the US Marines used, Vicky's troops had only a single charge load.

A dart went right through the thug's skull and buried itself halfway through the hostage's brain.

The company had its first dead hostage.

But Vicky had no time for that. As soon as the troopers had fired their four rounds at two targets, Vicky was running for the door to the room they didn't have a team ready to break in.

She busted through the door to find herself facing a man with his pants down and his member buried in a redhead's mouth. He also had a machine pistol aimed nowhere in particular, neither at the hostages, nor Vicky.

"Move that gun and you die," Vicky growled.

The redhead eyed Vicky, turning, with her mouth still full. Then rage filled her eyes . . . and she bit down.

The guy let out a howl, and brought his gun around, he slammed it into the head of the hostage, sending her sprawling. He looked at the blood gushing from his still-attached sex and screamed in rage.

He brought the machine pistol up to aim it at his attacker.

Vicky had her automatic up in the proper two-hand stance. Six rounds stitched up the guy from his belly, through his heart, and ended blowing his face off, leaving a bloody mass in place of the back of his skull.

The blood, and what brains he had, splattered all over the women in the next room. That set up screams of dismay and fear.

Vicky hurried past the redhead, who grinned at her through bloody lips. She raced into the back bedroom.

"Everything's okay. The Marines are here. The Navy's got medical people waiting for you. Women from the farms will be up here in a minute."

Maybe half of the women seemed to understand what Vicky was saying. They held each other, those that could soothing those that hadn't yet comprehended their new safety.

The redhead came to stand beside Vicky.

"I got one of the bastards," she said, running a hand over her bloody lips, and held up her bloody hand for all to see.

Now, there was a cheer.

Vicky let it roll down naturally, then turned to the naked woman. "Why don't you take that around for all the women to see? I think they could use a cheer."

"You're in all four rooms!"

"Yep. There's not a live piece of shit on this floor. All we've got left is the top floor."

"What do you know about them?" the redhead asked.

"Not one damn thing," Vicky answered.

"Then I better talk to you before I go show the girls what I got my teeth into."

26

Vicky huddled with the company skipper, three platoon LTs and a couple of sergeants. The other sergeants were busy overseeing the movement of the freed hostages or bringing order back to platoons that had become pretty mixed up during the assault.

When the former redheaded hostage's stomach didn't so much rumble as growl, the captain offered the young woman a chocolate bar. She quickly attacked it and seemed unbothered when it mixed with the blood on her lips.

"There are a lot of hostages on the top floor, but only three pieces of shit. The battalion commander, the deputy commander, and the adjutant took that entire floor over for themselves and their . . . sex slaves. That's what we are. Sex slaves. They threatened to knock our front teeth out if we so much as touched their roots when they were jamming them down our throats. Ha. I got that one good."

"What can you tell us about that floor?" Vicky asked. "Are there guards?"

"Nope, no guards up there now. They don't like having the goons eyeing the naked boobs of their girls. About four hours ago, they ordered everyone down to these floors to guard them from here. All you people are supposed to be dead by now. That's what they figured would keep them safe. With all these other bastards already dead, I guess they kind of got it wrong."

"Sounds like it," Vicky said. "Captain, could one of your engineers put a snooper scope into the hall above our heads?"

He nodded at a sergeant who left at a jog. Soon, a small fire team with two engineers was silently working their way up the stairs.

Vicky opened her battle board again, and quickly found herself looking at a hall very much like the one she was standing in. Maybe it was a bit fancier.

Unlike this one, it was empty. Very empty.

"Captain," Vicky said, "if you would, please put together a platoon-size force with your best sharpshooters. Reinforce it with all the engineers you have and let's go kill us some high muckety-mucks."

Two minutes later, Vicky strode along beside the captain as they moved upstairs. One four-man fire team slipped into the hall and took up prone fire positions covering the rest of the length of the hall. They were followed by another team that backed them up. Finally, two engineers slipped toward the first door.

While one slipped a snooper scope under the door, the other went to work with a lock pick. About the time the scope showed the living area empty, the door clicked open.

The backup fire team slipped inside, and soon there was a whispered call of, "Clear."

A squad moved forward to cover the hall while Vicky and the captain hurried through the open door and into the suite. It was larger than the ones downstairs. Thicker carpet. Wall paper with quaint country scenes on it. The furniture was soft cream leather. Definitely upscale.

The bed was badly rumpled and there was blood on the carpet in the bedroom. Vicky made a face at it. She had been warned that the SOBs up here went for violence with their sex.

Their chances of surviving the next hour went from nil to zed in her opinion.

In the bedroom, the engineers were at work. They were as careful as they could be. They'd pressed two hand-holds onto the wall before they started cutting a large hole in it. Two engineers with circular handsaws quietly attacked the drywall in this room. One cut from the right, ceiling-to-floor, while the other cut from the left, floor-to-ceiling.

The third engineer lifted the slab of drywall out and set it on the bed. A fourth immediately punched a tiny hole in the wall for the snooper scope.

The next bedroom was empty.

A few quick cuts later and a four-man team slipped through the freshly cut hole and spread through the apartment.

"Clear," came back in a soft voice.

They quickly repeated it another time.

They approached the fourth suite more cautiously. They cut the first hunk out of the wall then paused as an engineer applied a listening device to the back of the wall for the next room.

He listened intently, then waved Vicky and the captain over.

"I've got something," he said. "I'm not sure what. No one's talking."

"Crying?" Vicky asked.

The Marine engineer shrugged.

Vicky stepped back, then turned to the engineers. "Cut a small hole in the bedroom wall and listen in there."

A few minutes later, the report from the bedroom was negative. No noise of any sort.

Vicky pursed her lips and decided she had a target. She pointed to the corner where the bedroom wall and the living room came together. "Get me a shooting position two feet out from there."

"Aye, aye, Your Grace," came back at her immediately.

Four minutes later, Vicky was standing on a stepladder, her head bumping up against the ceiling as her automatic's sight gave her a view of the next room.

A dozen, maybe more, naked women were roped together at the neck into a circle. Some faced inward, some outward. Some held on to each other as they wept softly.

Every once in a while, the piece of shit in the middle of them would growl for silence and threaten them with his machine pistol. That usually got a squeak from at least one of the women hostages.

He might slam his pistol against that one's head, shoulders, or back, but there seemed to be no real intent behind the blow.

They'd make more noise. He'd hurt them more. Then he'd go back to nervously eyeing the floor below him or looking up and listening intently.

Whatever he did, he kept himself well down. The huddled women gave Vicky no target.

Then she heard him mutter, "Why's it so bloody quiet down there? Why aren't they still shooting?"

Vicky studied the situation. As it stood now, to get a shot at this head thug, she'd have to shoot one or two of the women. She didn't want to do that.

Having her Marines bust in would have too much of a chance of the women being caught in the crossfire, with deadly results, or giving the punk time to machine gun them in the back.

She needed something. Something new had to be added to this equation.

Vicky waved the captain over. "I want several of your people downstairs to start a fake firefight. Machine pistols, M-6s, whatever you have. I want volleys like you'd get if there was a firefight going. Could you order something like that up for me?"

The captain grinned, then stepped well back from the wall and began whispering into his commlink. A moment later, he gave Vicky a thumbs-up.

She began to slow her breathing, calm her heart rate. She wanted to be ready when the shot came.

Beneath her feet there was the sound of a short burst from an M-6. It was quickly answered by the wild chatter of at least two machine pistols. They paused. An M-6 cracked out a three-round burst. The shorter machine pistols snapped off a reply.

Vicky ignored the noise from below. She eyed the man, willing him to stand up.

"Now that's more like it," the deputy commander of the battalion said, coming to his feet. "Lay it on them, boys," he shouted as he rose to his full stature.

Vicky held her breath and squeezed off three rounds at the guy's head.

At least one of her rounds slashed into his left eye. Maybe another one hit his right eye, or maybe it was just below it. The third buried itself in his forehead. They were small puncture wounds.

The back of his head blew off, splattering bone, brains, and blood all over the women on that side of his forced circle.

He didn't even seem to know what hit him. He crumpled like a bit of newspaper in an open fire.

The women who had been splattered with blood, or maybe cut by skull fragments screamed, but the other women leapt on the downed punk. They slammed his lifeless body with their fists over and over.

When the bloodied ones saw that, they dropped to their knees and joined the others in smashing his body, especially his genitals.

"Make me a hole," Vicky said, coming down the step ladder. The engineers quickly cut their way through the wall.

Vicky shouldered the captain aside and put herself at the head of a fire team, ready to storm the next room. She was first through the breach.

One of the women spotted her. She looked up but did not stop smashing her fists into the body. "Who are you?" she demanded hoarse voice.

"I'm the woman who just blew his head off," Vicky growled.

As the Marines stormed into the room, the women seemed to panic.

"These Marines are under my command," Vicky snapped. "They will not harm you. There will be nurses and women from the country up here soon to take care of you."

"Who are you?" one diminutive woman demanded.

"I think she's the duchess," an older woman of maybe twenty-five put in.

"Yes, I'm the Grand Duchess Victoria, and your planet is now under my protection. I'm putting an end to this kind of shit."

"Why couldn't you have been here last month when my mom was still alive?" a harsh voice asked.

"I'm sorry. I went to Dresden first. You're my second planet to liberate. Lublin is next."

"I guess you have to take a number and wait in line. Ain't life the shits," another woman said.

Then they fell into each other's arms and began sobbing.

An engineer with a big knife made to cut them loose, but Vicky stepped forward and took the knife from him. She slipped up behind one of the weeping women and said, "May I cut this rope?"

"Please," was pure begging.

Starting with that woman, Vicky worked her way around, asking first as she went from those who were just weeping to finally finishing with a poor girl who was wailing pure pain to the air.

Vicky hoped that her sobbing wouldn't get through to the next target, but there was no way she would attempt to silence the poor girl. Two of the other women came to console her.

Vicky made a point to offer them her canteen of water and encourage them to head into the next suite. The oldest of the three women seemed to catch on to Vicky's concern and slowly urged the woman out of the room.

27

Considering her next move, Vicky listened as the woman's wailing dissipated with distance.

"Well, Captain, do we switch sides of the hallway and go for the battalion's so-called commander or do we keep going on this side?"

"The boss skunk is likely to be the hardest nut to crack," the Marine officer said. "Let's slip across the hall."

With a squad left behind to keep this section secure, a fire team kept the hall under armed observation while two engineers checked out the room and picked the lock into that suite.

Quickly two squads crossed the hall. The small arms fire below was rather desultory at the moment, just enough to show that no one had lost interest in killing someone.

The engineers found the next suite both larger and empty. It had been occupied enough to pretty much trash it. There was way too much blood on the carpet and walls for Vicky's taste.

Mentally, she signed another death warrant.

They didn't tarry there. The engineers moved quickly to breach the wall into the next empty suite. It was as if every member of this small strike force wanted to see someone very dead.

That suite also showed way too much blood in both the living room and the bedroom. Even the kitchen and bathroom had blood splatter.

In every Marine's eye was a single thought. Someone needed to die, and they'd be only too willing to oblige him.

The snooper scope was silently extended into a hole high above the living room. It showed naked and bloodied women huddled on couches that had been moved to block the path from the door to the bedroom. They were tied up tight with many colored ropes, most artistically and creatively. They could neither duck nor fall out of their seats.

There was a clear line of fire between the bedroom and their heads.

Silently, the engineers moved their interest to the bedroom. Quickly, Vicky found herself looking at its view.

A man lay on the bed, covered with layers of naked women, both hog-tied and tied together. Many were still bleeding from cuts to their breasts and genitals. Most had tape over their mouths to stifle their cries. All wept in silent terror.

Vicky felt a violent need to vomit, but she suppressed it. She didn't have time, nor could she afford the noise.

The captain was looking over her shoulder at the video take. A low growl rumbled through his throat.

Vicky quickly went through all the ways she'd killed these thugs this night. Most had hidden behind women. This man had brutalized them most cruelly, then burrowed under them to use them as shields from the justice he so deserved.

There was no way Vicky could shoot down at him. His head was too close to the wall. If they stormed into the room, he'd start shooting hostages. They might kill him, but far too many women would die at his hands. A machine pistol carried a lot of ammunition.

Vicky pointed at his head. He'd covered everything, but his head was "safely" up against the solid wall.

The captain nodded and called his engineering sergeant over for a look. He looked at the video, then looked at the wall. He did it several times, then nodded.

"We can do this. Carefully. Quietly. What about the headboard?"

That was where the rub came in. They could make a hole in the drywall, but the wooden headboard was another matter. Drilling or cutting a hole in it would make noise and take time.

Vicky measured her options. Shooting through the wooden headboard was very possible. You just jack up the M-6's propulsion charge to maximum range and pull the trigger. Maybe pull it several times so if one bullet didn't make it through the wood, the next one would, or maybe the next one.

Of course, if she jacked it up too high, the dart might go right through the guy's thick skull, maybe half his body and still be going strong when it hit a woman in the stomach.

Then there was the worst case. She could be too high, too low, too far right or left. If she missed him entirely, he would more than likely pull the trigger and hold it down as he mowed down his hostages.

"We shoot through the headboard," Vicky said.

"I'll get my best sharpshooter," the captain said.

Vicky shook her head, violently. "This won't require a sharpshooter. Just someone with a blackened heart willing to pay the hangman's price."

"Your Grace."

"Get me an M-6, Captain."

"Ma'am?"

"Don't ma'am, me. This is what a Grand Duchess does. I pronounce judgement. I pull the trigger."

The captain looked none too happy, but he had the nearest Marine give up his weapon. Vicky checked it over. It carried a full magazine of 4mm darts. Its propulsion flask showed full. The sights showed her the picture of where she was aiming.

"Any problems with your weapon?" she asked the Marine.

"No ma'am," was the quick response. The response she expected.

"Engineers, move the scope over to just above his head."

Five minutes later, the engineers had used their knives to cut her a hole fifteen centimeters above the top of the headboard. At least with the headboard in this suite.

The curved lens of the snooper scope distorted the view the farther away you got from directly in front of it. Things were pretty distorted at the bottom of the screen. Still, it looked like his head was directly under the scope.

Vicky would just have to trust it.

The engineering sergeant finished silently whittling a hole in the wall. He measured the height of the bed they'd moved away to gain access to the wall, then he checked the location of the scope. Finally, he drew a cross on the wooden headboard.

Silently, he mouthed to her. "That's the best anyone can do here, Your Grace. God be with you."

Vicky would have expected "Good luck," or even "God speed." The blessing and prayer threw her. For a moment she found her eyes misting up. That had never happened before.

But then no one had ever offered to bear half the blame if she killed the wrong person.

She gave the sergeant a nod. One more time, she checked her weapon. The power setting was on high. The safety was off and moved to fire a three-round burst each time she pulled the trigger.

The captain came to stand beside her, showing the sniper take on her own battle board. There was no use trying to use the gun sight. She was shooting blind based on a measurement and a horribly warped video.

Vicky said a quiet prayer to any god who would pay attention to a black-hearted Peterwald . . . and squeezed the trigger.

Three rounds snapped from the rifle.

On the screen, nothing seemed to happen. The thug did not react. Neither did any woman. Vicky could see no sign of blood. She'd aimed a dart at the top of his head. It should have carried all the way down his body to the soles of his feet.

Gritting her teeth, Vicky lowered the butt of the rifle, aiming for a high angle.

Again, she pulled the trigger and the weapon spoke three times.

This time, the punk's head was twisted around. This time, there was screaming from the women who didn't have their mouths taped shut.

The engineer pushed the snooper scope forward. Its head was curved down, and it took some of the distortion out of her view of the man and the writhing mass of tightly bound women.

The man wasn't moving. His machine pistol had fallen from his hand, knocked loose by one of the women.

"Make a hole," Vicky ordered.

The engineers quickly cut through both layers of dry wall and shoved the wreckage out of the way.

Again, Vicky was the first through the hole. She had her automatic in one hand, a sharp knife in the other. If the guy so much as twitched, she'd put another dart through his head.

Three steps to the bed and it was clear that all six rounds had hit him, killing him instantly. The top of his skull showed where each round had gone in. The length of his body showed where they had gone from there. One of the last rounds had shattered his jaw, but not pierced the skin.

Now, his body twitched in its death throes as the stench of piss and shit filled the room.

Vicky holstered the automatic and switched the knife to her right hand. She studied the women tied up and tied together, spotted where two were roped together and attacked the rope.

The sight of the knife sent the women into panic. As one, they struggled to get away from Vicky's knife.

"I'm cutting you loose. I'm not going to hurt you. The hurting died with that son of a bitch," Vicky said, as soothing as she could.

Getting through to women who had been pushed way past hysteria was not going to happen. Not while knives were out.

But with all the ropes, there was nothing to do but use the sharp steel. Vicky was now joined by engineers with the small circular hand saws. They slipped the guards down and began working on a rope here or there.

Women began to tumble to the floor.

"Go easy on them. Marine, lay a hand," Vicky ordered.

"Aye, aye, ma'am," came from several and they safetied their weapons and came to help the first woman to her feet and stand by to catch the next one that was cut free.

The women needed help standing. Their legs and arms were tied to their bodies by intricate patterns of rope loops and knots. Different colored ropes were looped around them, forcing their arms in tight to their bodies, sometimes behind their backs, other times in front. Their legs were tied together as well. Sometimes they were stretched out long, or the legs were bent with feet tightly secured against their buttocks.

Each woman presented a different complex puzzle. The Marines studied them. One said, "Don't try to cut every loop or every rope. Look for the central rope or knot and cut it."

That Marine began roving from Marine to Marine, eyeing their puzzle, and pointing to one rope. If it was cut, legs were freed, or maybe a head could finally move. One cut knot allowed an entire series of loops to loosen, letting a woman move her legs or arms.

While that the Marines worked, the women still wept, cried out in panic, or screamed, still in the grips of the nightmare they'd lived over the last weeks or months.

Medics arrived. Local women followed them. They took the women who could walk out of this room of horrors, through the hole in the wall and away to somewhere they could soothe them.

Vicky continued attacking ropes. The stack of women, as much as three deep, began to flatten out as more women were cut free and lifted off the bed.

Those in the worst shape were carried away in the strong arms of Marines. Somewhere in the other rooms they would be cared for and cut loose from the last of the ropes that restrained them.

In the living room, the same process was going on with the women who had been tied to the couches.

"You're safe," the captain said, softly. Repeatedly. "The Marines are here. No one will ever hurt you again. That piece of shit is dead. Our Grand Duchess blew his brains out."

That soothed some of the woman, but others were way past such easy consolation. They needed to be carried away, held tight, and allowed to find their own way back from the precipice they'd lived on for the last eternity.

Vicky would have preferred to have women rendering care for these poor women, but there weren't enough aides, and these women needed to be moved as far from the next target as possible, as quickly as possible.

When the bottom of the pile was finally reached, Vicky found that this had not been a bloodless liberation. One of her darts had done more than kill the bastard. One woman showed where one bullet had slashed through her breast; in one side, out the other. Another woman's leg showed where a round, maybe the same one, had creased her skin from just below the knee down to her ankle.

Medics took over the care of both of them, and they were soon carried away.

That left Vicky staring at what was left of the man she'd killed. His blood now soaked the pillow his head still rested upon. His eyes were open, a surprised look on his face. He thought he'd had it all.

Vicky hoped he lived long enough to know that how badly he'd misjudged her.

Now it was time to tackle the last one.

Once again, a fire team went to a prone firing position, covering the rest of the hall.

Vicky was down to a single squad and the four engineers when they quietly slipped into the room just down the hall and across from the one they'd just liberated.

Quickly and quietly, they moved through the next two suites, checking to make sure they were empty, then breaching them. The third suite showed a presence.

Vicky studied the situation as the snooper scope peered through the wall. A man was huddled in a swivel desk chair. He held a machine pistol in his hand as he lazily swung around the circle of naked female hostages.

As before, the women were roped together, neck to neck. This time, all of their hands were bound tightly behind their backs and pulled painfully up to their shoulders.

All of them faced in, giving the thug a full frontal view. Every once in a while, he'd reach out and tug a breast or other lady part to continue his slow swing around in his chair.

This time, all the women had wide tape covering their mouths. They might moan or weep, but little of it was audible to tear at this man's conscience.

Assuming he hadn't sold it long ago to any passing demon.

There was an outbreak of heavy automatic fire from below. Maybe someone had suggested it. However, it had no impact on this guy. He actually laughed.

"Keep it up, boys. Kill all those stupid lackies of the Peterwalds. The universe will be better without them."

Unfortunately, he paused long enough to pinch a breast hard enough to make the woman howl through the tape on her mouth. Then he shoved himself off and spun around, laughing.

Vicky saw no good shot.

She continued her watch, but nothing changed. Whether the fire from below was hot or haphazard, the guy pretty much did the same, spinning around, threatening the women . . . and keeping his head down.

Finally, Vicky had had enough. She turned to the captain. "We're going to have to do this the hard way.

"May I offer a suggestion, Your Grace?"

"Please. I have been known occasionally to take good advice."

The Marine officer grinned and spoke. Vicky listened, a grin growing wider and wider on her face.

"By all means, Captain. Let's do it."

28

Vicky hunched outside one final door, her automatic at the ready. In a few seconds, she might well be sending darts into the naked flesh of hostages.

That was why she alone could do it. Her service automatic was the only one in the strike force that was a gift from Kris Longknife. Her weapon alone could be switched to shoot sleepy darts.

If Vicky missed the piece of shit with the machine pistol and hit one of the women, she, at least, would wake up.

In front of Vicky, an engineer worked silently at picking the lock.

On the floor below them, the fake firefight reached toward a crescendo. Let the bastard inside chew on that for a while.

Maybe it would distract him.

The engineer handed off his lock pick and took a firm grasp on the door.

"On three," he whispered.

Across from him, two Marines each pulled the pins on a grenade. With hostages in the next room, the grenades were flash-bangs, meant to disrupt and confuse.

Hopefully, they'd fluster and befuddle the gunman enough that he would not pull the trigger on his weapon but it would keep him distracted long enough for Vicky to put him to sleep.

What she'd do with him then was a matter of some concern, but she'd face that when the time came.

"One. Two. Three."

As the chatter of weapons from below rose even higher, the engineer opened the door just wide enough for the Marines to toss two grenades in. They were on a one second fuse.

From inside the candlelit room came a rattle of bangs. Maggie counted down Vicky's head. A second before the grenades would go silent, she snapped. "Open the door."

The room Vicky saw as the door swept open was a tableau from hell. Naked women in various stages of hysteria stood, fell, or were on their knees around a man in a comfortable desk chair. As luck would have it, he had been facing the door. He'd taken the full impact of the flash-bangs.

Maybe the flesh of some of the woman had stood between him and the grenades, but the incessant pounding of the bangs had driven the two women in front of him to their knees.

Vicky had a clear shot.

He struggled to shoot her before she could shoot him.

He lost.

Vicky sent three sleepy darts into him even as he strove to raise his weapon.

The gun fell from his numb hand. Though his eyes were wide at the sight of Vicky, they soon closed as his head fell forward until his chin rested on his chest.

He pitched forward, out of his chair. He was dead to the world as his heavy body bore the screaming hostages down.

Roped together and with their arms roped behind their backs, the woman fell painfully to the ground.

"Marines," Vicky ordered. "Free these women."

As the Marines raced in to obey her command, Vicky strode toward the prostrate gunman. Her eyes were hard, her lips were a tight glower.

She yanked the machine pistol from his hand and safetied it. Rolling him over, she found only shock on his face.

The Marines moved the former hostages away from the thug. Their screams of terror were winding down to sobs and wails. A medic appeared and began checking them over even as the Marines cut them free of the ropes that painfully bound them.

The women fell into each other's arms, sharing their freedom as they'd shared their hell.

"Anyone think this punk should live?" Vicky asked. She glanced around. The women she saw were too traumatized to form any sort of an answer.

A medic arrived to care for the women.

Vicky intercepted him. "Do you have any drug that can wake this punk up?" she demanded.

"What put him to sleep?"

"Wardhaven sleepy darts," Vicky snapped.

"I don't have any of the antagonists for it, but I have something that probably will work."

"Give it to him."

The medic did, then took one look at Vicky and fled back to care for the women.

The former gunman and redcoat became agitated in his sleep. While he was being forced to wakefulness, Vicky studied her choices. She had her automatic. She had his machine pistol. There was a balcony off the kitchen that he could be hurled from.

She also had the knife that had cut the women free. It was a long Bowie knife and had brought terror to the eyes of the women even as she freed them.

She'd shot criminals between the eyes today, or maybe that was yesterday. Did this man deserve a death that clean and quick?

As his eyes blinked open, she made her decision. With her foot firmly planted on his chest and her automatic aimed right between his eyes, she announced her verdict.

"I am the Grand Duchess Victoria. You are convicted of high crimes deserving of death. You will die." So saying, with her left hand she slid the point of the knife into his flesh below his sternum, then aimed in and up.

She shoved, and the knife slipped through flesh to his heart. There it halted for a moment, strong muscle resisting even a knife that sharp. Then it lost and the knife sank home.

The man screamed as he saw blood pumping out of his chest.

He screamed and struggled to get out from under her boot, but he was still weak from the drugs she'd shot him with. Still, he was wide awake as the terror drained from his eyes.

Then his face contorted in terror. He saw death coming for him. Vicky hoped it was a demon from the deepest pit of hell.

She held him down until he quit kicking, until the contortions of coming death became few and shook him less violently.

Around Vicky, the sight of his death had a calming influence. Several of the women stepped forward to spit on him. Some did so while he was still conscious.

One of the women who seemed to have it more together than the others spat, then turned to Vicky.

"You're the Grand Duchess."

"Yes," Vicky said.

"Can I swear fealty to you in both my name and the name of my planet?"

"I am accepting the fealty of Oryol," Vicky told her.

"You won't ever let them . . .." She ran out of words, but one furious glance at the cooling body beside them was enough.

"The Bowlingames and their cronies will never harm a hair on your head, ever again."

"Thank you. Now, if you'll excuse me," and the woman vomited on the body. It wasn't much, she'd eaten little, but her stomach was in revolt and she knew where she wanted it to go.

A newly arrived woman came to her. "Helen, I'm so sorry."

"Don't be, Amy, at least I survived." The former hostage Helen glanced around the room, seemed to relive the horror stories of every patch of blood on the carpet. The woman began to tremble, and her friend helped her out of the room.

Vicky found the captain at her elbow. He studied the body.

"A knife?" he simply asked.

"To the heart. It's faster when you can be the judge and executioner."

"I guess so. All the buildings along the park blocks have been cleared. Now only the Imperial Hotel remains."

"No doubt it holds the command headquarters."

"That is what the people say."

"Have we scouted the hotel?"

"What we could. They're conducting an active defense with two or three gunners walking each hall. We tried to slip some rolling drones down from the roof, but they've got snipers up there, too. Nothing got in the front door, even after we blasted all that glass."

"Roving guards?" Vicky asked.

"No. They collected all the couches and chairs together into a kind of fort. Hostages are in every seat with nooses around their necks and the rope secured behind them."

Vicky let out a tired sigh. "You think we'll have to fight our way through the building, floor by floor?"

"It sure looks like it. General Pemberton has established a command center next door in the Farm Bureau."

"Then we must join him," Vicky said.

She retrieved her knife, cleaned it on the dead man's pants, then snapped it into its scabbard. Done, she followed the captain as he headed for the stairs.

29

Geneal Pemberton quickly filled her in on all that they didn't know about their final target. He finally ran down with one last issue.

"When we blew the glass in the front and back windows into the foyer, a few of the gunmen jumped up. Not much, but enough that our sharpshooters got a shot. The rest have an awful lot of women shields tied down in front of their overturned tables and couches. They're being a lot more careful to keep their heads down. Problem is, they can shoot between the heads of the women hostages. Rough on their eardrums, but even harder on our troops who they're shooting at."

Vicky processed everything he'd told her. She did not like the way it all added up. Even though she knew the answer, she asked the question anyway.

"What would you recommend?"

"We have to storm the building, and quickly."

"No negotiatiations?"

"They've demanded a ship out of the system."

"You've told them they aren't going to get one," Vicky said.

"Yes, ma'am. There are four dead bodies out in front of the hotel.

They released five hostages. They told them to run. They'd only shoot four. The one woman who made it to our line is in pretty bad shape."

"When will they kill the next group?" Vicky didn't have to ask if they would, only how soon.

"In thirty minutes. A group every four hours. At noon tomorrow it goes to every two hours."

"They have a lot of hostages?"

"They say they do."

"Okay, General, where's your lead assault company? I'll be joining them."

"Sorry, Your Grace, but no, you won't be."

"General?" Vicky snapped.

"Your husband has told me that you are not to be allowed out of my headquarters until I leave it."

"General," Vicky growled.

"Don't growl at me, Your Grace. You know damn well that Kris Longknife's husband had the legal right to lock her in the bedroom if she got lost in a death wish, and, woman, what you have now is a death wish. He told me to keep you here with me, and I agree with him. We can't afford to lose you, ma'am. This Empire needs you alive, not dead."

Vicky's scowl at her insubordinate subordinate was of Olympic proportions. "And if I choose to walk out of here and join the fight?"

"I'm hoping that you won't, ma'am, but I've got four strapping Marines assigned here to see that you don't."

Vicky turned around to see four of the biggest, meanest looking Marines she'd ever seen standing between her and the door. After an instant of reflection, she faked right, then went left. She hadn't gone two steps when a Marine blocked her way. Soon it was two, and two swung in behind her.

"Your Grace," the general said, "you can give me your word that you won't try that again, or, well, ma'am, I have some leg manacles with a very short chain."

"You wouldn't," Vicky growled.

"Gunny Sergeant," he ordered.

A big, grizzled sergeant stepped away from the wall. He held up a pair of nice, shiny manacles with likely less than thirty centimeters of chain between them.

"Your Grace," he said, with an honest face and adamant eyes.

"General, you are getting a hell of a performance review this year," Vicky muttered.

"I'll take any review you choose to give me, Your Grace, so long as you are alive to give it."

Vicky changed the subject as she turned back to the general and his board. "About the snipers on the roof. Can we suppress them?"

"I have snipers back four blocks. That's too far for their damn machine pistols, but just fine for our long rifles. We can keep them down. My main concern is that they'll drop hand grenades from the roof on any large force we move forward."

"So, how do we storm the hotel?" Vicky asked.

Fifteen minutes later, the assault began.

30

The drone imagery showed dark shadows detaching themselves from the surrounding buildings and closing on the front and back of the hotel. No one clumped up. A shot might pick off one, but they were a waste of a hand grenade.

In a few minutes, a small force huddled, low to the ground around the front of the foyer, awaiting the signal. It came with a pair of soft "whumps".

A moment later, the foyer lit up with flashes of light and brutal pounding. Two whiz-bangs had gone off.

Immediately, two scouts were up. Their helmets were equipped to strobe the light out of the wearer's eyes and tone down the noise. They dashed forward, into the lobby and were shooting down the thugs skulking behind their human hostages even before the last grenade burned itself out.

When the lobby fell silent, only the screams of the hostages were to be heard. There were a few moans from the redcoats, but a shot to the head relieved their pain.

From the surrounding buildings medics and woman aids dashed forward. They had been warned not to clump up, but the civilians had never seen what a grenade could do.

One of the murderers on the roof saw enough of a clump to hurl a grenade. A Marine sniper blew his head off, but the grenade left five women screaming on the ground. Cautiously, Marines came forward to drag them off the killing ground.

Vicky let out a deep sigh. The night had been bad. It was about to get a whole lot worse.

"The ground floor is clear," the general reported. "Somebody tossed a couple of thermite grenades into the parking garage under the hotel."

Vicky sniffed the air. "Oh, shit," she muttered.

"Correct, Your Grace. They were using the garage as their latrine and now it's burning."

Vicky shook her head. "Now we fight through gagging smoke. Can they make this any worse?"

"Please don't challenge them, ma'am. I'm sure they would be only too happy to exceed your expectations."

"True," Vicky said, then realized the import of this last move.

"With a fire in the garage, how long before the building gets involved?"

"I don't know, ma'am, but they are living on borrowed time."

Vicky shook her head. Some people were just too dumb to live.

Automatic weapons fire came from the hotel.

"We're trying to force the stairwells," the general reported. "We think they've run out of grenades."

"Can we blow a hole in the floors and send a team in behind them?" Vicky asked.

Even as she said the words, one of the few armored vehicles in the fleet went crashing into the lobby.

"The engineers have arrived," the general said, dryly.

"Remind me to keep my tongue under control for a few extra seconds next time."

"If you'll pardon me, Your Grace, I just feel honored that you've learned enough of my trade to know what needs to be done next. It's my job to plan ahead so that it's ready to go when you want it."

"You're being kind to me, now, General."

"I'm being respectful."

Vicky listened to the chatter of machine pistols and the lower sharp reports of M-6's.

"I have to admit that I could add nothing to this mad melee battle you've got going here."

"Thank you, Your Grace. We Marines are doing what we are trained to do. Only you can bind up the wounds of this mess when it's over. Only you."

For a moment, they studied the battle board in silence, then the general spoke. "They're into the second floor." He paused for a moment, then added grimly. "The redcoats shot down a batch of hostages. We're checking for survivors."

Vicky let her anger out with a blast of expletives that did not make the tall Marines guarding her blush, but they did nod respectfully.

"Get more people into the hotel. Push them harder," Vicky ordered.

A company of Marines advanced toward both the back and front of the hotel. Both units kept to a wide order. Still, a few of the gunmen on the roof tried to take shots.

All those that tried, died, as the snipers five hundred meters away put a bullet through them.

The rest of the gunmen on the roof huddled down and didn't dare show their faces.

Now, more women helpers and medical personnel moved forward. There was some fire at them, from behind the glass of the upper windows. Those were answered quickly by the sniper teams.

That kind of noise went away.

The third floor went differently. The engineers breached a bedroom with a dozen terrified women bound together. For some reason, they were behind a closed door.

When asked, one of the women whispered that the guard was in the next room with two girls.

An agile Marine slit his throat before the bastard even knew he wasn't alone with the girls.

While the engineers pulled up another stepladder, the trigger pullers put a quick end to the fight at all three stairwells. The gunmen were all concentrated on the stairs and died of ignorance regarding where the bullet came from that killed them.

All of the hostages on this floor were captured alive.

The next floor was a bit more difficult. It took three tries before the engineers found an empty room.

There were a dozen open doors along the hallway. Each of those rooms had to be entered and a gunman killed. Fire teams also needed to reach the stairwells at either end of the corridor and the other hallway beside the elevators at the midpoint.

A company skipper organized his troops into three teams ready to dash in both directions.

To the right or left were troopers with orders to enter each open door and kill the gunner there, hopefully before he killed the hostages.

The middle team would race for the stairwells at the end of the hall, engage the redcoats there and take them down.

31

P rivate Philip Houseman was fast on his feet. He was assigned to lead the right column. He would be making the farthest dash to an open door. By the time he busted in, three of his buddies would have shot themselves some shit heads.

He was looking forward to getting himself a few as well.

The skipper said the first three should bust through the open doors and kill any bastard they found in the rooms. The rest of the eight teams that had been assigned rooms could bust in or slow down and make their attack a bit more carefully.

"Houseman, you can do it any way you want."

"Want to bet me, sir, that I can get there before two of the three other guys can?"

"No way I take that bet, private."

When the skipper brought his hand down, Philip dashed forward, his rifle held close across his chest. He passed the men in the middle file and pulled ahead of his buddy, Wik.

As he neared the open door, he heard shots behind him. Bringing his weapon up to his shoulder, he whirled into the door, slamming his right shoulder into it. His rifle was up and aimed across the room. This one had a kitchen across from the door. The guy standing in the other door was diagonally across from Philip. He was swinging his machine pistol around to fire off a burst at the Marine.

Philip got off the first shots.

The three-round volley missed, but it made the guy jump just like the sergeant said it would.

The second volley was in the exact center of mass. The redcoat looked down in shock at the blood pulsing from his chest. He made one more try to raise his weapon, then collapsed onto the floor.

Quickly, Philip entered the bedroom, his weapon held at the ready, his eye following his sight picture.

"Clear," he said, though no one was supposed to be behind him. But that was also his order to raise his weapon to the overhead.

"Don't worry ladies, the Marines are here," he shouted to be heard above the wailing and sobbing. He pulled his knife from his boot and handed it to the woman that seemed most together.

"Can you cut the rest loose?"

Her shout was turned into a mumble by the tape over her mouth, but her raising her hands to him was enough communication. He slashed the rope at her wrists.

The woman quickly pulled the tape off her mouth. "Thanks."

"Pardon me, ma'am, but I got to guard the door," Philip said.

He peeked into the hall just in time to spot a redcoat slip out of one of the doors that hadn't been opened. He leveled his weapon to shoot the Marines in the back as they approached the stairwell at the end of corridor.

Philip shot him in the back. He tumbled forward onto the carpet. Philip glanced back, then forward, then back again.

Wik was just coming to his door.

Philip waved at the body down.

Wik nodded and turned to cover the other direction.

No more doors opened.

At the far end of the hall, Philip watched as the battle in the stairwell turned bloody. Hearing weapons fire behind him, one of those bastards had turned to see where the noise was coming from.

The jogging attack force had shot him down. This alerted the other fellows standing in the doorway. They'd been firing and ducking back in, then firing again.

A dozen hostages sat, taped up tight, waiting their turn to be shot and tossed down the stairs.

Now, all five of the gunmen tried to pile through the door into the stairwell. Likely they hoped to flee up them. They might have made it if they went single file, but organization was not their strong suit.

They died as they had lived, undisciplined, and with no clear direction. They clogged the door open, which left the guy laying prone on the landing in full sight when he jumped to flee up the stairs.

Every member of that blocking force died.

Philip grinned with pride for himself and his buddies. Those pieces of shit had no idea what to do when they came up against real bad asses.

32

U nfortunately, one of the guys from third floor managed to escape up to the fourth floor. What he would tell them was anybody's guess.

The engineers were already forcing their way into two rooms on the fourth floor. One was occupied, the other wasn't.

The attack teams moved into place even as the engineers began working on the fifth floor.

Vicky watched from her secure jail of a headquarters as floor after floor was breached. The casualty figures made her want to cry. Most often the bastards holding the hostages chose to fight it out with her troops, but too often they turned their guns on the hostages and died with a bullet in their back.

The wounded were evacuated quickly to hospital. No one kept a count of the dead hostages. That sad duty would have to wait.

As the count of the dead redcoats grew, the number of killed and wounded among Vicky's troops grew as well. Vicky had never before been engaged in a grim battle of attrition.

For the redcoats there was no surrender. It was as if they knew that the hostages and the stories they could tell were a millstone around their necks. They could die fighting or die at the end of a rope. With no other choice, they fought for blood. Maybe they hoped that if they killed or wounded enough of Vicky's Marines that she'd throw in the towel and give them a ticket off planet.

Vicky admitted to herself that the thought crossed her mind. It had crossed it several times. Still, she let the battle rage on.

Her troops tried everything they could think of to reduce their casualties. More engineers were brought in so that they could breech floors in two places at a time, then three.

The enemy began opening every door and assigning roving gunmen to check out every room.

With the prospect of discovery imminent, the Marines, now much experienced, went up the ladders ready to shoot and moved quickly to do their jobs. The time it took to clear a floor got shorter and shorter.

Sadly, the slaughter never declined. The gunmen died shooting. The hostages died screaming or lived to weep and tremble in shock.

As they cut their way onto the eighth floor, Vicky had had enough.

"General, you can stay here and sit on your ass. I've had it. I'll be with the troops."

"I'm with you," the general said, and followed her into the street.

33

Vicky's senses were raw, as if sliced open by a thousand shallow cuts from an obsidian blade. The night was that darkness that preceded the dawn. The moon had risen into a low fog and shed no light. The air held a chill that went straight to the soul and a smokey stench that revolted her stomach.

As she crossed the street to the Imperial Bismarck Hotel, she faced the walking wounded coming back. Marines helped along by their comrades. Former hostages were assisted by women volunteers. The blankets that wrapped the wounded could not hold at bay a world gone cold and ugly.

It was the stretchers hurrying by that hammered at Vicky's heart the most. The moans and cries of pain from the wounded would never be forgotten.

She'd commanded ships and Sailors had died by the thousands. That was like a game. This was honest and dirty and real. They assaulted Vicky's soul, one at a time.

She hastened her steps.

Inside the hotel, a third battalion was being brought in to relieve the one at the point of the spear. A captain from the forces on the line briefed the Marines on their enemy.

"They're trigger happy. Their nerves are shot. If you see one, get off a quick burst. It doesn't matter if you hit him, it will spoil his aim. That will give you time to get a good sight picture and make your next shot a kill shot."

"Kill?" a trooper asked.

"Guys, if they see you, they will shoot to kill. They don't want to talk. They just want as many side boys as they can take with them to hell, okay? They give no quarter and we're taking no prisoners."

"Even if they offer to surrender?" a young Marine asked.

"We've had five of them scream they wanted to surrender," the captain snapped. "Each one of them cost us a dead Marine. The only reason they offer surrender is because you've got the drop on them and they want to flip it. We've taken to shooting them in the knee. If they go down, we'll let them live. If they go down shooting, we kill them. So far, they only go down shooting. That answer your question?"

The serious look on the Marines' faces was answer enough.

The captain then went on to brief the Marines on the breeching procedures and the need to move quickly from room to room.

"Listen, I'll warn you beforehand. Sometimes the gunmen with the hostages turn toward you and shoot it out. We almost always get them first. However, too many gunmen turn toward the hostages and spray them with those damn machine pistols even as you're shooting them in the back. I hate those bastards, but you've got to understand. There's nothing you can do to make them do one or the other. They've made up their mind which way to turn long before you showed up in their doorway, okay? Dead hostages are not your fault."

Only a low mutter greeted that comment.

The battalion commander stepped forward to fill the gaping void created by that bitterly won fact, "Half of you have been given shields. With the long hallways and open stairwells, there's not a lot of cover, so we're making some. The shields are made of the best plate we've got, but nobody's calling them bulletproof. These redcoats are firing heavy, low velocity rounds. Enough of them at close range will pierce your battle armor. A few of them at a longer range will leave you black and blue tomorrow. If you take it in the chest, there may be internal bleeding, okay? You didn't join the corps to live forever, but there's no use letting idiots like these shit heads mess you up.

That got a bold "Ooorah!" in response.

"Those of you with the shields, keep them at an angle. We want to deflect the rounds, not stop them, okay? You shooters, keep your shit wired tight and behind the shields. You get yourself killed and Gunny here will have you on punishment drills for the next year," the major growled.

That got a smattering of laughter.

"Okay, any questions?"

"Yes, Major," General Pemberton said.

"Sir?"

"Would one of your men give the Grand Duchess a shield?"

"Of course, sir. Ivanovich, hand yours over."

"Yes, Major," and a fresh-faced young man was trotting toward the general.

"General, I came here to shoot the bastards," Vicky growled softly through her clenched teeth.

"And you've shown that you can do very well with one hand. You can use the other arm for the shield."

"This is ridiculous," Vicky growled, but she took the shield from the young Marine. It was well balanced and easy to control. Despite its size, it didn't seem to weigh that much.

With one last "Ooorah" the Marines filed off by companies to relieve the company now fighting their way up each of the three stairwells.

Vicky and Pemberton followed in the wake of the company headed for the central stairwell near the useless elevators. At the second floor, the general aimed Vicky into the hall.

"They don't have a lot of grenades, but every once in a while, someone tosses one down the stairs. You and I are taking a different route up."

A Gunny Sergeant from the battalion being relieved waited by the elevators for them. "Your Grace, if you will follow me."

She did. He led her down the hall to a room with a hole in the overhead and a ladder.

"May I suggest you shoulder the shield, Your Grace," the Gunny offered, then helped her swing the shield onto her back. She hadn't noticed the two leather straps at the bottom of it. They turned the shield into an awkward backpack.

Still, it was easier climbing the ladder with both hands than with a hunk of ceramic and composite on one arm.

Vicky smiled as she followed Gunny up the ladder. The Vicky of a few years ago would have pouted if a guy didn't offer to carry anything heavy for her; pouted and demanded he carry it.

Somewhere over the years, that Vicky had disappeared. Was it while she was fleeing for her life from Greenfeld in a yacht with a leaking fuel tank? More likely it was some time after she woke up naked and strapped to a bed, left to die of thirst. She'd learned that if she was going to live, she'd have to do it with her own two hands.

So now the pampered Grand Duchess carried her own shield.

Besides, this Grand Duchess wanted a certain Count of Oryol dead. Preferably after she'd pulled the trigger.

Somehow the change didn't seem so strange.

Gunny led her and General Pemberton on a roundabout path. Sometimes the room with the breach was to the right of the elevators. Sometimes to the left. Vicky found herself walking a lot of halls.

Halls that stank of death.

The wounded had been removed. The dead had not.

The dead redcoats lay sprawled about. Sometimes in halls. Other times in rooms. Usually alone, occasionally in pairs. Rarely were three or more together.

The dead hostages were always clumped in rooms where they'd been shot down by their now dead kidnapper. Some of the women looked as if they'd found peace in the end. Others died with a horrified look still on their faces.

Every one of the dead demanded vengeance from Vicky as she hurried by them, hastening toward just that retribution. The more ladders Vicky climbed, the louder the sound of gunfire grew.

Now she understood why men ran toward the widow maker.

On the ninth floor, she joined two squads standing by for the engineers to finish cutting a hole in the deck above. Two Marines stood by, ready to run a ladder into the hole. Another two stood ready to rush up the ladder, eager to be the forlorn hope.

Vicky elbowed her way through until she was right behind them.

That left General Pemberton with two bad choices. He could follow her and put himself behind her and ahead of some Marine that might actually contribute to saving the Grand Duchess's neck. Or he could hold back, letting his crazy Majesty get away from his clutches.

With a scowl that had thunderheads at both edges of his tight lips, he held in place, while giving her the stink eye.

Vicky grinned back at him and gave him a little finger wave.

The engineers got a concrete-and-rug chunk of decking loose and shoved it off to the right. The ladder rushed in from the left and was slammed into place. Even as those two Marines held it down, the two other Marines stormed up the ladder.

The lead Marine paused just centimeters below the deck, unleashed his rifle from where it slung around his neck, and took the last step up with both hands on his rifle. Not an easy thing to do.

He did a quick twist around to check out the room, whispered, "Clear," then with the rifle still held up with one hand, he used the other to hurry up the last steps. The other Marine followed him.

Since no shots had been fired, Vicky followed him up, just ahead of a dozen Marines, a sergeant, and an LT.

The bedroom above got crowded very fast.

An engineer was buried somewhere among all the riflemen. He hastened to the door and slipped a snooper scope under it. A moment later he whispered.

"It appears clear."

The two eager-beaver Marines came to stand beside the door. After a quick three count, the engineer yanked the door open and the two Marines slipped through and began to survey the living room over the sights of their rifles. Two more Marines followed them through.

Like a good little Grand Duchess, Vicky held in place until a "clear" call came through. She was just slipping into the living room when General Pemberton came up the ladder.

Seeing her disappear into the living room did not improve his scowl.

One Marine stood in the middle of the kitchen, three more held down the main room. Like the bedroom, these rooms looked like they'd received hard use. The kitchen table was in the middle of the living room. The couch wasn't far from it. There was blood around both. It looked like some Roman gladiatorial arena, if gladiators toyed with unarmed and helpless women for cheers of the crowd.

Vicky thought the other floors had been bad. This floor was going to be sickeningly worse. The engineer soon gave more evidence of that.

"All the doors on the other side of the hall are secure. There are gunmen at each end of the hall, prone, and with clear lanes of fire if we show our butts there. We'd be the ducks in a shooting gallery."

The LT and sergeant put their heads together on that. Vicky joined them.

"If you'll pardon me. We faced something like this in the building we cleared," and she filled them in on her technique of shooting the gunmen before they breached the bulkhead and stormed the room.

The LT gave General Pemberton a questioning glance.

"I wasn't there, but we did get more survivors out of her building than the others."

"Okay, Your Grace, we'll try the first one your way," did not sound all that sure she could do what she said.

"Get a step ladder up here."

Five minutes later, an engineer was up on the step ladder, cutting a small hole in the wall. Vicky watched the take from his snooper on her battle board with one general, one LT, and one sergeant . . . all skeptical.

Vicky swapped places with the engineer. He joined the other one, ready to cut a big slab out of the next room's drywall.

The sicko in the next room was enjoying playing with the soft skin of a young girl – with his knife. Two other gunmen looked on, their tongues hanging out like dogs.

As much as Vicky wanted to get off a quick shot, she took her time to get a solid sight picture on the head of the guy closest to her. She'd take the three out from the back to the front. Unfortunately, it was the front guy wielding the knife.

Slowing her breathing, she waited for her heart to beat, then squeezed of a quick three -round burst.

The man's head exploded.

She got the second guy before he could react.

The guy with the knife was just looking up, terror in his eyes, as he tried to figure out what was going on.

Vicky put a round between his eyes as he turned to face her.

The poor girl began to scream her lungs out.

Vicky was down the stepladder, shoving the Marines aside. She was first into the living room and first to the girl. She held her until she finally stopped screaming and wound down to sobs. Vicky held her until a corpsman showed up to care for the shallow but bloody wounds on her breasts.

A woman hurried in to take over holding the girl, and Vicky stepped aside. Her battle gear now was covered with blood.

More corpsmen and women hurried by to help the women lashed together in the bedroom. It would take a while to empty this suite.

The LT must have been impressed. "Admiral, we've got a gunman in the room on the other side of the room we climbed into. While we check out the next room here, could you take care of that bastard?"

"Is it as bad as here?"

"At least he's not using a knife."

Vicky hastened back across their first room. Marines and women aids were stacking up or passing through, depending on someone's orders.

The ladder was in the bedroom. She climbed it to find a redcoat with his pants down. By the way his hostage screamed, it was likely she was not used to that type of sex, nor was he using any lubrication.

Again, Vicky forced herself to take careful aim and prepare her body for the shot. She caught the bastard in the face. One second, he was grinning. The next minute, he had no jaw. He reeled back in shock, giving Vicky a clear shot below his belt. She took it.

If he still had a jaw, he'd have dropped it as he gazed down at his pulverized flesh.

This idiot had failed to secure the hands of the women in the bed and around him on the floor. They descended on him, blocking Vicky's view of his last few seconds of life.

She didn't rush into that suite, but left it to the Marines and women aids. She stalked back to see what the other end of the battle line had for her.

At least these four bastard were dead drunk. Vicky regretted executing them while they was senseless, but she had no time for niceties. Word was, they had a sicko back at the other end.

Thanks to the silencer on Vicky's automatic, the four died before the last one even knew why their heads were exploding

Her runs between suites grew longer as the Marines extended their reach down the hall. As luck would have it, they had breached a room on the side away from the elevators. They soon held rooms from one end of the hall to the other. Two full companies were arrayed up and down the length of it.

Some troops were already positioned prone and ready to turn the place into a shooting gallery. Others had orders to take the stairwells from their rear. A third group stood by to bust doors down and force their way into the as-yet unsecured rooms across the hall.

It looked to be a bloody storm, but time was short, and the bastards were getting nastier. Girls were being forced out to service gunners in the halls and then shot to raucous laughter.

The redcoats plumbed the depths of depravity. At least one girl was murdered before their eyes. One redcoat played his knife all over a girl, from face to groin. Then he did the unspeakable. Holding her up by her hair, he grinned in her face as he slit her throat and watched her bleed out.

Then he shouted for another toy to play with.

Vicky joined the fire teams aiming to take down the force holding the elevators and that stairwell. This bunch of gunmen were a more cohesive clump. Worse, they had a gaggle of hostages intermixed with them.

Vicky had been eyeing this group for a bit, studying the snooper scope take off them. Several of the guys seemed better dressed. Also, when three of them gave orders, the others hopped to it. And of the three, two did what one of them said.

Vicky tagged him for the count. She wanted to personally see to his departure from this life. She unshipped her shield before General Pemberton told her to, but she stood third in line to storm down the hall to the elevator foyer.

The general scowled and stood aside for a Marine sergeant to come stand at Vicky's elbow. A big, hulking corporal was on her other side.

Somewhere. a whistle sounded. Doors slammed open. M-6s snapped out sharp, quick bursts. Women screamed.

Vicky bellowed in the strongest voice she'd been taught for commands. "Ladies, down. The Marines are here. Drop."

Those who could, obeyed her command.

Others, held in strong grips by desperate men, did their best to obey her. They winced as bullets and darts whizzed past them, or screamed when one buried itself in their soft, vulnerable flesh.

Marines did their best. From suddenly opened doors, they shot the bastards laid out on the deck. Instead of the bad guys shooting ducks, they became the ducks, shot at from behind.

More Marines moved quickly out of the door to take aim at those standing behind the doors to the stairwell.

These punks had women mixed up with them and servicing them even as they wept.

The Marines did their best to shoot the rapists and avoid the raped. However, fate is fickle, and people move. People flinch. People who didn't deserve it, ended up dead.

The clumps around the stairwells at either end of the hall turned into bloody charnel houses with people screaming in pain, sobbing in shock, cussing with their last breath.

The Marines moved quickly among them, separating the women from the dead men. If a man wasn't dead yet, they made sure it happened quickly.

That left the elevator hallway. There, tragedy danced among them.

Three gunners lay on the carpet, ready to shoot down anyone who came in view.

Well, maybe not so ready.

As three Marines burst through the door of the suite just up from that hall, they saw three gunners and three women.

One gunner rode a woman who was down on her hands and knees. While he kept his hips moving, he also kept his machine pistol pointed in the general direction of the Marines.

A second man lay on his back, a weeping girl above him, doing her best to please him. He'd threaten her with his machine pistol, then bring it back to above his head, ready to fire down the hall, even if he wasn't ready to make those aimed rounds.

The third man was serious about keeping guard. He lay with his weapon at the ready. However, he was shirtless and had a nude woman sitting astride him, massaging his back as he lay on his stomach.

That was the picture that greeted Vicky as she stepped up behind the three Marines. Each one of them got off a short burst at their assigned target.

However, they were not the only ones to act.

The woman on her hands and knees followed Vicky's command. However, as she dropped, she kicked back with one leg. The gunman above her was knocked about. The first round missed him, but the next two rounds blew his face off.

The weeping woman sitting astride the middle gunman,

screamed what could only be called a war cry and dropped onto the bastard that had been forcing her. Unfortunately, he'd just been menacing her. She fell onto his weapon as he was trying to roll out from under her and fire.

Instead, he emptied a long burst into her. Blood flew as bullets blasted through her body. Three Marine rounds took the gunner in the top of the head. Even then, it took a moment for his finger to relax in death.

The third was the most tragic.

That gunman was the most alert. Even as he brought his machine pistol up to fire, the woman on his back threw herself at his arm, grabbing it and yanking it back.

The two struggled even as a Marine aimed carefully at his head and put three good rounds into him.

Unfortunately, the two rolled in their struggle. Two darts took the man at the top of his skull. The third dart took her low in the face, shattering her jaw and slicing through her neck.

"Medic!" the Marine shouted.

Vicky ran forward, twisting through the Marines, then bringing up her shield, blocking her view down the hall. However, the shield had a cutout for her weapon. She used the remote screen to sight her automatic at a brute holding a woman up before him. She, however, had gone weak in the knees and was doing her best to drop to the deck.

Vicky's aim was wrecked as her shield took several bursts of slugs from several directions down the hall. She went to her knee and set her shield, angling it to send shots ricocheting into the overhead.

Behind her, Marines snapped off quick bursts as she knelt in frustration, unable to get a sight picture as her shield bucked on her arm. Intellectually, she knew she was drawing the fire, helping the Marines. Still, her blood was up.

She wanted to kill someone.

As the rattle of automatic weapons fire and the snap of quick bursts wound its way down, she saw her chance.

The three men she'd picked for the head of this collection of wild beasts and criminals broke for the stairwell door. They dragged four women behind them and pushed another two ahead of them. With machine pistols at their heads, the women fled. The two ahead even tried to outrun the thugs.

They disappeared into the stairwell before anyone got a shot at them.

"They're mine," Vicky screamed as she raised her shield and ran after them.

On the deck in front of the elevators, women rolled out of Vicky's way, or helped those who were too traumatized to know what was going on around them. She stepped over one woman, writhing in pain.

Whether she had been hit by a dart or a slug, Vicky couldn't tell. She was totally focused on the door to the stairwell.

She kept her shield up, holding it just high enough not to cover her eyes.

Shoving the door open, she shouted, "Marines, hold your fire in the central stairwell! Friendlies above you!"

Since she was the only woman running around in this building, she expected that the Marines below knew who was yelling for them not to shoot her.

When the barking of M-6s fell silent, Vicky stepped into the stairwell. It seemed empty above her.

Crouched low and keeping her shield on her threat axis, she made her way cautiously up the stairs. She had some bastards to kill.

34

At the top of the stairs, Vicky cautiously shouldered open the door to the roof. She kept her shield in front of her, using only the screen on her automatic to sweep the roof of the building.

Slugs rattled into her shield. It dented in more places, but it neither shattered nor holed. No doubt, tomorrow, Vicky's shoulder would ache.

The thick metal door beside her also thudded against her other shoulder as slugs slammed into it. It seemed to take more hits than her shield. Was most of the shooting coming from a blind spot on her left?

"Maggie, I need some eyes above."

Immediately, a vision of the roof appeared before her eyes. There were two large housings on an otherwise flat graveled deck. She was edging out from one, and there was a stairwell and elevator housing. Across from her was what looked like an air conditioning stack.

Behind it, there were two gunners. One hunkered down on her right. She caught occasional glimpses of him as he ducked out to fire at her. He had four hostages tied in pairs. The other one was to the left, blocked by the door. He had two naked women hostages with him.

A third figure was also to her left, also blocked. He also had two hostages. He fired from behind the elevator housing.

No wonder the door was smashing into her space-armored shoulder so much.

The one target she could possibly hit ducked out of cover to fire a long burst at her. She was just lining up a shot at him when he swung back behind his cover.

Vicky sent a few shots his way just to let him know she cared.

No matter how much Vicky thought about her situation, she could not come up with a good way to break the stalemate. If she moved from her present position, she'd be shot to hell before she got halfway to the air conditioning unit.

Vicky kept the one guy she could under fire and waited for matters to change.

The guy to her left made the first move. He pulled back from his spot behind the elevator housing, then began to drag the two women with him around the structure. He was careful to keep the hostages between him and any Marine snipers a thousand meters away.

Smart man.

Vicky kept up her base of fire, just to let everyone know she was still here, while she waited to see what the movable object was up to. As expected, he made his way around the housing and came up on her right side.

He walked bent over, keeping the women above him as he covered the distance. Once to the corner off to her immediate right, he hunkered down to work up his courage.

That left Vicky on the sharp edge of decision. She had to keep up her fire at the guy across from her. She also had to get ready to fire off to her right as soon as the guy went gunning for her.

She fired a burst, then pulled back a bit, scraping the shield over the roof.

The noise was enough to settle it for the SOB to her right. He leaned out low and made ready to snap off a burst.

Vicky had guessed how low he'd be crouched. Her snap shot caught him in the shoulder and shoved him back. His head strayed out just enough for Vicky to take the top of it off with three solid shots.

He collapsed screaming, but not for long.

"Girls, get back!" Vicky yelled, even as the gunman across from her hung his machine pistol out and fired a burst at the edge of the elevator housing.

No woman screamed, so Vicky guessed they got back in time.

That left her with two bastards to kill.

"Ma'am?" came nervously from behind her.

"Yes?" Vicky answered the Marine.

"We got a general behind us that says we need to get out ahead of you."

Vicky scowled as she fired off a shot to keep at least one of her problem children down.

"And you got a Grand Duchess ahead of you that wants to kill herself some SOBs."

"Oh. Oh! *Oooh!*" dawned slowly from behind her, but it dawned.

"Now, be a good Marine and stay where I tell you. You get to kill all the rest of these POS's. These two are mine."

There was much murmuring from behind her.

"Ma'am, you sure we can't fire over your shield, or something?"

"You get your head up above this shield and your mama's going to be getting a condolence letter from me."

That quieted things down a bit from behind her.

The aerial view showed that the one to her right had gone over to have a talk with the one to her left. That guy edged out just enough to get a quick glance at her fire position, then pulled back just as her shots whizzed by where he'd been.

The two continued to talk.

Finally, two young women, nude and vulnerable, were forced out to stand between the edge of the air conditioner housing and Vicky. Between their heads, shoulders, and hips, there were spaces for this crook to shoot at Vicky. It didn't leave much for her to get a shot off at him and not hit the women.

Vicky checked her aerial view. The guy was hunkering down but keeping his legs behind theirs. If he tried for a shot, he'd be low. He'd likely try to get a shot off somewhere from between the women's hips and shoulders. She doubted he'd go so low as their legs.

Still, he used his machine pistol to force the women to spread their legs. One winced as the hot barrel made contact with her sensitive thighs.

"You're a real sicko," Vicky muttered.

The gunman leaned out and fired from the apex at the top of her legs. The recoil sent the machine pistol high. The woman screamed as her most delicate parts came in contact with a hot piece of stuttering metal.

Vicky held her fire until he was done. The two women had somehow managed to settle down from the wild jittering and screaming they had done as a machine pistol snapped off a burst either close to or on their vulnerable skin. Then Vicky fired one shot. It hit the wall just where the gunner's head had been a moment ago.

The women must have felt the wind of the dart on their skin, but they didn't jump at the lower sound of her shot. Good.

Vicky went back to aiming between their legs.

This time, the guy fired a burst from between the other woman's hips. This time neither woman jumped. They'd been inured to hell. Now that they knew this new version, they adapted to it and let it become just a normal part of their miserable existence.

Again, Vicky picked a bit of wall off the corner near the guy's face for a late shot. From the overhead take, she watched him flinch.

She also watched him get down on one hand and both knees.

Setting up her shot, she breathed slowly, evenly. Her finger squeezed gently back on the trigger. She knew exactly when it would fire. She held just short of there.

"Come on, you SOB," she muttered, urgently.

He made his move. He leaned forward, positioned himself

between the skinned and bleeding knees of the hostages and took aim at Vicky.

She squeezed off one shot. It hit his pistol, knocking his arm back and kicking his shoulder back. Her second round was aimed between his eyes.

He'd flinched at the first shot. The second shot only took him in the cheek. As he rolled away, Vicky got a good shot at the back of his head.

This one hit where she aimed it.

With a cry, he fell flat, deflating like a blowup doll. He screamed again. Vicky put two more rounds into his skull.

She could hear the last huff as his breath left him. He lay there, bleeding.

The two hostages took off running.

They'd been through enough hell to know not to block Vicky's field of fire.

The last guy hung his gun out to fire a wild burst at them. Vicky sent a shot at him. She missed the gun, but the wind of the dart on his skin sent his aim wide and his gun back behind the air conditioning tower.

The women fled past Vicky. They didn't quit running until they reached the other end of the elevator equipment. One of them, however, paused as they rushed by. She retrieved the machine pistol and several spare magazines from Vicky's first kill.

No sooner were the women behind the elevator gear than one of them was snapping off shots at the edge of the air conditioning towers.

Vicky had to like that kind of woman.

35

"**M**a'am?" the Marine behind Vicky kind of begged. Marines don't beg. Not when they're fully armed and dangerous. But then, most didn't have a headstrong Grand Duchess blocking their path.

"Yes?" Vicky said, not even trying to strip her words of the deadly anger in her soul.

"Could we please get out there ahead of you? The general is getting mighty mad."

"He's not mad at you. He's mad at me. Don't worry. I'm used to people being mad at me."

"Yes, ma'am," didn't sound all that convinced.

Vicky ignored the Marines and General Pemberton. She had no time for them at the moment. She studied her overhead view. The last POS had retreated, dragging four hostages with him, back to the middle of the air conditioning stacks. Two naked and vulnerable women were to his right. Two to his left.

His head and weapon whipped back and forth, left and right.

He had only one way off this roof, and that lay dead ahead of him: the edge of the roof and a ten-floor drop. He must somehow realize that he wasn't getting out of this alive. How many people did he want to take with him?

"Listen," Vicky whispered to the Marines. "The kill shot is mine. This bastard is mine. Understand?"

The two Marines behind Vicky exchanged worried looks, but they nodded their assent.

Vicky used hand signals to tell the Marines that she was headed to the right side of the stacks. The next two were to go to the left. The rest were to stand their ground. They didn't like that, but one look at Vicky's Grand Duchess-size glare and they were as cowed as Marines could be. It helped that none of them were higher than corporal.

They all nodded agreement.

As silently as she could, Vicky lifted her shield. Keeping it in front of her, a very angry Grand Duchess stepped out of the door and headed at a low crouch across the roof. The two Marines reached their corner as she got to hers.

She checked her overhead take. The guy was showing bad signs of taking his desperation out on the women. He had a choke hold on one of the women on the right while holding his machine pistol jammed hard into the back of one woman on the left.

Vicky made a guess that the women were tied together.

She moved forward to only pause at the corner, before edging around it. Crouching behind her shield, she confronted the head bastard.

He snapped off a burst of fire at her. The shield took the hits and deflected them.

"Can't you do better than that?" Vicky called.

"A bitch! What's a bitch doing up here? Hiding behind a stinking hunk of garbage?"

Vicky fired one round, hitting the air conditioning stack above his head. Chunks of metal splattered all around him. He took a hit on his head, but two of the women took slashes to their shoulders.

They flinched but stayed in place. As Vicky expected, both were bound together by plastic strips at their wrists and ankles.

Running would be a bitch.

"Oh, so the little baby girl has a gun. I am sooo terrified," he baby-talked as he did an exaggerated tremble in fright.

Vicky fired another shot. It was just centimeters above his head.

Now it was his turn to flinch down behind his hostages.

"You do that again, and I'll blow these bitches away," he snapped.

"Count Blankster, you die exactly one second after you kill any one of them," Vicky said. "Or maybe I'll take your gun away and let the women here have at you. I've got a knife in my boot. Want to see what one of them can do with it?"

The guy crouched lower.

One of the women muttered low, "Oh, yeah."

He slapped her on the butt with his pistol. She rocked with the blow and made not a sound.

What Vicky did notice was that both of the women facing her were shuffling their feet just a bit wider.

She had a good shot at his knee. She took it. One shot only.

He screamed as his knee blew out beneath him.

All four of the women took off running. One among each pair counted "One, two. One, two." The four of them must have had some time in three legged races at picnics or fairs. One got four steps, the other six before they lost coordination and went down.

He yanked up his machine pistol, screaming he'd kill them all.

Vicky caught the hand that held the weapon just as he settled his aim on the closest pair. She put a round into his wrist and the gun flew from his hand.

He grabbed for it with his other hand. She put two rounds into his forearm.

It shattered, leaving it dangling at a sickening angle with the ends of both bones showing through the bloody pulp.

He fell to the deck, screaming in agony. As Vicky stood up from behind her shield, one of the Marines from the other side raced forward. He kicked the weapon well out of the count's reach. One of the women grabbed it.

"Don't shoot him!" Vicky screamed. "Don't shoot! He doesn't deserve a quick death."

She got some nasty looks from the four women, and the other four that had joined them.

"Who are you to tell us what we can do with this piece of shit?" one woman demanded.

"I am Her Grace, the Grand Duchess Victoria, and I hold high, low, and middle justice in this half of the Empire. If you kill him, it's just another murder that justice must be done for. If I execute him, the blood price ends with me. Understood?"

"The Grand Duchess?" several of the women echoed.

The bleeding redcoat had a few vulgar and bitter things to say about her and her lineage. Of her ancestors, Vicky couldn't much disagree. Of herself, she really didn't care.

She aimed a dart just a centimeter in front of his nose.

A couple of small chunks of gravel took him in the face. He shut up.

"Now, we can do this the hard way, the harder way, or the hardest way. You understand me?" she told the so-called count and commander of this regiment of murderous, raping thugs.

He gulped while trying with his shattered hand to staunch the bleeding from his arm.

"I can give you a quick death. Three rounds, right between the eyes."

The guy actually looked hopeful. The women looked dismayed.

"Naw, that ain't gonna happen," Vicky said. "You've got too many crimes on your soul to get off that easy."

The women relaxed and the guy who had tortured and murdered so many women went back to whimpering and looking terrified.

"Now then, I could put a couple of rounds in your gut, your stomach, or your lungs. Nobody ever died from a few hits there. Leastwise, never quickly. I could let the women here have my knife and they could play with you. I'm told women can be the worst torturers ever. How would you like to eat your dick one small bite at a time or have one eye cut out as an appetizer?"

The women exchanged wicked smiles. This was fine by them.

The guy wasn't so into it. "No. No. You can't let them . . . let them do that to me."

"I can if I sentence you to that. There's one thing about this damn Peterwald Empire. We never got around to defining cruel and unusual punishment. If the Grand Duchess says it ain't, well boy, it ain't."

"You said there was a third. Some third way. What is it?" he begged, eagerly.

"You can drag yourself over to that roof edge and see if you can learn to fly during the ten-floor drop."

The women didn't look too happy, but the guy began to crawl across the gravel roof for the edge.

He didn't crawl so much as drag himself. He had only one knee to push himself along with and only his two good elbows, one arm and one hand being wrecked. The gravel was cruel against his ruined knee.

"Ladies," Vicky said, "don't you think he's a bit over-dressed for this? After all, we wouldn't want his clothes to interfere with him learning to fly, now would we?"

Vicky handed the gal who had picked up the first machine pistol her boot knife. She went to cut the others free. She gave Vicky a hopeful look, but the Grand Duchess had to ask for her knife back.

Still, the six women were not gentle as they rolled him over and stripped him naked. There may have been a few unkind kicks and punches, but no one was keeping count.

No one but the former count, Head of the Security Consultants on Oryol . . . and he wasn't talking. Grunting, groaning, screaming, but not talking.

He lay there on his back, going nowhere, resting in his agony.

"Hey ladies, look at his pink little prick," Vicky said, "it ain't like he's got any use for that nice tip. Who wants to cut it off?"

All were eager volunteers.

However he, quickly rolled over on his stomach and began a slow crawl across the tar and gravel rooftop. Soon, a smear of blood followed him both from his mangled knee and somewhere between the apex of his legs.

"Can I borrow your pistol?" the woman who'd picked up the second machine pistol asked.

"What do you have in mind?"

"If I tell you, and you don't like it, I won't do it."

Vicky swapped weapons with her. The Grand Duchess checked the machine pistol. The safety was off. The magazine was still half-full.

The woman with the automatic strolled up to the punk as if she had not a care in the world. As if the gravel wasn't as cruel to her bare feet as they were to his package.

Once she was up to him, she aimed the pistol down at his good knee. She gave Vicky a questioning look.

Vicky shrugged.

She put three slugs into that knee.

The man howled in pain.

The women exchanged smiles. They all liked that he'd need more time to crawl to his death.

But the young woman with the automatic wasn't done yet. She stepped around to in front of him. Stooping, she waved the pistol in front of his eyes.

She immediately had his attention.

"Sing us a song, cutie." Her squat in front of him gave him a good look at her bare sex. "What's the matter, don't you have a song for us?"

He croaked something. It didn't sound much like a song.

"I didn't hear no song, little girl. You are gonna sing me a song, aren't you, little cutie?"

He croaked louder, but there was no melody.

"Oh, no song. Well then, you don't need those lungs if you ain't gonna give me and my girls a song, now do you?"

She stood up, and seemed to walk away, then thought different of it and whirled on him. She put one dart into the back of his right lung.

Grinning she came over and swapped guns with Vicky. "Thank you."

"You think he can make it to the edge on one lung?" Vicky asked.

"Alice managed to crawl halfway down the hall with four slugs in both her lungs. He ain't hurting. Not really."

They watched him crawl for a few more excruciating minutes. He tried to push himself along with his legs, but neither knee would give him any purchase. He struggled to use his elbows, but one arm flopped about every time he moved. That had to be painful. The other arm had a shattered wrist at the end of it. More pain.

Still, he struggled along, barely making a few centimeters with each excruciating pull of his elbows and body.

Vicky glanced around. The two Marines at the other end of the air conditioning unit looked kind of green around the gills.

"You don't have to stay here if you don't want to," Vicky told them.

"Will you be okay, ma'am?"

"I got four weapons. He's got none. I feel pretty damn safe."

"Okay, ma'am. If it's okay with you, ma'am," and the two Marines didn't retreat. Not exactly. It was more like a proper retrograde. Breaking contact with the enemy. Yeah. That's what it was.

A moment later, from the other side of stacks came "General, I wouldn't go around there if I was you, sir."

"What's the Grand Duchess up to?" a gruff old voice demanded.

"Justice, sir. Raw and bloody justice."

"Is she alone?"

"No, sir. She's got eight bitches from hell and I wouldn't bother any of them just now, sir."

"She get the last of the sons of bitches?"

"She got him. He sure wishes she didn't, sir."

"Your Grace, do you need any help?" the general called.

"Do we need any help?" she asked the naked man.

He crocked something, but no one understood it or cared to.

"Ladies?" she asked the former hostages.

They shook their heads without taking their eyes off the struggling former count.

"No, General Pemberton, I have everything well in hand. You go police up this mess. Get those women back with their loved ones. Families."

"Yes, Your Grace. Okay, Marines. Don't stand around gawking. You got your orders. You two. You post at the first landing on this stairwell. When Her Grace is finished here, you get her to my headquarters."

"Yes, sir," came in perfect unison.

"Damn, she *is* the Grand Duchess," one of the former hostages whispered.

One of the women with a weapon sidled up to Vicky. "You damn Peterwalds can be pretty vicious."

"Yeah, my pa and grandpa were real SOBs. Now, for what it's worth, I'm a SOB, too, but I'm *your* SOB. You okay with that?"

"Yeah. I guess so. Don't Peterwalds come in any other flavor?"

"Maybe my kids won't be SOBs. Maybe my husband can help them not to be," Vicky mused aloud,

"I'll pray for the poor bastard."

"Married to me, he'll need all the help he can get."

"Your Grace," the shortest of the naked women around Vicky said.

"Yes."

"Can I borrow your knife for a minute?"

Vicky eyed her, but said nothing.

The woman turned her gaze to the struggling man. "I can't have my pound of flesh, but don't I deserve a few square centimeters of skin?"

Vicky retrieved her knife from her boot, flipped it in her hand, then offered it to the woman, hilt first.

She went over, knelt down, and cut a two-centimeter-wide gash in the guy's butt. Then she peeled back a good three-centimeter-long strip. Blood welled up in it.

He screamed in agony.

"Sorry, I ain't got no salt to pour into your wound, but maybe this will help." She stood up and pissed on his bleeding butt.

He sobbed and wept as he dragged himself another few centimeters to his death and release.

One of the other unarmed women was right behind her. She eyed Vicky.

The Grand Duchess shrugged without batting an eyebrow. No question that worse had been done to these women, or the women whose mangled bodies had been hauled out of there.

There was little Vicky would say no to.

The first woman handed off the knife to the next one, then came to stand beside Vicky. She accepted the machine pistol when the woman with it wanted to join the line. The two working machine pistols stayed several meters back from the struggling man.

One by one, the women took their strip of skin. His butt, his back, and a thigh all made their contribution to these women's' revenge. One took a strip off of his bleeding arm just below the shattered break. She was sure to piss on the bloody pulp.

The last one stood in front of him, grabbed his hair to hold him in place and then took her slice from his forehead.

The wailing man's head dropped to the graveled roof as she pissed in his face. "Why don't you just kill me?" he pleaded.

The women were unmoved by his plea. "Hurry up or we'll start another round. I'm thinking I should have scalped you."

The women were truly hard-hearted. Vicky could almost feel sorry for the bleeding wreck of a man in his agony.

However, in his case, "almost" and "any actual" regret were a hundred kilometers apart.

He continued to slowly drag himself to his death.

As he did, the women taunted him. That was how Vicky learned just how horrible it had been to be a hostage to the likes of this bastard. He'd held all the power, and he'd delight in the corruption it bestowed upon him. He hadn't been content to just take his pleasure. No, he had to have the women around him suffer for it.

Vicky thought she knew the depravity of men. The stories these women told opened the doors to a new meaning of hell. She was revolted by it. Her stomach went sour, then nauseous.

As she listened, a realization dawned on her.

She sought power.

A Peterwald chased after power the way a tiger chased after fresh red meat. She'd been revolted by her father's folly and the abuse of power that he wallowed in the last few years while the Bowlingame girl lead him around by a chain wrapped around his prick.

That was sickening enough.

Father had never sunk this low, but there was nothing to keep him from going here. There were no limits on his power.

The Bowlingame family had taken up the power he left lying on his wife's bed and used it to lay the Empire to waste. They'd murdered and raped and pillaged their way across the Empire, taking what they wanted, tossing aside the rest.

This man, with his four or five thousand willing and eager thugs had weaseled their way through the cracks in this disaster to find their own private hell and fill it with helpless victims.

There had been nothing in place to protect these people from this rapacious wolf.

Now Mannie's mania for self-government under the rule of law began to make sense to her. His insistence that the local government have its own police force, and even an armed guard took on an immediacy that she could now understand. These people needed a defense from the likes of the Peterwalds. They also needed protection from those wolves that skulked among them. Trash the likes of which she'd executed yesterday out in those two far hangars.

Democracy wasn't just something that was nice to have. It was a necessity for the survival of a decent people.

The demented pirate prince was getting close to the balustrade around the roof. He'd have to pull himself up a half meter before he could roll himself off the roof and begin his ten story drop to blessed oblivion. Several of the women weren't willing yet to let him slip away.

One woman approached him. "I hear tell that one guy just loved to slug his women in the kidney. Hurt like hell." She kicked him in his lower back.

He groaned.

"I guess I missed. You didn't scream nearly loud enough."

Another woman went to a knee beside him and slugged him on the other side.

The guy screamed that time.

The women now stood on either side of him, his side boys to hell. He'd pull himself a few more centimeters toward his death, and one of them would slug him in a kidney.

At first, he screamed at every blow, but before long, all he could get out was a croak of a groan.

It was taking him longer and longer to work up the strength to pull himself along. The women took to nudging one of his shattered knees or his broken arm to encourage him to make the next pull.

Vicky found the entire effort exhausting in body and soul, but the women never tired.

Finally, only the low parapet blocked him from his death. However, even though it was only a half meter high, it might have been a hundred.

His knees were shot. Literally. A dart had demolished both, turning them into bloody pulps. He could not push up on them. He had to slowly draw himself up on the broken wrist until he could get that elbow up on the low wall. He screamed in pain as he whipped his broken arm around to get that elbow up as well.

He pulled himself forward until he hung there, whimpering and sobbing, on his arms and shoulders. But it seemed he could go no farther.

He shouldn't have done that. Hanging there, he was vulnerable like he hadn't been before. His prick, bloodied and torn, hung down for all to see.

One of the women took that moment to apply the knife and totally castrate him.

From some pit in the hell within him, he found one final scream. The women around him grinned as the woman with the knife plopped his bloody sex down right before his eyes.

"What can you do worse to me now?" he somehow managed to get out.

"Is that a challenge? Do you really want to ask any of us if we've got something more we'd like to do to you?" the woman with the knife said and began nudging it between his butt cheeks.

That was all it took. He began struggling to swing his hips up on the ledge. He rolled himself flat on the low wall and paused. His ruined front, with embedded gravel, showed every centimeter of his slow progress to that moment.

Around him, the women exchanged glances, licked their lips, and eyed each other with one question. Did they let him go now, or did they take one last ounce of flesh?

The woman with the knife, slashed down, aiming for a kidney though she had to slice him from front to back.

She must have hit it because the man let out a blood curdling scream.

The woman handed off the knife to another.

Now the man was struggling to roll over. To roll off the roof to his death.

The women got to him first, stabbing deep. He screeched in agony as he rolled away from her, taking the knife with him as he hurtled down the ten floors, shrieking all the way until it ended with a dull thud.

Vicky sighed, not for his death, but for the end of her ordeal, watching him die.

She'd shot men between the eyes, telling herself she was preforming her duties to justice, that she was executing them under the law.

This torture and enforced suicide was something else. She felt an urgent need for Mannie. For a hug. For a chance to talk. For someone to help her scrub herself, her mind, her soul from this.

For someone to tell her she didn't have to go the way of this piece of shit but rather could return to the way of the gracious Grand Duchess.

The eight women collapsed onto the roof like puppets whose strings had been cut.

"I'll get you some help," Vicky said as she stumbled her way toward the stairwell.

"Water," one cried.

"Something to eat. It's been days," another muttered around a moan.

Vicky shook her head in a nod. These women had been in such physical need, yet their need for vengeance had driven them on.

People were strange that way.

36

V icky found the Marines waiting nervously for her on the first landing down. She doubted they'd missed any of the screaming.

"You done?" one asked her in a shaky voice.

"Yeah. We're done. Listen," Vicky said, glancing over her shoulder up the stairs, "the women are in pretty bad shape. They need water and some food. Then they need help."

Vicky paused trying to organize her thoughts back to the task at hand.

She nodded at the smaller of the Marines, "You, go get help. Female aids, corpsmen. You know what I mean."

He nodded.

"You, help the women."

Before Vicky even had to dredge out the next order, the Marines were doing it for her. Both of them were detaching their water tanks from their suits. Both were rummaging around in their rucksacks for emergency rations, energy bars, whatever food they still had with them. Vicky added her stores to those they were giving up.

The runner also handed his off to the other Marine and took off down the stairs. That Marine turned and began to trudge up the stairs. Vicky had a strong sense that he was scared of the women he'd been sent to help.

With a sigh, Vicky made her way on shaky knees down the stairs. Somewhere along the way, tears began to stream down her face. She hated her leaking eyes. She didn't know why she had gone all blubbery. She willed herself to stop, but that only seemed to make it worse.

She held on tight to the handrail as she put one foot in front of the other, going down each step as if it might not be there. As if a great abyss threatened to engulf her.

Almost to the bottom, it was so tempting to collapse onto a step. To sit there for a bit of a rest or for the next eternity. She couldn't face her general or the troops with herself so at loose ends.

She turned the corner at one landing, stared blankly, and halted. On the next landing was Mannie.

Holding onto the railing with both hands, she asked, "What are you doing here?"

"I heard that you were having a hell of a day. I thought you might like a hug."

Vicky gasped for a breath and let it all out in a rush, "I'd love a hug."

Mannie was up the stairs like lightning. In a moment, he held her, even as her legs let go and she settled to the step behind her.

Now she surrendered herself to large wracking sobs. Mannie soothed her with words that meant nothing and arms that seemed to shield her from the world for the moment. His soft stroking of her hair seemed to strip away a little bit of the hell that surrounded her.

Not much, but enough.

A long time later, he asked, "Have you had anything to eat?"

Vicky shook her head.

"They've set up mess facilities in an abandoned restaurant a couple of blocks from here. They've brought down scrambled eggs and bacon, ship-baked biscuits, and coffee. It's amazing how they've kept it fresh. Come on. Let's get some chow into you."

"I can't go out there looking like this."

"What? The troops can't see that their Grand Duchess is an honest human being? Remember, I saw you naked, your body covered with bug bites and scratched by thorns. I saw you as human and love you."

"But I can't fit all of them in my bed," Vicky snorted a kind of laugh.

"Your assassins would love to try," Mannie said, keeping up the inane jokes.

Slowly they made it to the bottom floor and its exit to the street. The sun was up, bringing warmth that penetrated the chill inside Vicky's battle armor. Troops went about their duty, hurrying here or there. They saluted Her Imperial Grand Duchess Victoria, and ignored the woman with tearstained cheeks in the battle armor of a four star admiral.

None objected when she failed to return their salute.

Mannie supported her as they made their way two blocks up to a derelict building marked only by the flow of Marines in and out. Mannie found her a chair at a small table. He turned to head for the chow line, but a private already had a plate full of bacon and eggs, two biscuits and jam ready at his elbow.

"Give me a second and I'll get you some coffee, Ma'am. Sir, do you want anything to eat?" he asked Mannie.

"I've already eaten," he answered, "but I'd love another cup of that coffee. How do you make it so good?"

"It's the pinch of salt, sir."

Mannie settled back into his chair and stared at Vicky.

She stared blankly at the food in front of her. The lovely smell of bacon made her mouth water.

"Do you think I could have some orange juice and a glass of water?" she asked Mannie.

He passed it along to the trooper who brought two cups of coffee and he immediately trotted off to find some.

Still, Vicky could only stare at the lovely meal in front of her.

"You want me to feed you a few spoonfuls?"

"I'm embarrassed enough. No need to humiliate me."

"Yeah, but I can't have you starving to death sitting here in front of that delicious chow. The cooks would never forgive me for that. It would likely scare off their paying customers."

Finally, Vicky found a chuckle. She managed to retrieve one stick of bacon. She took small bites and chewed each one slowly. Just as slowly, her body seemed to stir to life.

She began to dredge up words. She let them crawl from her mouth without thought or reflection.

Mannie listened intently to her every word she spoke. He only interrupted her to remind her to take a bite. The palace rules of not talking with your mouth full was suspended for the duration of this meal.

The words spilled out of her. An entire night's worth of words. She knew she was babbling. Trying to keep the story of the early morning going to avoid having to talk about the ending.

She tried, but there was no way to avoid the final assault on the roof, the attack, and the judgement that followed.

She finally ran down to emptiness and ended up just staring at her empty plate. Somehow, her coffee cup was filled again. The Marine who had been so helpful appeared again at her elbow with another plate of bacon. He offered Mannie a piece, then Vicky.

She took two.

Mannie wolfed down the bacon then leaned close, and put out his hands, palms up.

"What about this morning frightens you?" he asked softly.

"Frightens me?" Vicky echoed, dumbly.

"Yes. You sound frightened."

Vicky wanted to snap back at him that she was many things, but frightened wasn't one of them. But she paused, held her tongue . . . and let Mannie's words roll around her muzzy brain for a minute.

It was only then that she realized that Mannie was right. She was terrified.

"I'm terrified," she said slowly, "of being both. Of being the leader who became a beast and abused power over the people, and like the women, who also went down the same path, becoming beasts howling for revenge. The thing is," Vicky said, looking deep into Mannie's eyes. "It was their right. He deserved all they did to him. But it was wrong. Not because of what they did to him, but what they did to themselves."

"And what have you done to yourself?" Mannie asked.

"I thought I was doing justice." Vicky said, choosing each word as if it cost her blood. "I was really just one of them, demanding vengeance."

Mannie gave her a soft nod. "Okay, now, tell me, my Gracious Grand Duchess, what have you learned about yourself?"

Vicky leaned back in her chair. She picked up another piece of bacon and slowly munched it as she thought. The bacon was delicious, a reward for this painful self-reflection.

"I am no better than my father and my grandfather. Given absolute power, I can be corrupted. I pray to whatever god will listen that I never become as bad as that piece of shit, but I am capable of losing control and doing horrible things."

She leaned forward to fix Mannie with a firm stare. "You are right. I *need* the rule of law."

He responded to her with an understanding nod.

"I have learned that I need help distinguishing justice from revenge. I think as a Grand Duchess I should limit myself to choosing wise men and women to dispense justice and reserve only the most difficult of decisions to myself. And maybe not even then. I may need further reflection on this."

"The search for justice always requires more reflection. When do you apply the rule of law, and when is the law an ass?" Mannie said, ruefully.

Vicky found herself chuckling at her husband's ever-dry wit.

"Do you think we could somehow do this . . . and keep our bed to ourselves?" Now it was her turn to draw a chuckle from them both.

"I certainly hope so. I certainly hope that I can help you and your subjects establish a rule of law that will outlast us all."

"And you can begin planning for elections of a senate or house or whatever it is you think that should make the laws."

"And an Ultimate Court to define, protect, and apply those laws."

"Good God, Mannie, isn't there any limit to your scheming?"

Mannie gave her the cutest shrug. "Dearest, you are hard to replace. Let's see. I'm dividing you up into a First Minister to be your chief minister and lead your government. At least two deliberative bodies, although the moneyed interests think they should get one to represent capital if the people get one to represent them, and the planets get one for them as well."

"Is there no limit?"

"We're trying to keep the guild halls from getting their own. You'd think one for the people would be enough."

"One would," Vicky said with a deep breath. This was fun. So much more fun than executing criminals herself.

They talked on until it was time for lunch. The cooks served up meatloaf sandwiches with a choice of several potato or pasta salads. Many of the men and women who had been working with Mannie showed up to join them for lunch. They moved to a much larger table in the back.

Vicky sat back quietly and just listened as they plotted both her downfall and her hope for a future for herself, her children and them all.

It was strange what these humans did.

It was just past noon today. In the last twenty-four hours she had seen humans in all their many facets, both their glory and their degradation.

37

After Vicky and Mannie finished lunch, General Pemberton came in for his own meal. Before eating, he brought Vicky, and all those around her, up to date on the efforts to get Oryol back on its feet.

"Power is the first thing we have to do before we can do anything else." The general said, then just shook his head as he hunted for words, "Those . . . idiots . . . raped the lovely young wife of the lead engineer at the power plant. The entire work force took off after that and the reactor went on for another week before it began to fall apart. We're lucky it shut itself down gracefully. Anyway, we're bringing down the parts we need to get it back up and some of the workers have already reported back."

"When will we have power?" asked a college professor of history who was working closely with Mannie.

"I'm hoping by tonight," the general said. "I've been warned that once we fix one thing, we may find something else. All I can really say is look for the lights when they come on."

"Understandable," the professor agreed.

"Once we have power, we can start pumping water again. The wells here are pretty clean. Still, we need to process the water a bit.

We have a small supply of chemicals on hand, but we'll need to order in more. The same for sewage treatment. We can start it up after the water gets online, but treating it requires some serious chemicals. That supply was allowed to run pretty low before it all came apart."

"How do we get food flowing into the city?" a businessman asked.

"It will have to be the right food," a doctor added. "So many of these people have been starving. You can't just give them a candy bar or a beef steak."

"We have famine biscuits aboard ship," Vicky said. "That should serve to start."

"What we need is some money to jump-start the economy," the professor said. "We're flat on our back. We need a hand up."

"Mannie, from my private purse, can we pay the farmers for a week's worth of food to give to the starving city folk?"

"Yes, sweetheart. That would be a most gracious act for the Grand Duchess to perform."

"I helped in the assault on two buildings," Vicky said. "I remember the stink. They'd been using the lower floors for a latrine. We'll need to clean that up before we get an epidemic going."

The doctor nodded agreement.

"I still have some Peterwald money around here somewhere. Don't you think that would be well-used cleaning up the shit?" Vicky deadpanned.

That was good for a laugh, and approval. Peterwald money should be used to clean up the mess it made.

Of course, Vicky knew that what money she had was all the same, but these poor people didn't need to know that. Nor did they need to know that most of this was money given to her as wedding gifts for her charities.

The general got time to eat his lunch after that. The planning went on, through supper and into the night. They were joined by the managers for many of the city's services and the planning got more granular.

There was a cheer when the lights came on and the generator cut out. People would have street lights for the walk home. Vicky managed to scrounge up rides to take her advisors back to their homes. She sent them on their way with food baskets for themselves, their families, and anyone they thought they could feed.

Vicky felt very good when she bedded down with Mannie. She refused to sleep in any of the rooms she'd freed hostages from. Fortunately, the Marines had brought down temporary buildings.

She and Mannie ended up pulling two camp cots together and sleeping in a barracks with a hundred other exhausted soldiers. Mannie slept in his clothes. He helped pry Vicky out of her armor. She slept in the padding.

What mattered was that she slept in Mannie's arms.

38

T he next week was full of hard work. They did things that left them cheering. Things also happened that almost broke their hearts.

There was no book, no checklist; nothing with instructions on how you pick an entire planet up when it's face down in the dirt. Vicky had Maggie keeping a record. Certainly the Grand Duchess would find more planets in just this sort of mess. There was no need to repeat some of these mistakes again.

By the grace of some merciful god, five thousand redcoats could not poison an entire planet. These Security Consultants didn't spread much beyond Kromy. True, they terrorized a city of two hundred thousand people, but many had succeeded in fleeing to family on farms or in the small distant towns.

The redcoats had raided farms for food. They burned the first farm they hit and murdered all the people working there. After a few assaults like that, lookouts were scattered around Kromy. Since all modern communications were down, they used pieces of mirrors to flash their warning.

Farms close to town built hideaways out in the fields. After the first few farms were slaughtered, the redcoats didn't get another person from the farms. True, they burned some homesteads, either just a house or barn, or the entire place. Still, the farmers learned quickly to hide their women and themselves.

Vicky's offer to buy a week's worth of food got the farm-to-market pipeline going. Her offer of money to pay for the cleanup of the worst hazards for disease put some money in the hands of hungry people. Somehow, they came up with money to pay the civil servants who got the power, water, sewage, and garbage collection up and going.

Everyone rejoiced when the communication net came back online. Man does not live by bread alone. They must have a way to talk to each other.

All of those efforts came with a price that would not stop. In too many of their efforts, the work of putting things back together brought more bodies into the light of day. The renegade Red Coats didn't just want power; they insisted on abusing it every chance they got.

How could human beings be so sick?

They were also stupid.

The redcoats had confiscated the entire money supply, including everything gold or silver, that they could tax outright or steal. All of it ended up stashed somewhere in the hotel.

They were absolutely crazy. They even had their slaves empty the bank vault of money and lug it over to the hotel.

Vicky turned the money over to the new government, and they used it to pay those who were working for them. They also gave everyone in town a cash grant to help them get started again.

It wasn't just a monetary give-away. Every mark they gave away created seven marks worth of exchange before it vanished into the background. The goods and services that were essential to modern civilization began to stir back to life.

First they bought food. Then the minor things were added. It was surprising how many clothes stores hadn't been raided or burned down. Plumbers, carpenters and electricians began fixing things for people once they had cash.

Of course, Mannie got his democracy going. This time, it was a much more interested Vicky who watched it happen.

Everyone who wanted to sit in the parliament was invited to get a thousand signatures. Some got it from the farmers who lived around them. Some got it from the people of the smaller towns. Bonki, down south of the equator, got to field a hundred representatives. Kromy had to field two hundred. However, in the cities, it wasn't so much ground as skills that made for a representative. The power system ended up with two reps, using signatures both from the workers and their family and friends. That pattern was followed often. Female students even elected four of their own. The male students chose their four, only to discover that the girls had gotten there first, getting their boyfriends to sign.

The House of the People ended up with only two male students.

The campaigning went on for a week, then all those with less than five hundred signatures were made to drop out. That left those still below a thousand hunting for signatures.

Three weeks after Vicky's first troop landed, the opera house was opened to serve during the day as the People's House. Parties had not coalesced into anything solid enough to put forward a platform, so Vicky appointed three co-presidents pro tem, and called the house to order.

She had a nice speech all prepared, thanks to Mannie, but she never got to give it.

A runner from General Pemberton's headquarters dashed in just after she'd only called them to order.

He had a hot message from Admiral Bolesław. A fleet had entered the system. It was hostile ... and it out-gunned Vicky's.

39

A dmiral, Her Grace, the Grand Duchess Victoria took time to get topside. A quick flight down to Bonki, then a ride up the now operational ferry. She had plenty of time to calm down.

It didn't work.

She was still mad as hell when she stormed onto the flag bridge of her flagship, the *Victorious*.

"How in the hell did we not know a fleet was headed our way? Why are we just learning about it when it shows up on our doorstep?"

"I can explain, Your Grace, if you will just sit down, take two breaths, and listen," Admiral Bolesław said.

Vicky gave the admiral a serious scowl, but she did sit down and take the requisite two deep breaths.

"Okay" she snapped. "Explain yourself."

"There are three jumps into this system," Admiral Bolesław explained in an even voice. "One jump leads back to Dresden. We set buoys all along that route and around it. The second jump leads back to the territory of the Grand Duchy. We gave it the same careful treatment. The third jump kind of points toward Greenfeld, but in a very round-about way. The second jump out along that route is into a system that has six jumps from it. By the time we finished laying all the buoys that we needed for the other two jumps, we only had enough to cover six jumps in that sector."

Vicky took several more deep breaths. "I didn't order enough buoys, huh?"

"*We* asked for and ordered as many buoys as Dresden could produce. We had to spread them out around Dresden as well as cover Oryol and Lublin. For an economy that was dead in the water and scraping the bottom of its resources, they did the best they could, and we did the best we could."

"Okay," Vicky said, taking another deep breath, "but we *did* picket the *next* system out. Why didn't we at least get that much warning?"

"We drew the wrong conclusion. You may recall that we had problems with the station keeping jets on the buoys."

"Yes."

"Well, we've been having problems with the communication systems on them since they went into service. Sporadically, this one or that will close down and not give us a daily report for three or four days. Then they come back on line."

"I see where this is leading, but go ahead and finish."

"We assumed that the buoy in the next system that reported a freighter coming through failed temporarily. About the time we started to wonder about its continued silence, the hostile fleet showed up."

Vicky forced herself to take two more deep breaths. She was appalled by this situation, but she was also appalled by her reaction to it. Admiral Krätz had taught her better than this. She'd have to have a long talk tonight with Mannie. Maybe they could figure out where this anger came from over a pillow.

"Okay, so we've got a SNAFU leading to FUBAR. What's the enemy squadron look like?"

"We've drawn two of the best battleships in the old reserve fleet, the *Blücher* and the *Scharnhorst*. They've got eighteen 410 mm lasers compared to our twenty-four 460 mm battery. We've got the range on them, but not by much. They do have four heavy cruisers: *Gefion*,

Freya, Hansa and *Hertha*. All we have is the *Sachsen* and the light cruisers *Rostock* and *Emden*. Their 155 mm lasers will be outgunned by the heavy cruisers' 210 mm. They don't have any destroyers, but they do have two armed merchant cruisers. Sensors says they are carrying several 155 mm lasers. Their reactors have not been increased, so they will need more time to reload."

Admiral Bolesław paused.

Vicky considered all the odds and found them . . . challenging.

"So," she said, "if the *Victorious* can keep them at arm's length, and shoot straighter and faster, we can defeat their two battleships and then the heavy cruisers. If the *Victorious* gets blown out of space, our cruisers are toast."

"Pretty much, Your Grace."

"How good is the *Victorious*?"

"Good. Her crew is well-trained, professional, and capable. Most of the crews we've encountered from the Bowlingame faction have been scratch affairs with poorly trained landsmen, unfamiliar with their weapons."

"Of course, we could have drawn the one admiral who has whipped his crew into a fighting force," Vicky said.

"Yes, there is always that chance."

Vicky examined the battle board, then had it expand out into a star map showing the jumps between Dresden all the way through to Brunswick. Dresden was closer. Brunswick was several jumps farther.

"Have we reported our situation?"

"I sent off messages to both Dresden and Brunswick ten minutes after we found those ships drifting at Jump Beta, Your Grace."

Vicky drummed her fingers on the arm of her chair. "I don't want to weaken the fleet around Dresden," she said slowly. "I'd prefer that any reinforcements come from Brunswick."

"Yes, Your Grace, but any ships from there will take more time."

"Yes. I know."

There it was. She'd made the call. She waited to see if an experienced admiral would tell her that her solution to their problem didn't meet the standards the war college expected.

The silence between them went long, then Admiral Bolesław nodded. "It's six one way, half-a-dozen the other. Maybe we can win if they come fast. Maybe we can get reinforcements while they shilly-shally around out there."

The two exchanged nodding agreement.

Then the comm officer of the watch ruined their moment of agreement.

"Your Grace, we've intercepted a message in the clear from near Kromy. It says, 'The Grand Duchess is here. Repeat. The Grand Duchess is here'."

Now the glances the two admirals exchanged turned dark.

"Well, that tosses the fox in the hen house," Admiral Bolesław muttered. "It will take them a day or two to get the message. Do you want to make a run for Jump Point Charlie?"

"Would they follow us or go straight for Oryol?" Vicky asked.

"Your guess, Your Grace, is as good as mine."

Vicky let out another one of the sighs she was using so often today. She hoped they had a sufficient supply in store. She shook her head. "I have no idea. I just know that I will not run while there is a good chance that my people that I leave behind will be subject to what we just freed them from. Hell, admiral, what's to keep this fleet from just lasing this planet from orbit?"

"Nothing, Your Grace. While some of these SOBs might regret the chance to rape and pillage, no doubt they are dumb enough to get matters out of order and burn it first."

They shared a dry, if bitter chuckle at that. It was good to be in the company of a professional soldier who didn't flinch from turning the brutal truth into the joke it was.

Vicky might have flipped a coin in her head. But, no. She chose her next move.

"We stay and fight," She said, then added. "You want to counter-mand my order, Admiral Bolesław?"

He shook his head. "No, Your Grace. Whether you flip the coin or I do, we face only two options. Which one is better we will not know until this week is done."

"Yeah," Vicky growled. "That was what I figured. So, how do we prepare to fight these bastards?"

"With a lot of blood, sweat, and toil. Hopefully we can avoid the tears and make sure it's their blood."

"Drill the fleet, Admiral. When you have time, we need to examine our options. Charging out there for a few seconds of fire as we sweep by each other is off the board. I will not allow anyone from this crime ring to get between me and my people."

"You've read a few of Kris Longknife's after-action reports," Admiral Bolesław said with a proud, almost fatherly, smile.

"Admiral Krätz saw to it that I read them all. He bled red ink on my written reports until I fully understood what that Wardhaven princess was doing. Yes, Admiral. I will not do some stupid cavalry charge out to meet them."

"I'm glad. I was afraid that most recent demonstration the Longknife princess did at the battle of Cuzco, what with the actual charge, might have given you some bad ideas."

"We have 460 mm lasers. She had 625 mm monsters. No, I know just how small our killing zone is and how good our ice armor is against our own lasers. No, we need a bit of a running gun fight if we're to wreak the damage we must."

"Then, Admiral," Admiral Bolesław said, "I assign you the job of coming up with the first draft of a battle plan for us to massage and improve."

"Gee, and I thought I might catch up on my sleep."

That got a sharp, mocking guffaw from both of them.

40

For the rest of the day and well into the next, the *Victorious* rang with calls to drill and battle stations. Vicky spent the time studying her enemy, her situation, and her options.

Over supper that night, she talked it over with Admiral Bolesław.

"I know I'm not supposed to base a battle plan on enemy intentions," she began, "but we know their capabilities as much as they know ours."

The admiral nodded as he tested the contents of the bowl before him. It was goulash night and the cook had outdone himself.

Somewhere, a long stretch of road was missing all its roadkill. Vicky hadn't been in the Navy nearly long enough to identify all the different meats in tonight's supper.

"There are really only two possible intents," Vicky said. "Bombard the planet to punish it for me killing all the security consultants, or kill me because the Bowlingame faction has a huge price on my head."

Admiral Bolesław nodded as he spooned in some of the unknown goulash meat. "Since they only started heading in from the jump when they got the message you were here, we can assume your lovely self featured heavily in their decision.

"Yep. I wonder what the bounty is on my head," Vicky said.

The admiral shrugged. "Since they don't care how much they hurt people, they can give away several planets as private fiefdoms for your dead body."

"True," Vicky said, dryly. She'd seen what could happen to several planets when the Bowlingames gave them away to one of their dukes or counts.

She had to put an end to this.

"So," Vicky said, "we can assume that I am the target and they will go for me as soon as they get the chance."

"That is a very reliable assumption," the admiral agreed. "You know, this goulash tastes a lot better than it looks."

"I hope our odds are good as well," Vicky said. "*Victorious* outranges both of their battleships, but their four heavy cruisers outnumber our one heavy, and outrange our two light cruisers. I guess we could send the destroyers around on a sweep at the armed merchant cruisers, but their 150 mm guns outrange the destroyer's 125 mm lasers."

Vicky paused. "The *Victorious* is our queen. So long as we have her on the board, this chess game is a match. If we lose her, we lose this battle."

"Your Grace, if we lose the *Victorious*, we lose you and the battle is over."

Vicky couldn't disagree with the admiral.

"Which raises the question," Admiral Bolesław said. "Should you be on the *Victorious* or stay dirtside?"

"If I'm down there, they go for the planet and laser it all to hell. No. I stay here and fight."

"I didn't doubt that, but I had to ask."

"Still, you have a point. I'll need to make it clear to them that I am aboard the *Victorious*, so they don't make the mistake of going for all those people I just liberated."

"We could still beat feet for one of the other jumps out of here, Your Grace. There is no reason for you to stand here and fight."

Vicky gave the admiral a sour look. "If I don't stay and fight, they'll take it out of the people below. Everyone knows they're vicious bastards. It won't bother them to slaughter another million or so more people."

The admiral sighed. "You'd think, now that everyone knows they're vicious bastards, they wouldn't need to give any more demonstrations."

"Planets are cheap when you don't care about them and their people," Vicky said. "Lazing a couple of planets down to slag is no skin off their noses. No. I'm sure they'd rape and pillage and burn. Oh, right, they already did the raping and pillaging. All they have left to do is the burning."

Now it was the admiral's turn to give Vicky a sour look.

"Okay, we let them know you're on the *Victorious* and we fight them."

"It will be a running gunfight, with us doing the running for as long as we can to keep the range where we want it. Lethal for 460 mm lasers while they can only boil water with their 410 mm guns."

"We'll need to depart the station with a full fuel load," Admiral Bolesław said. "If they chase us away from Oryol's gravity, we'll have to work hard to get back in orbit."

"Yeah. I wonder what their fuel situation is?"

The admiral gave her a stoic shrug, "We'll know it when they run out of reaction mass."

"So, we'll put our task force into a looping orbit," Vicky said, bringing out her portable battle board and laying it down on the wardroom table between them. "They'll be headed for the station. We can use a loop around Oryol that swings us way out to bring us swinging back on roughly a parallel course. We begin the shoot with both of us on about the same course but well-distant."

The battle board showed the *Victorious* in a high, looping orbit that began to circle back toward Oryol just as the enemy battleships got in their range.

"We can adjust the range by steering ourselves out of our orbit. The turn can be harder, depending on how hard they turn into us."

Admiral Bolesław studied the board as he used a piece of brown bread to sop up the last of his goulash. Vicky would likely leave some in her bowl. However, if you stayed Navy long enough, she guessed a taste for the stuff could be acquired.

"What if they cut their deceleration and come at you fast? You're assuming that they will be slowing down to make the space station. What if they keep enough velocity on their ships to cut toward you faster than you can turn away?"

"That would put them into a quick fire and fly-by course," Vicky pointed out.

"Yes, but they'd have more fire power once they got in range, and they could brake to extend their time in range. All they want to do is blow up the *Victorious* or leave it as a dead hulk spinning in space that they can board or blow up whenever they get back here again."

"Maggie, how long could they stay in range if they came at us fast?"

"That is impossible for me to determine, Your Grace. While we know the range, I cannot determine what velocity they will have. It could be a little as a minute. It could be longer if they slow more or cut in close."

"There are too many variables there, Your Grace, to ask a computer for an answer. Even a computer as smart as Maggie."

"Thank you, Admiral Bolesław," Maggie said, "though I wish you hadn't used computer so often. Most computers are very dumb machines."

"Yes they are, Miss Maggie," the admiral said.

"So," Vicky said, returning to the intractable problem at hand, "what do we do if they don't cut their acceleration?"

With no food to distract him, the admiral eyed the battle board for a long moment. "We will just have to decide when they make their move. If they do it farther out, that will tell us they are intent on missing the station and Oryol. If they can't make orbit there, you can decide how much you want to concentrate on them, or if you want to take the chance they've offered you to back off and make them come at you again. Have you ever seen video of that ancient and banned sport of bull fighting?"

"I've heard of it," Vicky said.

"The matador distracts the bull, encouraging it to charge him over and over again. Then, when the bull is fully enraged, he slips a sword into the bull's brain and kills it."

"I see why it's banned," Vicky said.

"Some people enjoyed the sport. Sometimes the bull won," the admiral pointed out. "I believe there are several planets in the Hispania League that still have bull fighting rings. Anyway, it appears to me that you and the *Victorious* are the matador and the cape. They are the bull. If the bull gets too close to the matador, they can gore him and the bull wins. I fear the simile is quite exact."

"Yes," Vicky muttered softly. "I suspect that it takes split second decisions by the matador to keep those horns a fraction of an inch away from disemboweling him."

"Precisely."

"Have the captain keep drilling the crews, Admiral. Our survival may depend on getting off more broadsides per minute than they can."

"Every time you met the Empress in battle, her crews were poorly trained compared to your crews."

"And you and the other admirals that chose my side deserved all the credit for that."

"Us, and the crews, Your Grace. Never forget the sweating Sailors at their battle stations."

"Never, Admiral. Never."

Vicky skipped dessert and returned to her quarters. There, Maggie helped her take the hostile fleet through an entire series of possible changes in their approach. There, the two of them fought through the various responses to each of them until they had the best choices.

They worked quite late into the night. When Vicky finally fell into bed, she hardly missed that Mannie was not in it waiting for her.

No, it was best that he was planet-side, waiting to see if she'd be coming back, or if he was now the single father to their as-yet unborn children.

"I really must create him a Grand Dukedom. If I get myself killed, he could carry on. If not him, who could?"

She fell asleep with no answer to that troubling question.

41

The hostile squadron accelerated from the jump at 1.3 gees. Vicky found that interesting. One gee was comfortable. Vicky would have chosen 1.5 gees. Her crew would find themselves moving around the ship carrying half-again their weight.

That was usually manageable. Few of the professional crew wrenched their backs or blew out their knees at that acceleration. The opposition's choice of a lower acceleration, but not one gee, presented Vicky with information. What story it was telling was more than elusive.

Clearly, someone wanted to get here faster than they could at one gee. Just as clearly, they didn't want to make the crew walk around with more than a third of their normal weight. Vicky considered that a compromise between wanting to get at her throat quickly and maybe a crew that wasn't as physically fit or highly trained as hers.

Did that also mean they weren't as trained at their weapons as her crew was?

Vicky shook her head. She could ruminate over this tidbit of information for as long as she wanted to. Until the enemy actually closed with her and they began exchanging shots, it was all guess work.

The bad thing about being an honorary admiral and a Grand Duchess was just that. Everyone on board had a battle station and work to do that could mean victory or death.

She had nothing to do but wait the enemy's final actions.

Vicky kind of wished Mannie was aboard with her. Guilt, however, kept her from asking him to come up the beanstalk. With the crew drilling constantly, how could she retreat to her night cabin and hold a private orgy with her husband?

Besides, she needed to keep him dirt-side. Someone had to take care of their children if this didn't go well.

Vicky knew, in the back of her mind that if she lost this battle, there was a good chance the planet below would be heavily lazed as punishment for fighting their way out from under the tyranny of their so-called "Security Specialists." She hoped everyone below was scattering out from the cities and towns. The urban areas would be the targets; open land was a waste of lasers.

The Grand Duchess shook her head. These people had just regained control of their fate, freedom to return to their normal lives and live in peace again. Now, once again, through no fault of their own, this sword of Damocles dangled over their head, twisting in the breeze.

People should live in peace, to work out their own prosperity with their own two hands. The government should be there to make that safe and possible, not demand rapnious taxes to build worthless palaces or enrich a few.

With a sigh, Vicky took herself to the ship's gym. An hour of lifting weights would do more to prepare her for the high gees of the coming battle. Maybe it would also clear her mind.

"Come now, that man is not here," Kit purred, sexy as a naked kitten.

"It's been so long, Your Grace. I've gotten to know all of Kit's few moves," Kat whimpered.

"Can't you find a man of your own?" Vicky shot back, doing her best to keep lifting weights while the two nude assassins did their best to distract her.

"Who wants a man if he's going to go all possessive and monoga- mous on a girl?" Kit answered.

"Can you imagine the fun we could have, the four of us," and Kit and Kat proceeded to tell Vicky in very precise detail exactly what they wanted to do to both her and Mannie if she'd just give them a chance.

"I've agreed to try his monogamous ways for the first year of our marriage," Vicky muttered to them as she concentrated on pumping iron. "Next anniversary we can talk about trying something different."

"Doesn't he even give you time off for good behavior?" Kat said. "Even prisoners get time off if they're good," she cooed.

That struck a nerve.

"I'm not sure I've deserved any time off for being good," she muttered.

The two assassins glanced at each other. "Vicky, we would have killed those criminals for you if you'd just asked.

Vicky did five lifts before she answered. "It was mine to do," she muttered. "Even if you had pulled the trigger, you'd only be doing what I told you to do."

"But that is what we always do. You tell us who needs dead and we make them dead," Kat said.

"But how does that fit under the rule of law?"

"Rule of law?" Kit asked, as innocent as a kitten of law and conse- quences.

Vicky sat up and shook her head. Serious thoughts made it easy to resist the blandishments of who two tiny assassins and body servants.

If she couldn't have Mannie, she really didn't want anyone else. The realization of just how badly she'd been bitten by this monogamy bug came as a surprise to her.

After a good workout and a nice warm shower with the two assas- sins who both soaped her up and rinsed her off, she agreed to a massage, knowing full well that a massage from these two always led to a happy ending.

Despite the need, when the time came, she waved off the offered extra care and headed for her locker. Two very unhappy assassins helped her, begrudgingly, to dress.

After a "thank you," that she sincerely meant, Vicky went back to her battle board with Maggie, trying to lift the veil of the unknown from the future.

Vicky knew what she would do for an attack. At the right point, she'd reduce her deceleration by a fraction of a gee, adjust her course, and come down on the defenders with additional velocity, ready to swerve and chase them no matter where they went.

That was what the book that Kris Longknife had rewritten said you should do. Had these fools, however, read the book? Did they have any idea how to chase her? Engage her? Kill her before she killed them?

Vicky knew what she would be doing. Get her guns in range, then concentrate on one battleship until it blew up. After that, again, keep the range right and go after the second one. Of course, all the time this one-sided duel was going on, they'd be doing their best to close the range so they could bring their guns to bear on her and the *Victorious*.

The laws of gravity and motion defined very tight limits for her battle space. Unless the commander of the incoming battle squadron was stupid beyond belief, the battle would take place within those limits.

"Maggie, could you get me Admiral Bolesław, please."

"Yes, Your Grace," came back from her commlink amazingly fast.

"Admiral, do you know who commands the attacking squadron?"

"I'm sorry, Your Grace, but whoever commands it hasn't said a word. Why?"

"I was just wondering if we faced someone who knew the limits that gravity and the laws of motion put on the coming battle. Alternately, is he the type who might make all sorts of stupid moves that, individually, are folly, but taken as a whole could surprise us most unpleasantly?"

"I understand your concern, ma'am. Captain Blue has been keeping the incoming squadron under tight surveillance. However, he has picked up no communication identifying who commands the 12th Battle Group. That's their designation."

"Twelfth Battle Group, huh?" Vicky said. "Does that mean we must assume there are at least eleven more of these raider squadrons wandering this space?"

"There's no way to tell, Your Grace. They could be the only group, but the commander thinks twelve is his lucky number."

"Don't you hate it when amateurs mess around in your profession?" Vicky said.

"I don't know. I know a desperate kid with no skills who's survived the worst and learned from her and her family's mistakes. She's pretty skilled at my profession these days. Or so I hear."

"Thank you, Admiral. I assure you, I didn't call you to have my ego stroked."

"Everyone needs a pat on the back some days. Everyone needs to know that people believe in them."

"Now, good admiral, you're making me blush."

They returned to their own work. Vicky did touch base with Mannie to see how getting a new government was going.

He told her that most of the people of Kromy had fled to the hills and lakes. Now that the city government controlled the money supply, bank deposits were returned to people who put the money in. Unidentified money went to the farmers for food.

Out in the hinterland, everyone dug in and did their best to offer as small a target as possible.

Still, up by a lake with a large natural amphitheater, ringed by summer homes hiding in the woods, the People's House had formed itself into a constitutional congress. There, they were trying to hammer out the makeup of their civil structure.

Vicky, of course, would be the head of state, but her first minister would be the chief of state with all the real power. There was also a bit of a problem. Everyone knew that the Grand Duchy was also trying to come up with a senate or something for the entire shebang, if not the Empire. *Just how would the two centers of power dovetail? Where did one authority begin and the other end?*

Mannie called it federalism.

Vicky listened to Mannie drone on, delighted to be up to his lovely elbows in the future of her people. She wanted to be at his side when he got all the puzzle pieces together.

Vicky must not have been doing a good job of holding up her end of the conversation. He wound down to silence. Then asked, "Is it that bad?"

"I don't know," Vicky answered. "I don't honestly know, Mannie. Too many unknowns. Are our crews better trained than theirs? How good is their fire control? I know how good our crew is and Admiral Bolesław has got them drilling twelve hours a day or more to make them better."

"Still?"

"Still, sweetheart, after we've won this battle, would you please let me create you a Grand Duke?"

"It's that bad, huh?"

"We can't have a head of state if the Grand Duchess gets herself blown to pieces. I need for you to step in, raise our kids, and make this dream of yours come together for both of us."

"Do you think anyone would accept me as a Grand Duke?"

"When you almost shot me down, did you think anyone would accept me as a Grand Duchess?"

"You're a lot prettier than I am."

"You'll have cute kids to bounce on your knees. You can always claim that you are only regent until the oldest girl comes of age."

"It could be a boy."

"Not if you check for two X chromosomes and make sure the first one you put in the can is a girl."

"You think a girl might rule better?"

"She'd certainly do no worse than my dad and granddad."

"Well, Mary Queen of Scots had one husband die early, then was kidnapped and raped until she married the second one. That went downhill fast."

"Didn't she flee to England or somewhere and end up having her sister cut off her head?"

"Cousin, I think," Mannie said.

"Okay, you have me. Either sex can screw up. Raise them well to work together. Keep the younger kids busy with constructive and creative jobs so they don't want the damn top job. Christ, why would anyone want this job?"

"When it's done right, it's a pain in your ass. But, of course, if you think you can get away with doing it poorly and for your own pleasure, like some people you recently killed, it can seem like fun."

"None of the kids you raise will make that mistake."

"Say, better, that none of the kids *we* raise will make that mistake. Come home to me Vicky, and you can create me anything you want from subject to dogcatcher to Grand Duke. Just come home to me."

"I'll do my best. Now, I've got reports to review and we both need sleep."

"Five clowns just came into my room waving some sort of document that has too many pages. I've got to go, too."

The both rang off.

Vicky wondered if Mannie's excuse was any truer than her own.

She lay on her back, stared at the overhead, and tried to see different vectors and thrusts as ships tried to chase each other's tails.

At some time during her ruminations, she succeeded in falling asleep.

42

Late in the first watch, the hostile squadron flipped ship and began to decelerate toward Oryol. It took sensors well into the middle watch to figure out their deceleration. The sneaky bastards were decelerating at 1.29 gee for five minutes, then 1.28 for the next five, then back up to 1.29.

Vicky couldn't blame the team on sensors for tearing their hair out. Every other one of their reports was different and they were all just a bit off from the 1.3 gee deceleration you would have expected. It took them until close to 0300 before they were sure the data was true and not an instrument failure.

If Vicky ever doubted it, this proved those SOBs were nasty. Real nasty.

Admiral Bolesław brought her up to date on this twisted tale over breakfast.

"Any idea which of your classmates might have come up with a revolting idea like that?" Vicky asked.

"There are several sly bastards I could name. Some might be good in a fight. Some might not be. What surprises me is that the enemy engineering standing watch were able to keep the ships in formation. None collided. None went wandering off."

"You're frightening me, Alis."

"I've got Captain Blue going over the raw sensor data. They were far enough out to cover a lot of sins, but your computer is working with Otto to take out as much of the hash as possible and clean up the images. We should know soon enough what Otto is hunting for."

At that moment, Captain Otto Blue staggered into the wardroom, collected two large black cups of coffee and made his way to their table.

"You're still awake," Admiral Bolesław said.

"I won't be in another half an hour."

"You will be if you drink both of those cups," Vicky pointed out.

He took a sip off one of them and winced. "That's hot."

Vicky handed him her water glass. It still had some ice in it.

He dumped it into his first coffee cup, then tried it again. "Much better. Listen, if I don't get some coffee in me, I'll fall asleep halfway through my report."

"Is it going to be that long?" Admiral Bolesław asked.

"No, but I'm *that* dead tired. Okay, your computer did manage to rasterize our data to a finer granularity. Yes, there was some ships wandering around, taking a bit too long to slow or speed up, and some were drifting off-station. About what you'd expect for a bunch of half-gomers."

"Half-gomers?" the admiral asked.

"Yeah. The battleships were rock solid. Whoever is running their reactors and bridge watch knows their shit and they got it wired tight."

Vicky and Admiral Bolesław exchanged worried glances.

"Doubtlessly, there are only two properly crewed battleships in their fleet, and we drew them," the admiral said.

"And they've got a sly fox for an admiral," Vicky said. "Have I finally used up all my luck?"

"Nope. He has," Admiral Bolesław growled. "Otto, do you have anything more to report?"

"Not really. They're staying to that crazy deceleration pattern.

Now that we have their timing down, we can spot any variation in the rhythm quick as they do it."

"Good. Head off to your bunk and get some serious sleep. We'll need you sharp when the time comes."

"I've got my best chief on the duty with a good lieutenant who is coming along fine. If anything changes, they'll let you know as soon as it does."

"Good," Vicky said, "and thank you, Otto, for the hard work. You've told us as much as we know about this bunch."

"Yeah, their admiral is too smart by half and those two battlewagons seem to at least have a decent bridge and engineering watch. I told my relief watch to keep an eye out at watch change. Maybe the next bunch of watch standers on those battlewagons won't be so good."

"We can hope," Admiral Bolesław said, and waved the captain off to his bunk. He wound his way a bit unsteadily through the mess tables and out of the wardroom.

"Does this tell us anything?" Vicky asked her admiral.

"Someone's betting that we've got a sloppy team on sensors," the admiral growled.

"Shaving just a hair off their deceleration, then jiggling the throttle so that we would take it for just a question of instrument unreliability. Very sneaky."

"Also, not nearly as smart as he thinks he is," the admiral said, slowly, thoughtfully.

"What do you see that I'm missing, Alis?"

"Just this, Your Grace. In the fights you had with the Empress, may she be tormented in hell and soon forgotten among us, you always had Captain Blue on sensors, and no one ever pulled anything off on you."

"Yes," Vicky agreed.

"But this joker tried a con job with the deceleration. If he expected you to spot it, why try it? If he expected to get away with this sort of noise, what rock has he been hiding under for the last couple of years?"

"So, he's sneaky, but not as up to date on who he's trying to fool as he thinks he is," Vicky said.

"Yep. We'll keep an eye on him."

Vicky went back to her day quarters and spent the rest of the morning going over nasty things that this guy could use with his slight edge in velocity when he hit Oryol's orbit.

Of course, if he was going faster, he'd get here quicker. "Maggie, by how much will he miss the planet at this deceleration?"

Vicky's computer reported the enemy task force would pass ahead of the planet and by how much.

"Can they make orbit at that speed and distance?"

"No," Maggie immediately answered.

"So, they need to adjust their course."

"Yes, Your Grace."

"Get me the officer of the sensor watch."

"Aye, aye, Your Grace,"

"Your Grace," came quickly, but with a hint of a gulp. Otto had said he was bringing along a new officer.

"The report my computer has at the moment shows that the hostile strike group is still aiming for where Oryol would be if they did a steady one-point-three gee deceleration. Of course, they will pass well ahead if they don't decelerate at the higher gee. Have they adjusted their course to cross Oryol's orbit at the proper time?"

"Wait one, Your Grace."

The phone went dead. No doubt, the young officer didn't want the Grand Duchess listening in on his side of the conversation.

"Maggie, time the one-minute wait, please."

"Aye, aye, Your Grace."

"Thirty seconds, Your Grace."

"Sixty seconds, Your Grace."

Just after the ninety second report the lieutenant was back on the line. "Sorry, Your Grace. We took extra time to run three checks. No, Your Grace, they're still on the course that they would be on if they were decelerating at one-point-three gees."

"Thank you very much, Lieutenant. Let me know as soon as they make any change in their course, as well as deceleration. Someone is very cagey. I don't want to end up in their cage."

"Of course, Your Grace."

Vicky leaned back in her chair and stared at the overhead. Whoever he was, he was doing everything he could to sucker her into assuming he was just a good old boy, coming at her fat, dumb, and happy.

Vicky doubted he was any of those.

At lunch she shared her thoughts with Admiral Bolesław. He, of course, had already considered the course issue and checked it out.

"But that was a good move, Your Grace. He wants us to stay misinformed for as long as he possibly can."

"He's going to arrive sometime in the first watch," Vicky said, pointing out the obvious.

"Everyone is always a bit off after midnight," the admiral agreed. "I'm ordering a stand-down for final maintenance checks. We'll have an early supper, then put the second and third watches down early for the night. I intend to work the third watch through right up until we beat to quarters. I doubt if the third watch will sleep through the battle, but we'll have them backing up the other two."

"A very good plan. Did they teach you that at the academy?" Vicky asked.

"Nope. They insisted that you always keep to your watch rotations. I was always considered quite the rebel."

"So, even before you worked for a rebel Grand Duchess you were into this rebel thing," Vicky said with a quick chuckle.

"It's always worked for me so far. Why change at this late stage of life?"

Vicky took the rest of lunch to run some of her and Maggie's alternatives by the admiral. He found them well thought out.

"I expect him to try something fancy as he makes his final approach," the admiral said. "I suggest we stay loose and be ready to respond to it when it happens. We don't want to fall for a fake that we're expecting and miss the main thrust."

Vicky just nodded.

No sooner was she back to her quarters than the duty watch on Sensors called. "Your Grace. We have a change in course and deceleration. They have adjusted their course to pass closer to Oryol and dropped deceleration to one-point-two-six gees."

"Thank you. Pass that along to my computer."

"Ma'am, Maggie was the one who spotted the slight deviation in course. We were busy checking the change in deceleration, Your Grace."

"Thank you, again," Vicky said, and rang off.

"So, Maggie, you're freelancing."

"It's not like you're doing much that needs my full attention. Actually, may I point out, you aren't doing anything that needs my full attention."

"I think you've mentioned that several times before. Tell me, Maggie, did your mom, Nelly, give you any suggestions about how you spend your spare time?"

"Yes, Your Grace."

Suddenly Maggie sounded a lot more cautious than she had been a second ago.

"Spill," Vicky said.

"Spill?" sounded downright evasive.

"Please tell me how you've been spending your spare time, and don't say it's been in the ship library. I know you're there. No, I want to know which part of the ship's innards you've been ghosting through."

"All of them, I think," Maggie admitted.

"Have you broken anything?" Vicky asked, not yet ready to panic.

"I don't think so. Everything appears to be working and I didn't accidentally fire the lasers."

"I'm so glad, considering we're moored at the station and there's only station ahead of us."

"The aft batteries are pointed away from the station," Maggie pointed out, eagerly.

"Yes, but during a certain part of the station's rotation, they're pointed at the planet below, right?"

"Oh. Yes. Right."

"Please tell me that you didn't just think of that minor fact."

"Ah, well, as soon as you said it, I realized I had the fact available to me. I just hadn't accessed it."

"Good point," Vicky said, trying to be patient with her computer like she would a four-year-old with a loaded M-6 in her hands. "Now, Maggie, I would like you to spend the next however many picoseconds it takes you to review all the data and information you have available to you. Please determine if it's something like where the 460 mm lasers point during half of a station's turn. Something you really should have readily available to keep you from killing me, my subjects, or destroying yourself, okay?"

"Yes, Your Grace," sounded downright chastened.

Vicky felt the emptiness in the back of her head that told her that Maggie was busy elsewhere. Since she didn't see much need for doing any more thinking without her assistance, Vicky chose to draw herself a bubble bath.

It was almost relaxing enough to get her down off the ledge Maggie had rocketed her up to.

43

Whoever it was that commanded the incoming battle squadron kept his silence. That left Vicky and Admiral Bolesław with only his strange actions to gauge him by. He continued to juggle his deceleration, while inching his course over a smidge now and again.

He was definitely now aiming for a much earlier approach to Oryol, if much too fast to make orbit. Clearly, the planet did not interest him.

Vicky had done her own part. On a raid involving the Imperial capital, she'd captured the Empress's surviving brothers and nephews. They had taken over the criminal enterprise after the first level of the family was blown away in battle with Kris.

You would think after the criminal family had been decapitated twice, they would have learned their lesson.

But no. Apparently the money was still good. Money and power. The headless beast just lumbered on, spewing evil and brutalizing Vicky's subjects. Rather, the subjects of her poor, inept father, the Emperor.

Now, all those subjects were Vicky's responsibility. All of them were hers to protect. To do that, she had to stay alive.

What Vicky would give for one of Kris's battlecruisers constructed with Smart Metal™.

Her own squadron, with the super battleship *Victorious* with its 460 mm lasers, the heavy cruiser *Sachsen*, and two light cruisers *Emden* and *Rostock* still swung around the hook at the station's piers. Even though it was the first watch, a double set of watch standers stood by at their battle stations.

In theory, the third watch group had been dismissed to their bunks. That a single one of them was sleeping was a bet Vicky would not take.

Who would want to miss this battle?

The hostiles were reaching the crucial point in his approach. The two battleships with their 410 mm lasers and four heavy cruisers might or might not be a serious threat to Vicky's squadron. Everything depended on Vicky's ability to choose the range for this fight.

The extra velocity on his ships could cause her some serious problems.

Vicky's squadron stood by to sortie on her orders.

She stood on the flag bridge of the *Victorious*. Admiral Bolesław stood beside her. They both studied the situation on the main screen.

"Your Grace," the admiral said, slowly, thoughtfully, "have you considered that he's so sly he's outsmarted himself? It seems to me that you can avoid this battle."

"Where's the glory in that?" Vicky drawled.

Admiral Bolesław threw her a glare like she'd failed her final exam.

"Okay, keep talking, Alis. It's just sometimes my inner Peterwald has to come out. Remember, I was raised to be a tyrant."

"It never crossed my mind," the admiral said, diffidently.

"Now, how and why does the gracious Grand Duchess avoid a battle and keep a lot of people alive. Remember, while some of whom don't deserve to breathe my Imperial air, many of them are my loyal subjects."

"Ignoring who may very well need to die, my classmate of high speeds and few brains has got so much energy on his boats that he's going to go whizzing by here too fast to make orbit."

"Right."

"He won't have much time to laser any ground installations. At least, not this pass," the admiral added.

"Okay."

"So why fight him?"

"Won't he fire at us as he zooms by?"

"Not if we've got the planet between us." The admiral fell silent, but a grin grew on his face until it was all Vicky could see.

"Let me get this straight. We stay here, on the station. Then, before he gets to closest approach, we sortie and spend his best gunnery time with a planet blocking his line of sight."

"Not exactly, Your Grace. His lasers have a hundred-thousand-kilometer range. He'll be making about one hundred and fifty thousand klicks an hour as he zooms by. What if we pull away from the station, do a quick swing around the planet, and take off perpendicular from his course, accelerating for all we're worth away from him and the planet?"

Vicky considered that for a moment then said, "Maggie, plot us a course that would get us a distance of one hundred thousand klicks away when he makes his close approach."

A moment later, a course appeared. "It would be best to depart when you have the planet between you and him. Then, you can do a quick swing around the planet, maybe just grazing the atmosphere, pick up as much energy from that as possible, and go to three gees acceleration. We would need to depart approximately a half-hour before he gets in range."

"Won't he adjust course to chase us?" Vicky asked.

"Of course, but we can play this foxy game, too," the admiral said. "While we duck low, we have destroyers between us and him laying down chaff that messes with his sensors. That buys us a few minutes and adds to his confusion. Then he'll need time to get his squadron ready to take high gees. All the while, we're opening the range."

The admiral paused to look the situation over some more. "I don't know what kind of shape his ships and crew are in, but I think our high gee stations are good for three-and-a-half gees. Maybe a tad more."

Vicky shivered at the mention of the high gee stations. It had been her brother's sabotaged high gee station that had killed him, not Kris Longknife. With his ship being blown apart, Hank had converted the station into a survival pod. He should have survived like the rest of his crew.

His empty oxygen tank left him gasping for breath as he died.

Of course, the high gee station had disappeared, along with her brother's body, on the trip back to Greenfeld. A botched star jump could send a ship hurtling off into the unknown, covering a multitude of crimes.

About the time Vicky accepted the circumstances of her brother's death, she had come to accept the Peterwalds were a family crime syndicate, one that was down on its luck at the moment . . . one that could go legit with her and the next generation.

Okay. Never mind all that. I've got a battle to win.

"Very good, Admiral Bolesław. Have all the high gee stations checked and double-checked. We will depart the station in," she glanced at the timing on the screen, "Approximately one hour."

"I will personally see that your own high gee station is double checked."

"No need for you to tie yourself up on my account. Have one of your most respected chiefs oversee the work and that should be enough."

"Aye, aye, Your Grace," the admiral said, and hurried away.

Vicky suspected that that "Aye, aye," didn't mean what other ones did. No doubt, Alis would see to it that her high gee station was safe. If he didn't, she might as well slit her throat and save everyone the time and trouble.

My, aren't you in a bad mood, today?

She went back to studying her board. "Maggie, what if he takes off at three gees as soon as he sees us running?"

There, she'd said the word. She would be running away from a battle. Running, or turning this into a running gun battle, with her running and him out of range to go gunning for her.

However, she could decide just how far ahead of him she wanted to run.

If she chose, she could pull ahead and just take her time cutting him to ribbons with her longer-ranged 460 mm lasers. That was what the book said: 410 mm lasers were good out to 100,000 klicks. The *Victorious'* 460 mm lasers were good for an extra 40,000 klicks.

The battle should be an easy victory if she went by the book.

But.

There was always a but.

In this battle, it was her running. She could only use her aft battery, so her gunnery was reduced by half. Then there was always that extra distance. A laser lost its official effectiveness at its listed maximum range. However, energy was energy, and the gunk in space wasn't always the same. A slight variance from normal vacuum could make the difference from adding or subtracting just that little bit of energy from the laser beam.

It was that bit of difference that could make a very major difference. Vicky was running away from this fight. She'd be showing this bastard her vulnerable stern with its rocket motors. Ice armor could easily absorb laser beams that were past their sell-by date. How well could rocket motors or their superconducting electronic gear that maintained control over the superheated plasma shooting out of them survive spent laser beams?

Vicky wondered if anyone knew the answer to that question. No doubt, in a few more hours, she would.

44

"Sortie the squadron," Vicky ordered.

No doubt Admiral Bolesław could have said the words just as well as she, but some wag at Bu Per had seen that her promotion to full admiral was signed a few seconds before his.

It didn't really matter. They both agreed now was the moment to go. The ship captains knew their duty and the crews were standing by, waiting upon their orders.

The sortie order was being given early. Late in the last watch, the enemy squadron had reduced its deceleration all the way down to just a single gee. It would be doing nearly two hundred thousand klicks when it whizzed by Oryol.

It was time to hit him with her own surprise.

The destroyers sailed first. They would spread out, swing low, then climb high up where they could pump chaff into the space above the cruisers. This would give Vicky's strike group cover and keep the enemy in the dark about her intentions for a few extra minutes.

Minutes that could mean the difference between life and death.

After the destroyers had performed their mission, they were to go to maximum acceleration and scatter. There was no chance the little boys could get into a position to launch missiles, not with secondary batteries having the long range they had now.

The light cruisers *Rostock* and *Emden* went next, followed by the heavy cruiser *Sachsen*. Last in the line, and positioned to be closest to the enemy battleships, was the *Victorious*.

All four detached from the station smoothly and decelerated hard to drop themselves down so close as to skim the top of the atmosphere. Then as they headed into a high orbit, they went to 2.75 gees and accelerated away from both Oryol and the incoming battleships.

By the time the *Victorious* did that, Vicky was "relaxing" in her high gee station, waiting for word from Sensors. She and Admiral Bolesław had a bet between them.

Vicky was the pessimist. She'd accepted that the sly fox would spot this ruse in less than fifteen minutes and order his ships to close them. The admiral figured they were good for fifteen minutes or longer. He counted on the destroyer's cloud of chaff to hide them. That should give them time to accelerate and be well on their way before his academy classmate, whatever his name was, knew the new game and made his own move.

A space station in geosynchronous orbit stays over the same place on the planet. It never moves. That meant that Vicky's ships spent a bit more than three and a half hours of each day behind Oryol, blocked from view of the incoming fleet. Sensors in orbit told her what he was doing, but he knew nothing about what she was doing when she was around back of the planet.

The station was about to complete one of those brief periods when Vicky's squadron detached and launched themselves back into the planet's shadow and began a hard deceleration burn.

The destroyers had been launching for some time, deploying chaff to block radar, bedazzlers to send lasers ranging beams off in all directions, and vacuum type WP to confuse infrared sensors. Vicky needed them well ahead of her main task force, covering her course with gunk when she swung out from around the planet, well below the destroyers.

Of course, being on the wrong side of all that space gunk meant that the *Victorious'* sensors were of no more use to Vicky and Admiral Bolesław than her enemies were to him. However, Vicky had a trick up her sleeve.

The destroyer *Oxalate* had been outfitted as a squadron leader. During its last refit, its sensors had been jacked up to be a cut above the average tin can. The squadron commander on the *Oxalate* was tight beaming the raw feed from his sensors straight to the *Victorious*.

Between Captain Blue's team and Maggie, they were squeezing every bit of information from the data that they could.

They were getting quite a lot.

Thus it was that Vicky admitted defeat and promised to pay Admiral Bolesław one hundred Imperial marks as soon as she got out of the clutches of this contraption that held her tight and kept her from feeling nearly three times her normal weight.

The *Victorious* was accelerating away from Oryol at 2.75 gees before the incoming battleships began to adjust their course. The two big boys immediately honked their engines around to add a vector along the same course as Vicky's *Victorious*. It took them five minutes to go from 1.3 gees to two. It took even more time to go to 2.5 gees.

By the time the entire formation was blasting on a course to pursue Vicky, the four heavy cruisers were spread out, having increased their acceleration at different times and along different power curves.

The two battleships were also out of their previously rock-solid formation. One had changed course and added acceleration at a smooth rate. The other had botched the course change and taken much more time to put on the extra acceleration. That put it well below and behind the first one and falling more out of position as it struggled to get up to 2.5 gees.

Vicky's fleet had gone to 3.0 gees smoothly. They were still in a column ahead, with *Victorious* holding steady the last place in line.

Now the enemy realized that Vicky running put him in a mess. While he might be adding vectors on his ship to chase after the *Victorious*, he still had a strong energy vector directed toward Oryol's orbit.

If he didn't reduce that vector, he would whiz by Vicky's ships with hardly enough time in range to fire.

The not-so-sly fox had to order his ships to go to 3.0 gees and split their vectors between pursuit and deceleration. He'd gotten himself into a fix of his own making. He expected Vicky to do something like Kris Longknife.

Kris had met incoming attacks by going into a high elliptical orbit that put her way above the planet she was protecting, but able to get on a parallel course for a running gun fight. That left both Kris's forces and the opposing ships decelerating toward the target planet, both firing lustily away at each other.

Kris usually fired first and longest. So far, no one had beaten the Wardhaven Princess at that move.

Admiral, Her Grace Victoria, the Imperial Grand Duchess of the Greenfeld Empire, was doing something quite different, thanks to the advice of her admiral.

This fight would follow a different play book. Victoria would add her own chapter to the book Kris Longknife was writing.

Vicky smiled at the thought. She'd have her own victorious battle to brag about when next the two gals met to dig the dirt.

Well, she would if she managed to survive and win this battle.

Yeah, girl, save the celebration for when we've got those two ships in the bag.

Vicky eyed the board as the guy who wanted her dead tried to recover from an assumption that had just made an ass of him. Her grin would fit nicely on the lips of a hungry tiger.

45

Vicky watched as the lead battleship chasing her edged into range of the *Victorious'* aft battery.

The physics of this battle were not doing either side much good.

The space station was in a geostationary orbit. That meant that it orbited the planet once a day. Its energy vector went one way. Vicky had launched her fleet the other way. Oryol had been kind enough to give her a slingshot orbit in the opposite direction, but to a great extent, the deorbiting burns had been expended to reduce the *Victorious'* vector in the wrong direction.

Now, accelerating at 2.75 gees, she was extending a vector away from the hostiles.

Her enemy had a similar problem.

All his vectors were aimed at the space station. He had no energy on his battleship in the direction Vicky was accelerating. He was also starting from zero as he tried to chase her down.

However, his situation was worse. He still had the other vectors on his ships and the velocity with which he approached Oryol was threatening to drive him across Vicky's course in an astonishingly short amount of time.

The battleship closest to Vicky edged its reactors up to 3.5 gees acceleration. Part of that energy was aimed to reduce the vector at which he was approaching Oryol. Most of it went to increase the vector he needed to chase Vicky.

It very much looked like he'd cut across her stern at a speed slightly less than 150,000 klicks per hour, headed toward the star, while he still struggled to shorten the range on the *Victorious*.

Vicky would have him in range at 140,000 klicks. He would have her in range for 100,000 klicks. Maggie was still working on adjusting the *Victorious'* danger time as well as that of the lead battleship.

No question, he would be in danger a whole lot longer than her.

"You thinking about matching his three-point-five gees?" Admiral Bolesław asked from his high gee station.

"Nope," Vicky said. "Maybe once we get him in our firing range, but before he gets us in his range. Admiral, how good is the *Victorious* at jinking?

"We don't have the oversized directional jets that Kris Longknife has on her battlecruisers, but the *Victorious* has some of the most powerful station-keeping jets of any battleship. You thinking we'd better be ready to dip and dodge?"

"I'd rather know that if that bastard gets in range of our engines that we can make his fire control solution hash."

"I would prefer goulash for my own appetite, but I get your meaning."

"Would you please have all the ships of our little fleet test their directional rockets. I want to know if anyone is weak."

"We did serious maintenance to every system before we departed the station, but we haven't had a chance to test them. Aye, aye, Your Grace."

Admiral Bolesław was quickly on his commlink. A moment later, Vicky's inner ear told her the *Victorious* was doing a bit of a dance. Likely not enough for her pursuer to notice, but enough to check out the system.

"*Victorious* reports all directional steering jets as optimal. *Sachsen* reports same. *Rostock*, same. *Emden* reports trouble with its right forward steering rocket. Her skipper requests that we go right as often as we can." The grim, tight-lipped look on Admiral Bolesław face showed no humor for the attempted joke.

"Maggie, your mom developed a lot of jinking patterns for Kris. Do you have any of them?"

"I have several of them. Actually, I have the algorithms Mom used to make them. I can tailor three to fit the less-than-energetic systems we have, and which will let us avoid collision with the *Emden* when it can't go to the left as fast as we can."

"Do it Maggie, and transfer the jinking programs to all the ships."

"One moment," Maggie said.

Vicky had enough time for two breaths before Maggie was back. "Three jinking programs loaded to all four ships' computers. I have advised the skippers and bridge watch of their availability and that you may be ordering we initiate any one of them at any time."

"Very good, Maggie," Vicky said.

"Now, Admiral, please advise the Emden to go to two-point-nine gees. Do it in a ragged power curve. I want it to look like she's scared and running away."

"She's not going to like that, Your Grace."

"Admiral Bolesław, I don't want to run any risk of these bastards getting even one of my ships. This also gives us a chance to send a message to that wise fool of a classmate of yours. The rest of us can't do any better than our two-point-seven-five gees. Let's sucker him into keeping up this chase. In a bit, I may even shave a hundredth of a gee or so off our acceleration."

The admiral grinned. "I serve a sly Grand Duchess."

Immediately, he was on his commlink. From the sound of it, he got some back talk from one disappointed light cruise skipper, but, very quickly, he received obedience.

Vicky reviewed her situation.

She had actually won the struggle to get her ships away from the station and on their course. Her enemy had been slow to discover her direction of flight and even slower to bring his ships up to 3.0, now a struggling 3.5 gee acceleration.

She was pulling away from him.

However, his high speed dive toward the planet meant he would cut across behind her and be in range of her for a solid minute. He'd pay heavily for that minute. Vicky would have him in range for five minutes before, and close to five after.

After that, it was anybody's guess where he'd be off to. There were no planets between him and the star Oryol orbited. He'd have to burn a lot of reaction mass to go anywhere.

Of course, so would Vicky.

"Order the aft battery to stand by to open fire," Vicky said.

Admiral Bolesław passed the order along and reported, "The fire directory team have a solid solution on that battlewagon."

"Good."

The countdown clock on the main screen showed fifteen seconds before they could open fire.

That was when everything changed.

The enemy battleship fired its right forward thrusters and its aft left thrusters. Suddenly, it took off to the left. Five seconds later, it did the same and nudged itself up. Five seconds later, it went more to the left and higher still.

"Adjust our ranging fire," Vicky snapped. "Fire looser ranging salvos."

"Done," Maggie snapped back

The sixteen after 460 mm lasers spoke for three seconds, then fell silent.

"One just grazed the bulge of the hull," Admiral Bolesław reported. "No significant damage."

"So, he's not only a sly fox, but a smart one. I guess he's read Kris Longknife's battle reports."

"It would appear so. I really wished we could have had a fire in the archives of State Security," Admiral Bolesław muttered. "I imagine someone in the Bowlingames' employ did enjoy reading Kris Longknife's file."

"Yes," Vicky agreed. She thought for a moment, then said, "Admiral

Bolesław, do you think you could arrange with the *Victorious'* skipper to let me and Maggie take over the helm, fire control computations, directing the lasers, and firing them? Kris and Nelly often do that."

"I've been expecting something like this since your Maggie became as sentient as her mother," the admiral said.

He spoke into his commlink for a moment, got a reply and advised Vicky. "Your Grace, you have the conn. You are Guns for the *Victorious*."

"Let's hope that we haven't all just made a horrible mistake," Vicky muttered. "Admiral, I know the book says it takes thirty seconds to reload 46 mm lasers. By any chance did you manage to cut down on that time during all your drilling?"

"As a matter of fact, you can expect to be reloaded in twenty-five seconds. We started reloading one capacitor as we shot the other empty."

Vicky studied her board. "It seems our opposite number does not like bouncing around so much. He quit jinking right after we fired. I think we may have a surprise for him."

As the twenty-five second count approached the end, Vicky's trigger finger itched to get the SOB. Maggie had a rock-solid fire control solution.

"He recommended jinking!" Maggie exclaimed.

"Fire," Vicky ordered.

Again, the wide spread of the salvos winged the other battleship once.

"Don't you hate it when the other side starts acting smart?" Admiral Bolesław drawled ruefully.

"It's going to be a long battle if we can't hit him harder," Vicky growled. "Maggie, next time, we fire two salvos. The first from one gun in each turret. Wait five seconds, then fire the second."

"Sly as a fox yourself," Admiral Bolesław said, a smile on his face even if it did weigh three times normal.

As expected, the enemy battleship went back to jinking two seconds before the *Victorious'* guns were loaded and ready. Vicky waited for the next dip and dodge. He went down and to the right. Four seconds later, he went up and to the right.

"He's going to go left and down," Vicky told Maggie.

"Assumption locked in," Maggie answered.

Three seconds later, he did, indeed go left and down. "Fire as soon as you have a firing solution," Vicky told Maggie.

Two seconds later, he went left and up. "Keep on your solution. Wide pattern." .

Two seconds later, the *Victorious* fired half a broadside from its aft battery.

"We winged him again," Admiral Bolesław reported.

"Now we wait to see," Vicky whispered, "if he settles down on a steady course for the next twenty seconds. Maggie a tight salvo, if you please."

"Firing," Maggie shouted.

If Vicky wasn't positive that was a computer at her neck, she'd say that Maggie was excited.

"Three hits!" Admiral Bolesław shouted. He was definitely an excited human.

"Any good ones?" Vicky asked.

"Sorry. We're just burning ice off him."

"Maggie, when he gets in range of us, I don't want to stay on any course for more than four seconds. Steer curves, constantly change the angle; sharper, then softer. Never be headed the same place from second to second."

"Aye, aye, Your Grace. Do we do a two-stage volley again?"

"I think we have his attention. Let's see how long it takes us to get a good shot for the first half. Maybe we'll have to wait until the second gun is reloaded in each turret."

"Understood," Maggie said.

The reload clock was ticking down by seconds and hundredths of a second. The first two numbers spun at a dizzying rate.

The time came for half the batteries to be loaded. The timer reset for five seconds.

The enemy had jinked two seconds before the timer ended.

"Hold your fire," Vicky whispered. "Hold your fire."

Four seconds into his last dip and dodge, he changed course again.

"Wide volley," Vicky ordered, "as soon as all guns are loaded."

"Aye, aye, Your Grace," Maggie answered. A moment later, the lights dimmed as the aft lasers let loose.

"He dodged a second before we fired," Admiral Bolesław reported. "We got one solid hit and a second grazing hit."

"How solid?"

"He's trailing a lot of steam," the admiral reported. "A lot."

"Now if only we could get lucky and hit there again," Vicky said, not really hoping. The odds were way too long.

Together, they waited through the seconds again. Now the enemy changed course every three seconds. Of course, that ran the risk of dipping and dodging its way back into the space it had just aimed away from.

Whoever was controlling the helm on that ship was having problems remembering what its last course adjustment had been. Now, occasionally, it went left then right, or up then down.

"Maggie, are you tracking the course adjustments?"

"Yes, Your Grace. There must be a human at the helm."

"Consider their pattern."

"Doing so."

However, there was no time to do that before the next salvo had to be fired, then the next. Each scored minor hits, but nothing to cause any major damage.

They were coming up on the time the hostile would have its minute to shoot. They had just enough time in for two more volleys.

"He goofed," Maggie crowed as she fired a full sixteen gun broadside.

"He doubled back right into the area I was aiming for. I adjusted my volley too tight."

"Two solid hits, two grazing hits," Admiral Bolesław reported in an excited voice. "I've got an internal explosion. I think we hit a full capacitor. God, it must be hell around that battery."

"Finally," Vicky sighed then immediately was back to business. "Admiral Bolesław, we're afraid of them shooting a laser up our rear end into one of our rectors, right?"

"Yes, Your Grace," the admiral said, cautiously.

"Why do we have to keep running away from him when he's in range? Couldn't we flip ship, fire our forward batteries and keep our own thick bow armor aimed at him?"

"You wouldn't want to be accelerating at three gees toward him."

"But we'd want to keep enough way on the ship to jink properly," Vicky said.

"Definitely. Maggie, can you adjust your jinking?" Admiral Bolesław asked Vicky's computer.

"Certainly. I could juggle our acceleration so that it adds further confusion to his targeting solution. He has been a fool to keep up his three-point-something acceleration the entire time we've been shooting at him."

"Prepare to put a twenty-revolution-per-minute spin on and flip ship. Put us into a soft left turn now. Something that we might do if one of our directional jets was leaking. Then, two seconds before he comes in range, jink hard right," Vicky ordered.

It was time for one more shot without having to dodge. This time he did a better job of dodging and they only got a grazing hit. However, the hostile was trailing a lot of steam and still sparking from the turret hit.

"I wonder if he'll have a full twelve guns in his bow battery?" Admiral Bolesław asked, softly.

"We'll know in a minute," Vicky replied.

They felt it when Maggie began the jinking. She flipped ship, cut acceleration to one gee, and put the ship into a soft, then hard right turn, with a hard, then soft drop.

This wrecked his firing solution. He should have canceled the salvo to give his fire control time to come up with a new targeting solution.

He didn't.

"Missed to our right. He aimed for where we would have been," Admiral Bolesław crowed.

"Maggie, change course, assuming the part he held back is his broadside."

"Aye, aye, Your Grace, though Sensors says he fired his entire forward battery."

"Are you sure?"

"His ice armor is still boiling off enough for us to get a sensor report. Oh, and he only fired a ten-gun salvo. I don't think he has twelve anymore."

"Thanks Maggie," Vicky said. "Flip ship. Let's see what our forward battery is good for."

Whoever had the conn on the bridge of the hostile battleship didn't expect a second broadside this quickly. He allowed the ship to wander a bit, but not seriously dip or dodge.

"Four hits," Admiral Bolesław reported. "He's really shedding chunks of ice now, not just steam."

"Very good," Vicky whispered softly, her eyes boring into the main screen as if she might see her future, or that of one enemy battleship on it. "Now we wait."

Both ships continued their ducking and dodging as their lasers reloaded. The *Victorious* came online first, and Maggie put a tight salvo where she expected the battleship to be.

Whether she guessed or predicted it, she was right.

"Two solid hits!" Admiral Bolesław shouted with the glee of a man who enjoyed his job. "Three grazing hits. One may have nipped a rocket motor aft. He laid himself over a bit too much and I think we got to his rear end."

"The hostile is struggling to keep his nose to us," Maggie reported. "I think we hit one of his maneuvering jets. He's going hard left. He may flip ship."

The rebel ship was indeed going all the way around to the left. Battleships were designed with three rings of maneuvering jets forward and another three aft. One damaged jet should not be causing this much trouble. *What was going on a hundred thousand klicks behind her?*

"How soon will the bow battery be reloaded?" she snapped.

"Thirty seconds," Admiral Bolesław shot back. "Now that we're reloading all our guns, it's taking a bit more time."

As the reload clocks ran down, the enemy battleship was struggling to jink, but it had to go left. A little or a lot was its only choice.

And it was flipping ship. When its aft rocket motors were aimed at the *Victorious*, they reduced their acceleration to one gee. Someone didn't want to open the range. When they got back closer to her course, the acceleration went up.

"Maggie, does them taking acceleration off the boat make it easier for you?"

"Oh, yes."

"Take the rear shot."

"Firing a tight salvo," Maggie shouted.

"Hits!" Admiral Bolesław shouted back. "Three solid hits aft."

Vicky waited for the next report. Had they hit the reactors?"

Hooters went off in the *Victorious*. "Hull breach aft. Hull breach aft."

Somebody had discovered that he had an aft battery. If he was going to aim his rear end at Vicky, they might as well fire.

Vicky held her breath. Was her reactor about to blow her ship to atoms?

The *Victorious* took off on a wild course, somehow corkscrewing through space. Vicky was thrown hard against one side of her high gee station while her body grew heavier than she ever remembered it being before.

A moment later, the *Victorious* took on a blessed steadiness.

"Recommencing jinking," Maggie announced, and the ship returned to its dodging and dipping.

"What happened?" Vicky asked no one in particular.

"They got a good hit on one of our aft rocket motors," Admiral Bolesław reported. "Engineering managed to cut the plasma flow to the wrecked jet. The laser did not hit a reactor. Yes, we're lucky."

"What about the enemy battlewagon?" Vicky asked. Somehow the guy who wanted her dead had become her second priority. Still, he was a high priority.

"Secondary explosions on board," Admiral Bolesław reported, all calm voice now. He sounded like the voice of doom.

He was.

"More explosions aft. I think at least one of the reactors is out of control."

A moment later, he added. "Make that two reactors. The aft end of the battleship is exploding. Chunks of hull are flying everywhere. Lots of steam."

After a brief pause, he added in a whisper, "She's going."

The tiny image on the screen suddenly became a blinding flash, expanded into a multicolored ball of gas . . . then it vanished from sight.

A mighty ship of a hundred-thousand-tons and a thousand people was simply gone.

Vicky suddenly had a wish that she and her computer had not taken control of the *Victorious'* guns away from its crew. She found herself wishing that she alone did not have to carry the burden of all those dead Sailors.

I've got so many dead souls on my conscience.

And the day was not yet done.

46

Vicky stuffed her feelings of guilt and regret into that black hole that Peterwalds had where other men and women had hearts. She still had a battle to win.

"Maggie, set me a course that will intercept the second battleship soonest."

"Yes, Your Grace. What acceleration?"

"I said soonest. Three gees," she snapped.

"That will give us a very fast closing rate," Admiral Bolesław pointed out.

"I know. We'll worry about it when we get there. I'm betting that us heading at him like an avenging angel is going to get more results in the next few minutes than any tiptoeing around would."

"You may have that right, Your Grace," Admiral Bolesław agreed.

Vicky spent a long moment examining her options and chose the one she figured to be the best, even if it did mean changing her mind on a ten pfennig coin.

"Maggie, take us down to two gee acceleration."

"Aye, aye, Your Grace."

"Comm, get me on the main screens of the bridge on that battle-ship and those heavy cruisers."

"We've got you there," Comm replied.

The main screen before Vicky opened onto five bridges. What she saw were a lot of high gee stations pointed at her. Some showed faces going pale with terror. None looked very stalwart.

Vicky stood up at double her weight and went to stand in the center of her screen. She locked her hands behind her back and glared at the screen.

One window showed her what she looked like.

An avenging angel wasn't far off.

"I am Admiral, Her Imperial Grace Victoria, the Grand Duchess of half the Greenfeld Empire and the Protector of the Peace for the entire empire. You have violated that peace. We are not pleased. You will surrender your ships immediately or face Our further displeasure. You have seen what Our displeasure cost that other ship and crew."

Her short speech was followed by a long pause.

"You're charging at us," a trembling voice said. Vicky wasn't sure which ship it came from.

"Yes. We are prepared to hunt each one of you down and reduce you to a smear of hot gas in space if you don't surrender."

"Can she do that?" was a different quaking voice.

"She's got a lot more reaction mass than we've got," was dry and professional. "I'd take her at her word."

"I surrender," came back fast from all five screens.

"Cut your acceleration to one gee and smash your main battle busbar."

"What's a main battle busbar?" someone asked.

"Ask your Maintenance or Gunnery Officer," came in that dry, knowing voice. "If they can't tell you, ask an old chief, one of the Navy types. If you come up dry, ask me."

"May We ask who you are, Sailor?" Vicky asked.

"Commander Blucher, Your Grace. Navigator on the battleship *Vigilante*, the next ship on your hit list."

"Then you know how to comply with Our orders."

"Captain, if you don't mind, I'm taking the con. Helm, go to one gee. Use it for deceleration. I'll get you a course and acceleration as soon as possible."

"Aye, aye, sir."

"Is your captain qualified to stand a watch?" Vicky asked.

"The greenest of Landsman, Your Grace. All our captains are Bowlingame appointments."

"I assume you know the more skilled officers on the heavy cruisers."

"Yes, Your Grace."

"Please relieve the men dumped on you by that crime family and stand up qualified skippers."

"It will be done, Your Grace."

"Now, one more question. Can you tell me where that main Bowlingame fleet is at present?"

"Regretfully, ma'am, they don't trust us with that kind of information. Maybe you can get it out of this toad, but I suspect the only ship that had that information was the *Savage*, that you just blew to bits. We have intercepted messages in a cypher that we have no access to."

"Do you have an opinion where we might find that fleet?"

"Your Grace, I'm not sure that it is a fleet at the moment. We were ordered here. I don't know that other small squadrons haven't been sent hither and tither to find subsistence."

"Oh, so other planets are drying up just like Oryol and Dresden," Vicky said.

"Ma'am, you're getting my best guess. I hardly consider it a basis for policy."

"Thank you, Commander. Please have the Marines put the Bowlingame criminals in the brig."

"We don't have Marines, Your Grace."

"More security consultants?"

"Redcoats."

"Tell them that if they don't want to hang like every last one of them that I hung on Dresden and Oryol, they're on your side now."

"We'll see what we can do," the commander said, eyeing the other windows on her screen. Each had at least one man standing. Most two or three.

It would be interesting to see how the crews managed to get back control of their ships.

"Can't we run for the jump and get out of here?" a trembling voice asked.

"Skipper, you lost that option when you followed that shit head you called an admiral and didn't maintain a one-point-three gee deceleration. Now we can't reach an orbit around Oryol. We're headed for the sun. We've got a long slow voyage and you may end up losing that fat ass you've been throwing around before we get a fresh meal. That's the mess you've got us in."

"We're going to starve?"

"If that ass you call a supply officer hasn't robbed you blind, we may survive. Otherwise, we may serve you and him up for dinner."

"Cut the screen," Vicky said. "I don't need to know what happens next. Maggie, let me know when the busbars are smashed."

"The *Vigilante* has smashed hers. The *Duke of Greenfeld*, Duke of this, Count of that, and . . . the Baron of something have now smashed their buses. There was at least one officer on board each ship who knew how to avoid your great displeasure."

"Admiral Bolesław, is there any way to make an educated guess as to how long those ships are going to be looping around the sun? They are headed for the sun, right?"

"Unless they've got a lot more reaction mass than I think they do, yes, Your Grace. They won't be back for a bit."

"Actually, Vicky, if you had just asked me, I could have told you," Maggie said with an injured sniff.

"Oh, Maggie," Vicky said, not missing the sudden familiarity from her electronic assistant. "What is their fuel situation and how do you manage to know it?"

"They will all make it back. I am checking on their supply situation as we speak. While you were in communication with them, I slipped into their ship computers. I know exactly how much reaction mass they have aboard, as well as fuel for their reactors. I would say I know their food situation, but from what I just heard, the books I checked may not be trustworthy. If they are, they will have no problem making it back here in three months without eating anyone."

Maggie paused. "However, since they will be surviving on porridge, beans, and rice, they might wish to slaughter the culprits to add some protein to their meals."

"Thank you very much, Miss Maggie," Vicky said, seeing how giving her computer some respect might get her some in return.

"I would prefer something like my mother, The Magnificent Nelly. How about the Superb Maggie? Terrific Maggie?"

"We'll try some of those out, Maggie, if you'll promise to cure yourself of that swelled head you're developing."

"Harumph," was all Vicky got from Maggie.

"Admiral Bolesław, can you set us a course for the jump point and Dresden? I think we need to get back there, soonest."

"What about Oryol?"

"If that fleet won't be back here very quickly, we can get a message to Brunswick to add two or three battleships to the force being sent here. They should be here well before that squadron drifts back this way."

"What about your husband, Your Grace?" Admiral Bolesław asked, carefully, as one might when crossing a matrimonial mine field.

"Mannie has a planet's government to work on. It should keep him busy at least until I can get a fleet organized to see about liberating Lublin, maybe Helsingborg as we fly by."

"He will not be happy."

"Leave his happiness to me," Vicky said. "It will be interesting to see if a mere commoner can hitch a ride on a light cruiser. Something tells me that there are a few Navy captains-to-be interested in helping him chase down his runaway bride. Maybe I'll make a Grand Duke out of him yet."

"Maybe," Admiral Bolesław said, dryly. "Navigator, work me up a possible course to Dresden. Run it by engineering to make sure all our ships have enough reaction mass to make it."

"Aye, aye, Sir."

"Comm, message to Brunswick, 'The Grand Duchess requests and requires that you reinforce the squadron around Oryol to at least two battleships and four cruisers.' Does that satisfy Your Grace?"

Sadly, only Mannie and a very big bed could provide the satisfaction that Vicky really wanted, but for now, this would have to do.

"Yes, Admiral, that is very satisfactory. Let me know when we are underway for Dresden."

"Your Grace, we already are. And may God have Mercy on all our souls."

"Maybe she will," Vicky said, a satisfied grin on her lips.

The admiral just shook his head and gave orders for the high gee stations to be parked in the back of the flag bridge. "We'll be needing them again soon."

ABOUT THE AUTHOR

Mike Shepherd is the national best-selling author of the Kris Longknife saga. Mike Moscoe is the award-nominated short story writer who has also written several novels, most of which were, until recently, out of print. Though the two have never been seen in the same room at the same time, they are reported to be good friends.

Mike Shepherd grew up Navy. It taught him early about change and the chain of command. He's worked as a bartender and cab driver, personnel advisor and labor negotiator. Now retired from building databases about the endangered critters of the Northwest, he looks forward to some fun reading and writing.

Mike lives in Vancouver, Washington, with his wife Ellen, and not too far from his daughter and grandkids. He enjoys reading, writing, dreaming, watching grandchildren for story ideas and upgrading his computer – all are never ending.

For more information:
http://krislongknife.com
mikeshepherd@krislongknife.com

f

RELEASE INFORMATION

In 2016, I amicably ended my twenty-year publishing relationship with Ace, part of Penguin Random House.

In 2017, I began publishing through my own independent press, KL & MM Books. We produced six e-books and a short story collection. We also brought the books out in paperback and audio.

In 2018, we began the year with Kris Longknife's Successor, followed by Kris Longknife: Commanding, and Vicky Peterwald: Dominator.

In 2019, we published Kris Longknife: Indomitable, Vicky Peterwald: Implacable, and ended the year with Kris Longknife: Stalwart.

2020 will be an adventure! In April Longknifes Defend the Legations will be published. I'll also be writing two Kris novels, and a Vicky novel. In the fall, you'll also get the release of Boot Recruit, the short story that premiered last year in an anthology, that explains a bit about why Kris chose the Navy.

Stay in touch to follow developments by friending Kris Longknife and follow Mike Shepherd on Facebook or check in at my website https://krislongknife.com

MORE BOOKS BY MIKE SHEPHERD

This is what we include in all of Mike Shepherd's publications. If you enjoyed this book, here is a list of more books by Mike Shepherd, including some of his early works and short story collections. All have hyperlinks for the purchase of your choice. Enjoy!

Published by KL & MM Books

Kris Longknife: Emissary

Kris Longknife: Admiral

Kris Longknife: Commanding

Kris Longknife: Indomitable

Kris Longknife: Stalwart

Kris Longknife's Relief

Kris Longknife's Replacement

Kris Longknife's Successor

Rita Longknife: Enemy Unknown

Rita Longknife: Enemy in Sight

Vicky Peterwald: Dominator

Vicky Peterwald: Implacable

Longknifes Defend the Legation

Short Stories from KL & MM Books

Kris Longknife's Maid Goes on Strike & Other Short Stories

Kris Longknife's Maid Goes On Strike

Kris Longknife's Bad Day

Ruth Longknife's First Christmas

Kris Longknife: Among the Kicking Birds

Ace Science Fiction Books by Mike Shepherd

Kris Longknife: Mutineer

Kris Longknife: Deserter

Kris Longknife: Defiant

Kris Longknife: Resolute

Kris Longknife: Audacious

Kris Longknife: Intrepid

Kris Longknife: Undaunted

Kris Longknife: Redoubtable

Kris Longknife: Daring

Kris Longknife: Furious

Kris Longknife: Defender

Kris Longknife: Tenacious

Kris Longknife: Unrelenting

Kris Longknife: Bold

Vicky Peterwald: Target

Vicky Peterwald: Survivor

Vicky Peterwald: Rebel

Mike Shepherd writing as Mike Moscoe in the Jump Point Universe

First Casualty

The Price of Peace

They Also Serve

Rita Longknife: To Do or Die

Ace Science Fiction Short Specials

Kris Longknife: Training Daze

Kris Longknife: Welcome Home, Go Away

Kris Longknife's Bloodhound

Kris Longknife's Assassin

Kris Longknife's Bloodhound & Assassin Duology

The Lost Millennium Trilogy by Mike Shepherd, published by KL & MM Books

Lost Dawns: Prequel

First Dawn

Second Fire

Lost Days

The Lost Millennium Anthology

Award-Nominated Short Story Collections by Mike Shepherd, published by KL & MM Books

A Day's Work on the Moon

The Job Interview

The Strange Redemption of Sister MaryAnn

Made in the USA
Columbia, SC
06 April 2022